What Wasn't Forgotten

A Secrets of Redemption Novel

Books and series by Michele Pariza Wacek

***Secrets of Redemption* series**
(Pychological Thrillers)
The flagship series that started it all.
https://MPWnovels.com/r/rd_wwf

Mysteries of Redemption
(Psychological Thrillers)
A spin-off from the Secrets of Redemption series.
https://MPWnovels.com/r/mr_wwf

Charlie Kingsley Mysteries
(Cozy Mysteries)
See all of Charlie's adventures here.
https://MPWnovels.com/r/ck_wwf

Redemption Detective Agency
(Cozy Mysteries)
A spin-off from the Charlie Kingsley series.
https://MPWnovels.com/r/da_wwf

Riverview Mysteries
(standalone Pychological Thrillers)
These stories take place in Riverview, which is near Redemption.
https://MPWnovels.com/r/rm_wwf

What Wasn't Forgotten

A Secrets of Redemption Novel

by Michele Pariza Wacek

What Wasn't Forgotten Copyright © 2024
by Michele Pariza Wacek.

All rights reserved. Printed in the United States of America. No part of this book may be reproduced or transmitted in any manner or by any means, electronically or mechanically, including photocopying, recording, retrieval system, without prior written permission from the author, except in the case of brief quotations embodied in a review. For more information, contact Michele Pariza Wacek, PO Box 10430 Prescott, AZ 86304. info@LoveBasedPublishing.com.

ISBN 979-8-89351-003-4

Library of Congress Control Number: 2024941090

For my family, for always believing in me.

Chapter 1

"Coffee first," I informed Oscar as I limped into the kitchen. "Then I'll feed you."

Oscar let out an impatient meow as he sat next to his food dish, his tail wrapping around his paws.

"I promise you won't die of starvation," I said as I dumped old coffee grounds into my composting bucket. Oscar didn't look convinced.

It had been almost two weeks since the night I freed Zelda and escaped from the Church of the Forgotten. Physically, I wasn't doing too badly—my ankle had healed enough to no longer require crutches, I had gained some much-needed weight, and most of the color had returned to my face. I was still suffering from headaches, but ibuprofen took most of the edge off the pain. The doctor said my brain was healing nicely, so I needn't worry about it.

My mental health, however, was a completely different story. Every morning, I woke from nightmares I could barely recall, covered in sweat and tangled up in my sheets. In those moments, I was sure that whatever dark presence I felt at the Church of the Forgotten had followed me home and was now residing in my room.

Watching me.

Waiting for me to drop my guard, so it could pounce and devour me with its sharp, shiny teeth …

In fact, being in my room at all was hard to bear. I was constantly eyeing every shadow, trying to discern any movement, and listening for any and every sound—including the soft inhale or exhale of breath.

I knew I was being irrational. But it didn't matter. Regardless of every effort I made to do so, I couldn't convince myself that there was no entity in my room … that it was just a figment of my imagination.

Even after retreating to the comfort of my kitchen to make coffee and feed Oscar, I was never able to shake the feeling of being watched.

Then there were the anxiety attacks that hit me at odd moments throughout the day. I had one at the grocery store two days ago and wasn't even able to finish my shopping. Daphne had to come fetch me from the parking lot, where I sat trembling uncontrollably. She drove me home and finished my shopping for me before she and Aiden brought my car home for me.

I don't know what I would have done without her. Chrissy was in school all day and still worked part time at Aunt May's Diner. But even if she had been available, I wouldn't have wanted to saddle her with what I was going through. She was a teenager who needed to enjoy her last year in high school, not babysit her hot mess of a stepmother. She had already been through more than most kids her age. She didn't need any more struggles.

And Mia ... well, she wasn't in any better shape than me. Physically, she looked great—her bruises had healed, and she was no longer a bag of skin and bones. But she wasn't the same. She was much quieter now, her attention often sliding away even in the middle of the conversation. I would often see her gazing at the wall, a glazed look in her eyes, as she wrestled with whatever demons haunted her. Even though she was now staying in what used to be my office, I knew she wasn't sleeping any better than I was. When I padded by her room before the sun even approached the horizon, I could hear her pacing. Sometimes, I would find her in the kitchen, waiting impatiently for the coffee to perk.

We never talked about it. Never discussed our nightmares or the things that haunted us. Instead, we simply allowed each other to muddle through it on our own.

I didn't know if that was the right decision or not.

"Morning."

I turned to see Chrissy shuffle into the kitchen, still yawning. She was dressed in tight jeans and a hot-pink long-sleeved shirt that perfectly matched the stripe of color in her raven-black hair.

"You're up early," I said, opening the cupboard to pull out a second mug.

Chrissy grimaced. "Biology test today. Which I'm not ready for. Ugh." She flipped a few strands of her dark hair out of her eyes and accepted the mug.

I offered her a sympathetic look as she prepared her coffee, doctoring it with a liberal amount of cream and sugar. "Science was never one of my strong suits. Or math."

Chrissy groaned as she took a sip. "Don't remind me. Algebra test is next week, and I'm nowhere near ready for that, either."

I winced. "Oh. Yikes. Sorry to hear that."

Chrissy rolled her eyes as she continued to drink.

"Do you want me to make you breakfast?" I asked, even though I knew she wasn't much of a breakfast person.

She shook her head and put her mug down. "I should get going."

"Where are you off to?"

"Library." She pulled her phone out of her back pocket and scrolled through it. "That's the best place for me to study. Otherwise, I get distracted. Oh, and since you're up, would you mind taking me?"

I frowned at her, even though she couldn't possibly see me, as her head was bent over her phone and her hair was swept around her face. "What's wrong with your car?"

She glanced up and gave me a strange look. "It's in the shop. We talked about this yesterday. Don't you remember?"

I put my hand to my temple, a whisper of a headache fluttering across my forehead. The doctor had mentioned that some degree of short-term memory loss wasn't uncommon after a concussion—especially seeing as I was not only dealing with physical trauma, but mental and emotional, too. Still, I found it worrisome. Especially since it seemed to be getting worse instead of better. "Oh yes, that's right. Sure, I can take you now. Do you need me to pick you up?"

She was still looking at me with that strange expression, but now, I could see the flicker of alarm, too. "No, Brittany can pick me up. Becca, are you sure you're okay?"

I rubbed my temple harder. "Positive. It's just early. I haven't had enough coffee yet." I forced a smile onto my face, trying to sound more confident than I felt.

She didn't look reassured. "Are you sure you should be driving? Maybe I should see if Mia is up."

"Leave Mia alone," I said, my voice sharper than I intended. Mia needed the rest just as much, if not more, than I did, and if she was still sleeping, we needed to let her.

Chrissy's eyebrows went up. "I wasn't going to wake her ... just see if she's awake."

"I'm sorry," I said with a sigh, running my hand through my hair. "I'm just ... I'm just frustrated it's taking so long for my concussion to heal."

Chrissy's face softened. "Concussions suck. One of our cheerleaders had one. It took months for her to heal."

My eyes widened. "*Months?*" Oh dear lord. I didn't think I could stomach months of headaches and anxiety attacks and memory loss.

Chrissy nodded solemnly. "Yeah, it was bad. It happened during practice. She was tossed up in the air, but no one caught her. She ended up falling on her head."

"Oh geez," I said, rubbing my temple again, the whisper of pain gaining strength.

Chrissy's eyes drifted to the scar on the side of my head. "I don't think what happened to you was nearly as bad, though, so I'm sure it won't take months."

I tried not to roll my eyes. "Thank you, Dr. Chrissy."

She grinned and went back to her phone. "So, you're sure you're okay driving me then?"

"I think I can handle a ten-minute drive at this hour in the morning," I said, reluctantly abandoning my coffee cup. "Let me grab my keys."

She didn't look up as I headed over to my purse and started rifling through. I didn't see my keys, but I did find my phone. Out of habit, I took a quick peek and saw that my mother had called. Again. She had also left a voicemail.

Chrissy was talking, but I had stopped listening. I couldn't tear my eyes away from my phone. Over the past couple of weeks, my mother had called and texted several times, begging me to call her back. I knew I should, but I just couldn't bring myself to do it. The last thing I felt like dealing with was her hurling a barrage of guilt at me for not calling or coming home to visit, which would then inevitably segue into when I was going to sell Aunt Charlie's house and move back to New York. It didn't seem to matter how often I told her that Redemption was my home now. She was insistent this was just a "phase," and any minute, I would come to my senses and go "home."

"Becca? Are you listening?" Chrissy asked.

I slid my phone back into my purse. I would deal with my mother later. Much later. "Sorry. I got distracted."

The concern I had seen on Chrissy's face earlier flitted across it a second time. "I was asking if you needed something for dinner. I'm assuming Aiden and Daphne are coming over again, but do you need me to cook something for you?"

"No, I can handle it," I said, trying to think where I had last seen my keys. Again, my memory failed me.

"Are you sure?" Chrissy asked. "I don't mind at all. I can whip up a casserole right when I get home from school."

"Honestly, it won't be an issue," I said, searching the counter for my keys. "I've got *all day* to make something."

I smiled as I said it, trying to turn it into a joke. But inside, I winced. As I was still supposed to be healing, not working, I had very little to do and a lot of time to do it. Puttering around the kitchen at least gave me *something* to build my days around. And with Aiden still living in a hotel and Daphne fussing over both Mia and me, making dinner for everyone was truly a no-brainer.

Still searching for my keys, I moved to the pile of mail to see if I had dropped them there.

Chrissy finally looked up from her phone. "What are you doing?"

"Looking for my keys," I said. "Have you seen them?"

She pushed away from the counter and tucked her phone back in her jeans. "No. When was the last time you had them?"

"I'm not sure," I said. "Maybe a day or two ago?" It might have been longer. I honestly couldn't remember, but I didn't want Chrissy to know that.

"Hmm," Chrissy said, picking up the cream and opening the fridge. "Did you check your office? I can run upstairs ... oh wait." She turned around and held up her hand, my keys dangling from her finger.

"Where were they?" I asked as my stomach sank and anxiety climbed.

She waved them at me. "On the top shelf of the fridge. Exactly where keys belong."

I picked up my purse and phone and reached for the keys, forcing a smile onto my face. "I don't know what I was thinking this morning. I guess I need to be more careful, before coffee."

She didn't smile back as she handed them to me. "Life is definitely better after coffee," she said softly.

At least she didn't ask *how* my keys ended up in the fridge, seeing as I couldn't even remember the last time I'd handled them.

Although it was quite possible that she didn't ask because she didn't want to know the answer.

Chapter 2

"You really don't have to cook for us," Daphne said. "Not that I don't appreciate a home-cooked meal, but honestly, you should be resting."

"I'm resting enough," I said, bringing the pot of spaghetti and meatballs with homemade sauce over to the butcher block table where Daphne, Mia, and Aiden sat. I had already set out garlic bread and a big salad along with wine for Daphne, beer for Aiden, and water for Mia and me. The entire house smelled like garlic, onions, and the snickerdoodle cookies I had made for dessert. "It's not like I'm making anything overly complicated. Besides, I appreciate you all coming over to check on us."

"It's the least we can do, especially since you're feeding us," Aiden said. His voice was normal, but his gray eyes were distant as he fidgeted with his beer glass.

"There are things you could be doing other than cooking for us," Daphne said as she helped herself to the spaghetti.

"Not many." I reached for the salad. "I'm still not supposed to be working, and there's only so much housecleaning I can stomach."

"What about painting?" Daphne asked, scooping up a couple pieces of escaped pasta and flipping them onto her plate.

I paused, suspending the tongs full of lettuce in mid-air. That was a good question. Why *wasn't* I painting? Even more importantly, why hadn't it even occurred to me to get back to it?

There was a time in my life when I thought I might be a painter. Back when I was a teenager and spending my summers with my Aunt Charlie in Redemption, I dreamed about becoming a successful artist. But then, everything changed. My friend Jessica disappeared, and I almost died, and that was the end of my visits to Redemption. That is, until Aunt Charlie died and willed me her house. By then, I had spent years burying my desire to paint. But when I first came back to Redemption, I thought maybe it was time to pick it up again.

Instead, I got sucked into re-starting Aunt Charlie's tea business, and painting got put on the back burner. Again.

Daphne hadn't noticed my stillness, as her attention was on corralling her unruly pasta. "I know you've had other focuses this past year, but maybe this is a sign to get back into it."

Mia looked at me sideways. "Everything okay, Becca?" She looked pointedly at the tongs.

"I'm fine," I said, quickly finishing up with the salad and pushing it toward her. "I guess I was just wondering why I hadn't even thought of it." I shot Daphne a small, rueful smile. "Although, I'm not sure recovering from a concussion is the best time to jump into creative pursuits."

A ghost of a smile touched Daphne's lips. "No one said you have to create a masterpiece. Maybe just have some fun with it and see where it goes."

Fun. The word practically felt foreign, it had been so long since I had done anything for "fun." Even before all the craziness of the summer, beginning with Penny's death, I hadn't pursued much fun. Instead, all my focus had been on taking care of the house and getting Aunt Charlie's tea business up and running. Not much fun in either of those.

The truth was, the last time I could remember having any fun at all was with Daniel. And the more I thought about it, the more I realized we actually had quite a bit of it.

My breath caught in my throat as a dull pain radiated across my chest. I looked down at my plate and forced the memories out of my head. There was no use thinking about what used to be. I wasn't getting back together with Daniel, and that was all there was to it. There was too much hurt and pain and betrayal hanging between us. I was sure we could never move past it. The only reason I was still hung up on him was because of the stupid concussion. I had way too much time on my hands, which meant way too much opportunity to mull over things I had no business even thinking about. Perhaps painting, if nothing else, would provide me with a better way to occupy my time.

"Speaking of fun," Mia said, this time eying Aiden, who still seemed lost in his own world. "What's going on with you, Aiden?"

Aiden startled, nearly spilling his beer. "What do you mean?"

"Well, for starters, are you going back to your job anytime soon?" Mia asked.

"Mia," Daphne interjected, her voice aghast. Even though Mia and Aiden's relationship had warmed up from its initial chilliness, they would probably never be friends. Still, that seemed abrupt even for her.

Mia raised an eyebrow as she met our gazes around the table. "What? I'm not trying to get rid of him ... of you," she directed the last part at Aiden, who inclined his head at the implied apology. "But you took a leave of absence from your job to come here, right? And you're living in a hotel. I assumed you would eventually need to make some money."

She had a point, and I was a little ashamed for not thinking, let alone asking, about it myself. He was supposed to be my friend, yet I was realizing I've rarely asked him about his life or what he has been doing with himself. Instead, I'd been mooning over Daniel like a silly sixteen-year-old again. Ugh. I needed to pull myself together.

Aiden put his fork down and reached for his beer. "Well, it's interesting you ask, because I did have some ... developments, around that."

Developments? That was an odd choice of words. I tried to read Aiden's expression, but he still wasn't meeting any of our eyes. I glanced at Daphne and saw the same concern reflected back as we both put down our forks.

"What kind of developments?" Mia asked.

Aiden took a long swig of beer. "Well, as you pointed out, I'm basically living at the Redemption Inn right now, and even though Lynne was kind of enough to give me a significant rate reduction, it's definitely not a long-term living arrangement. So, I'm going to have to make a change."

A change? A lump suddenly lodged in my throat, and I reached for my water, wishing it was wine. I had a bad feeling about where this was going, although I wasn't sure why. Aiden was living in a hotel; of course he was going to want to find his own place. So why did I feel emotional? I figured it must be the concussion.

"Are you going back to Riverview and your job?" Daphne asked.

Aiden continued to avoid looking at us, instead focusing on his beer bottle, which he was now spinning around on the table. "That's one possibility. I've also been considering *not* returning to my job and doing my own thing."

"Like opening your own business?" Daphne asked.

"That or consulting," Aiden said. "I could even work as a freelance insurance fraud investigator. There are a lot of possibilities."

I cleared my throat, trying to dislodge the lump. "So, are you thinking about staying in Redemption? Not at the hotel, obviously, but maybe finding an apartment?"

Aiden's eyes flickered up and finally met mine. "That depends."

The silence was thick with implication. Mia and Daphne glanced between us.

I was finding it difficult to force the words out. "Depends on what?"

His gaze didn't move. "On whether there's anything here for me."

There was another long silence. My heart had was beating so loudly, I was sure everyone else could hear it.

It was Daphne's turn to clear her throat. "So, you might stay here in Redemption then?"

Aiden's eyes didn't leave mine, even though he answered Daphne. "I could. There's a couple of people who are willing to rent me a room if I want to stay."

"Well, that's great to hear," Daphne said, her head ping-ponging between us. "I think we'd all love to have you here longer." I didn't miss the sharp look she threw at Mia to keep her mouth shut. Mia wisely decided to stay out of it.

"I wouldn't mind staying myself," Aiden said, his gaze still boring into mine. I was having trouble breathing. "But the fact remains I do have an apartment in Riverview I'm paying rent on. So, I feel like I need to make a decision, as it doesn't really make sense to rent a room here if I'm continuing to pay rent in Riverview. So, do I stay here, or go?"

The words seemed to suck the air out of the room. I couldn't see anything but him, and my only thought was around the question he was clearly directing to me.

Did *I* want him to stay?

And that was the problem. I didn't know.

On one hand, I absolutely didn't want him to leave. I considered him a good friend, especially considering everything he did to help me over the past few months. I looked forward to him coming over every night for dinner. If he returned to Riverview, it was possible I might never see him again.

But if he stayed … the question in his eyes was clear. He wasn't asking for a continuation of friendly nightly dinners with other people. He wanted something more.

And I wasn't sure I was ready to give it to him.

Nobody said a word. I could hear the silence pounding in my ears. Everyone was waiting for me to say something.

I just had no idea what.

My mouth was so dry, I wasn't sure if I *could* even get a word out. I licked my lips, my brain scrambling to come up with something … anything. I opened my mouth and …

The doorbell rang.

Everyone started. "Are you expecting someone?" Mia asked me.

I shook my head. "No. I guess that means you aren't either."

"Unless Chrissy forgot her key again," Mia said, getting to her feet. "I'll get it."

"You don't have to …" I started, but Mia had already left the room. I looked back at Aiden and Daphne and gave them an awkward smile. "It's probably the media. They're still hanging around, unfortunately."

"Well, they should be gone soon," Daphne said, her eyes still darting between Aiden and me. Aiden had straightened up and retrieved his fork, but he wasn't using it to eat. Instead, he was mindlessly tapping it against the side of his plate.

I could hear Mia's voice speaking to whoever was out there, but I couldn't make out any specific words. Whoever it was, though, seemed quite incessant. After a moment, I heard Mia's footsteps behind me. "Ah … there's been a development."

Another one? The first "development" wasn't going very well, and I didn't think I could handle a second in one night. I turned around in my seat. "What sort of development …" my voice trailed off.

Daniel, standing directly behind Mia.

Chapter 3

"What are you doing here?"

My voice was sharper than I intended, but seriously, what WAS he doing in my home? He was the one who wanted a break. He was the one who kept telling me to stop contacting him when I had leads on Mia. So why show up now? Especially in a pair of tight jeans and a dark-blue button-down shirt that emphasized his broad chest and brought out the blue in his eyes.

I always loved it when he wore blue.

But never mind that. He shouldn't be in my kitchen at all, much less wearing an outfit he would have worn not that long ago on one of our dates. Especially after I'd spent so much time convincing myself it was time to move on.

His eyes swept around the room, lingering a little too long on Aiden. "I'm here because I'm hoping you can help us. There's been an … incident."

Mia's gaze sharpened. "What kind of incident?"

"One of the Church of the Forgotten members is dead."

"Dead?" I burst out, unable to contain myself. My emotions were already stretched like a taunt wire inside, and it wouldn't take much to make it snap. "Seriously? You're calling someone's death an *incident?*"

Daniel's eyes shifted to mine. "It's complicated."

"*Complicated?*" My voice rose higher, and I wrestled with myself to get my emotions under control. Stupid concussion. It made everything worse.

Daniel's eyes were hooded, now. "If you let me explain, it will make more sense."

"Of course," Daphne said quickly, giving me a quick sideways glance before looking pointedly to Mia, who quickly got the hint and jumped to her feet while inviting Daniel to sit.

"Do you want something to drink or eat?" Mia asked. "There's beer and wine."

"And plenty of food," Daphne added.

Daniel's eyes swept across the table as he took a seat. "Water would be great, thanks."

I looked at my water glass, wondering if it was why Daniel refused a drink. And then I wondered why it mattered.

"So, what's going on?" Daphne asked as Mia got him his water, a plate, and silverware.

Daniel leaned back in his chair, as if it were old times … just hanging out and shooting the breeze like we used to. "Before I get into that, how closely have you been following the Church of the Forgotten case?"

"Why?" Aiden's voice was sharp. His fingers were tensely clutched around his beer.

Daniel stared at him, his eyes narrowing slightly. I could almost see his cop face sliding into place. "Because I need to know how much background to get into." His tone sounded more like a cop, as well—flat and professional. Still, it fell short of completely masking the iciness that frosted each word.

Daphne shifted forward, as if instinctually trying to insert her body between them despite the table. "We've been following it, as you might imagine, but not that closely. Our focus has been helping Mia and Becca heal."

Something unreadable flickered in Daniel's eyes. "That should be the priority." He glanced over at Mia, careful not to look at me. "How is it going? You both look much better."

"We're good," Mia said. "Slower recovery than we'd like, but isn't that the way it goes? Becca's is a little slower than mine, even, because of her concussion."

Daniel finally faced me. "What about your ankle?" His tone was perfunctory, like he was asking about the weather as opposed to actually being concerned about my welfare.

My spine stiffened as I straightened up, and I made an effort to keep my tone as flat as his. "Better than the concussion. I don't need crutches anymore."

He stared at me, an unreadable expression flickering in his eyes. But before I could figure out what it was, Aiden interrupted, banging his bottle down on the table. Hard. "To answer your question, let's start from the beginning."

Daniel jerked his head toward Aiden, his cop face instantly back. For a moment, the two men stared at each other, the faintest touch of hostility simmering between them before Daniel started to speak.

"The investigation has turned into … well, let's just say it's taken on a life of its own. Between processing all the former church members and combing through every inch of the Hoffman Farm, it's been a massive undertaking. And the more we dig into it all, the more questions we encounter. Unfortunately, we're not getting a lot of help from the former members, so it's become an uphill battle."

"What aren't the former members telling you?" Mia asked. "The Church of the Forgotten is dead, right? Eleanor is gone. Isn't it over?"

Daniel let out a tired sigh as he scrubbed at his face. I could see the faint stubble on his chin and cheeks and the dark circles that had started forming under his eyes. I wondered when the last time was that he shaved or had a decent night's sleep. Or a decent meal, for that matter. My hands itched to load up the empty plate in front of him with food, but I restrained myself, and then wondered again why I cared.

We weren't dating anymore. If he wasn't taking care of himself, it wasn't my problem. Not anymore.

"That's the problem," Daniel said. "It's *not* over."

It felt like a punch to the gut. All my nightmares roared to life in my head. I could almost feel that strange, dark entity that spent its night in my bedroom now settling itself into a shadowed corner of the kitchen, watching us as it chuckled. *You didn't think you'd get rid of me that easily, did you?*

Mia appeared to have been plagued with similar nightmares, as all the blood drained from her face. Her eyes were haunted as she stared at Daniel, her mouth and jaw working, but no sounds coming out.

Daphne glanced worriedly between us. "What do you mean, it's not over?"

Mia licked her lips and tried again. "Are you saying Eleanor is …"

Daniel quickly held up a hand, interrupting her. "I'm not saying anything like that at all. We have uncovered no evidence that suggests Eleanor didn't die in that fire."

From the corner of my eye, I saw Mia sag slightly in her seat, but I found myself stuck on Daniel's careful wording. No evidence that she *didn't* die in the fire? Did that mean there also wasn't any evidence that she DID?

"Although," Daniel continued before I could ask him more questions about Eleanor. "It might be easier if she was still alive."

"Seriously?" Mia's voice was exasperated, but there was a tinge of something else in it … something that sounded a bit like hysteria. "For what purpose? So you can try her and send her to jail? Don't you have enough cases to worry about other than this one?" She flapped her hands as she talked, her volume rising with every word. "Zelda is fine. She's *fine*. We got a happy ending. Why in the world should the taxpayers pay for her jail cell …"

"Eleanor wasn't the only one involved in Zelda's kidnapping." Daniel's voice was quiet, but it cut through Mia's rapidly devolving tirade. She immediately stopped talking, but her breathing was still too shallow and fast. I reached over to squeeze her shoulder, both to help calm her and to catch her, if she started to faint.

"There were others involved," he continued in the same quiet-but-commanding tone, though his expression softened as he watched Mia. "The ones who took care of her. The ones who brought her back when she escaped. That wasn't just Eleanor. Zelda identified some of them, but not all. And let's not forget about Pamela. Someone killed her and put her body in the woods. We need to find whoever is responsible for that."

"But the Church of the Forgotten is dissolved, right? Eleanor is gone, so what does it matter anymore?" As soon as the words were out of Mia's mouth, she winced. "Okay, that sounded awful. And it's not what I meant. I meant, even if someone other than Eleanor killed Pamela and kidnapped Zelda, they did it because Eleanor told them to. They were following orders. And with Eleanor and the Church of the Forgotten gone, there would be no reason for that person to kill or kidnap anyone else."

"Are you sure about that?" Daniel asked, his voice grave. "There's been another murder, after all."

Mia blanched. "Sorry," she muttered. "I ... the thought that Eleanor may still be alive gives me the creeps." Her mouth twisted into what I think was supposed to be a reassuring smile, but it wasn't at all. I found myself wondering again what haunted her dreams night after night. She hadn't seemed that scared of Eleanor when we were at the Church of the Forgotten together, but we also hadn't since discussed what happened there. Maybe she was hiding more than she let on.

"Do you think it's related?" Daphne asked. "That the same person who killed Pamela also killed the Church member?"

"And kidnapped Zelda?" I added.

"Unfortunately, we have no idea," Daniel said.

"You have no idea?" Aiden repeated, raising an eyebrow. "I find that hard to believe."

Daniel glanced at him, his expression unreadable. "Be that as it may, it's the truth."

Aiden narrowed his eyes as he met Daniel's stare. "How can that be when you have them all in custody?"

"Custody?" Daphne asked, looking between the two men. "The entire Church of the Forgotten?"

A muscle jumped in Daniel's jaw. "They aren't in custody."

A small smile touched Aiden's lips, but it didn't reach his eyes. "Oh, so they can leave Redemption at any time?"

Daniel's eyes hardened. "It's very common for us to ask people involved in ongoing investigations not to leave the area. The members of the Church of the Forgotten are not any different."

Aiden snorted. "Oh, is that what you call locking a group of people up with around-the-clock police guards? My mistake."

Bewildered, I looked between the two. "What are you talking about? You've arrested the Church members?"

"We haven't arrested anyone," Daniel said. His tone was neutral, but I got the impression he was gritting his teeth.

Aiden sat back and folded his arms across his chest. "Oh, so you're holding them without due process?"

"We're not holding them at all," Daniel said. "We did offer them a place to stay …"

Aiden raised an eyebrow. "You *offered* them a place to stay?"

"What exactly would you have us do?" Daniel asked, his tone still mild despite the tension radiating off of him. "They don't have money, or identification, or a physical address. Most of them are refusing to give us their legal name or even a family member to contact. And we're in the middle of an investigation of a crime, so the last thing we want is for them to disappear. So, yes, we offered them a place to stay until we can get this sorted out and they can get back on their feet."

"That still doesn't give you the right to withhold due process," Aiden said.

"That's true, which is why we aren't," Daniel said. "They aren't under arrest."

"No, they're simply under twenty-four-hour supervision by the police," Aiden said sarcastically.

Daphne stared at Daniel. "Is that true? You have the members under twenty-four-hour supervision? And someone was still murdered?"

Daniel pressed his lips together. "It's true we have been actively policing the area, but again, they are not under arrest. We have cops in the building at all times, but that was supposed to be for their safety." Daniel held up a hand. "I know how that sounds. Obviously, that wasn't effective in preventing this new situation. The officers watching should have been more … observant."

"Well, that's an understatement," Mia muttered.

Either everything was moving faster than normal, or my brain still needed a lot more healing. I held up a hand, hoping to slow down the conversation long enough for me to catch up. "Hold on. What area? I'm still not clear where you're keeping them."

Daniel sighed. "As they were all asked to remain in Redemption, we temporarily opened the community center for them ... at least until the end of the investigation. It was supposed to be temporary. Now, I don't know what we're going to do."

I stared stupidly at Daniel. "You put them in the community center? But there's like forty people. How do they all fit?"

"We've set up cots. Basically, we're treating it like we would a natural disaster," Daniel said. "I agree it's not ideal. But again, they don't have money or a place to stay. So, what else are we going to do with them?"

"And they are being guarded?" Daphne asked.

Daniel flashed a glare at Aiden before answering. "We have a police presence, yes, but they aren't under arrest. They're allowed to come and go. There are a lot of them in a very small area, though, and they may or may not have been involved in a kidnapping and murder. So, we are of course going to keep an eye on them."

What Daniel said made sense. The police should be watching the Church of the Forgotten members, and not just for what they had done, but for what they were planning to do—force Zelda to kill another child, all to try and "resurrect" a sociopathic ten-year-old who died nearly a hundred and fifty years ago.

But I could also see Aiden's point, as it did feel like something of a workaround to formally arresting the members. Although, considering one of their members was dead, they probably should have all been put in jail.

"Who was murdered?" Mia asked, seemingly having the same thoughts.

"She went by the name Edna," Daniel said.

Edna. It sounded so familiar. I felt like I should know who she was, but my mind remained blank.

Mia, however, didn't seem to have that issue. She jerked straight up in her chair like a live wire had touched her. "Edna? The person in charge of the laundry?"

Now, I remembered her. I had spoken to her several times when trying to locate my clothes that had mysteriously disappeared. I pictured her stick-straight, mousy brown hair, mud-brown eyes, and bony face as she repeatedly insisted that she had only taken clothes that were dirty, so she could wash them. She had even asked why I would possibly want to wear dirty clothes. She had frustrated me to no end, and I never was sure if she truly didn't understand or was simply pretending to be clueless. Regardless, she sure didn't deserve to be murdered.

"That's her," Daniel said. His mouth had flattened again. "I don't suppose you know her real name?"

"No one knows anyone's real name," Mia said. "Talking about our legal names was expressly forbidden. They called it your 'temporary name,' just to drive home the importance of forgetting your real identity."

Daniel bobbed his head in a faint nod. "Yes, a few of them talked about temporary names and seemed almost fearful of sharing anything but the name they were given at the church."

Mia's face was still paler than it should have been. "You have no idea how much of a head game it was, to be stripped of your name. Between that and the lack of sleep, food, and constant work …" she scrubbed at her face. "Sorry."

Daniel kept his expression neutral as he studied Mia, but there was a tinge of compassion in his eyes. "I'm the one who's sorry to bring up the bad memories. I wish there was another way. By now, I had hoped that at least some of the church members would have started trusting us and given us something to investigate, but with Edna's murder, everything has changed."

"Yeah, I know. I get it," Mia said. She gave her face one last scrub before straightening her spine. "What do you need to know?"

"What can you tell me about her?" He glanced at me. "Both of you?"

"Unfortunately, not much," Mia said. "She mostly kept to herself, although Becca had some dealings with her." Mia's mouth quirked up in a half-smile.

Even though I knew she was teasing, it still hit me the wrong way. The anger I had felt that day thinking Mia had deserted me was not something I wanted to joke about. I found myself scowling at her. "Not by choice. Although …" I winced at how crass that sounded and tried to soften it. "I am sorry she's dead. She didn't deserve that."

"What happened?" Daniel asked as he felt around in his pocket for his ever-present notebook and little pen.

"She took my clothes and wouldn't give them back." I cringed as soon as the words left my mouth. I sounded ridiculous.

Daniel raised an eyebrow. "She did what?"

I let out a deep sigh as I explained how all my clothes had suddenly gone missing, and I was forced to wear the Church of the Forgotten's signature dresses.

"Did you ever get them back?" Daniel asked as he furiously scribbled.

"No. Nor my suitcase or cell phone. I'm assuming they went up in flames." Eleanor had burned the main building down, presumably because that was where her offices were and she wanted to protect her records. But the laundry room was also located in that building, so I figured my personal belongings were gone for good.

"Probably, but I can check the evidence room," Daniel said, making a note. "We did recover a few things, and it's possible your items are there."

"Although they may not be in any shape to ever wear again," Mia said, wrinkling her nose. "Between the smoke and fire and who knows what else, that is."

Mia had a point. And even if they were salvageable, would I even want them back? I was having a difficult enough time convincing myself that no dark entity had followed me home. Wearing an item of clothing that had been in the belly of the beast for weeks and weeks? Not likely. "That's okay," I said to Daniel. "Mia's right. And it's not like I brought all that much with me, so it's fine."

Daniel eyed me. "If you're sure."

"I'm sure."

Daniel scribbled something down. "Do either of you know if Edna was a part of Eleanor's inner circle?"

Mia and I looked at each other. "No idea," I said. "But it seems … improbable."

Daniel raised his head to look at me. "Improbable? Why is that?"

In my mind, I could see Edna again, her expression confused as she kept asking me why I would want to wear dirty clothes. "She just didn't seem like the sharpest tool in the toolbox. Not that I'm trying to speak ill of the dead."

Daniel glanced at Mia.

"Again, I didn't interact with her much, but I can see Becca's point," Mia said. "I would also add that she had a tendency to get … hyper-focused on things, even to the detriment of everything else. It made trying to have a conversation with her … challenging. So, with all of that in mind, if I had to guess who was in Eleanor's inner circle, Edna would be pretty far down the list. But honestly, I'm not sure I even could guess. Eleanor was always careful not to play favorites and to talk to everyone equally."

Daniel frowned as he wrote something down.

"Is that why you think Edna was murdered?" I asked. "Because she was in Eleanor's inner circle?"

Daniel paused, but only for a moment before sliding his notebook onto the corner of the table. "Maybe not her inner circle. But yes, we do think Edna was killed because of something she knew."

Chapter 4

Killed because of something she knew? I kept picturing Edna's sharp, pinched face as she argued with me, and I just couldn't see it.

That same disbelief was mirrored in Mia's eyes. "What could Edna possibly have known that would have gotten her killed?"

Daniel sighed as he rubbed the back of his neck. "That's what we're trying to figure out."

"I'm not following," I said. "You don't know what she knew? Then why do you think she was killed over it?"

"As I said earlier, we've been questioning the Church of the Forgotten members about Zelda and Pamela. Nearly all of them have claimed they don't know anything … they were just busy doing their job, so they could create a better life free from the stress and overwhelm of modern society," Daniel said, making a slight face. "It's more or less the same script from all of them. In some cases, the exact same words."

"Like it's a script they memorized," I said.

Daniel nodded. "Exactly. That's why it's been so difficult to investigate."

"But Edna said something different?" Mia asked.

"Not at first," Daniel said. "Initially, she sounded like the rest of them. It wasn't until later that she approached one of the officers on site. She told him she had something she wanted to tell us. The officer asked her what it was, but she refused to tell him … said she wanted to tell the cop who initially interviewed her. She couldn't remember his name, and the officer she was talking to didn't know it either. He was …" Daniel's jaw tightened. "He hadn't been on the job long. Anyway, in the middle of him trying to figure out who she spoke to, Edna got spooked and changed her mind. It was late, and the officer didn't pursue it. He figured he would find the cop who did the initial interview in the morning, and he could then contact Edna to see if she would talk to him."

"I'm guessing by the time that happened, Edna was dead," Aiden said.

Daniel's face was like stone. "Unfortunately, that is correct."

Mia's expression was full of disbelief. "Seriously? He just let her go? Didn't even keep an eye on her?"

"To be fair, he's supposed to keep an eye on everyone, not just her," Daniel said. "But yes, he should have made different choices."

"Why *didn't* he keep a closer eye on her?" I asked. "Was he really that busy?"

"Partially," Daniel said. "But I got the sense he didn't ... take her seriously. What you said about her how she came across ... I think that might have played into what happened."

Now I felt a pang of guilt along with sadness that her life was cut short. She certainly wasn't the easiest person to get along with, but she definitely shouldn't have been killed.

Again, Mia seemed to share my thoughts. "Poor Edna," she said, shaking her head. "Such a shame."

"It is sad," Daphne said. "And you think it happened because she was going to tell you something?"

"Well, I think it would have to be a pretty big coincidence, if that wasn't the case. She was murdered just a few hours after telling one of the officers she had some information," Daniel said.

Daphne gnawed at her bottom lip. "It WOULD be a big coincidence," she agreed. "But you just said the officer in charge didn't take her all that seriously. Did she actually say she had information about Pamela or Zelda?"

"She wanted to speak to the person who interviewed her," Daniel said. "We were also spending a lot of time talking with them ... keeping them updated on the investigation and just chatting in general. We were trying to make them feel more comfortable with us, in the hopes they would finally say something."

"Was it working?" Aiden asked.

"Building trust is never fast or easy," Daniel said, inferring a "no." "But it did seem like we were making some headway, at least with a few of them. Of course, now that's gone. If anyone was willing to talk, they're definitely not anymore." His mouth twisted into a frown.

I was starting to wonder if the cops actually had anything at all, or if this case was destined to forever remain unsolved. "Was Edna one of the ones who was opening up?"

He nodded. "It seemed so. She talked about her job, the laundry, and how important it was ..." he flipped back in his notebook, searching for the right page. "And how she was basically completely in charge of it, which meant she had a great deal of responsibility. She didn't want to let Eleanor down."

"So that's why you thought she might be in Eleanor's inner circle," I said.

He inclined his head. "She also talked about how she knew things. About the things people would say in front of the 'invisible people.'"

"I'm assuming she considered herself one of the invisible people," I said.

"She didn't say it like that, but yeah, that's what we thought," Daniel said, sitting back in his chair. "There was some speculation that Eleanor might have used her as a spy of sorts. If people were ignoring the person who was in charge of the laundry, maybe they would be more likely to let something slip."

A cold shiver ran down my spine. All I could think about was Gertrude, the zealot who had disliked me the moment she met me, and what she had said when I had first met her:

The Forgotten are the ones with all the power, you see. No one thinks we do, though ... that's why they ignore and overlook us. But The One sees us. The One knows what we're capable of. That's why we serve The One.

"It's possible she meant that," I said slowly. "But it's also possible she was talking about what it meant to be a part of the Church of the Forgotten."

Daniel looked at me in surprise before clicking his pen absentmindedly. "What do you mean?"

"I was thinking the same thing," Mia said. Her eyes had a haunted look to them, and I wondered if mine did, as well. "That she was making a bigger statement about why she had joined the Church in the first place."

"It's the forgotten aspect of the Church of the Forgotten," I said softly as Daniel opened his mouth, probably to ask his question a second time.

Mia nodded. "They believed they were part of the overlooked, forgotten part of society. Much like Lily." Lily was the name of a ten-year-old girl who, back in 1887, had killed another ten-year-old girl. The townspeople were so horrified by Lily's actions, they burned her at the stake. Because of that, many believed the townspeople were cursed, which is why they all disappeared roughly six months later.

"So, the name of the church was a way to honor Lily?" Daniel asked.

"Not exactly," I said. "It's more about the concept of power. Society forgot about them, so it was assumed they didn't have any power. But that's actually not true. They are more powerful than anyone realizes, *because* they are constantly overlooked."

"*The One sees us,*" Mia murmured. "*That's why we serve The One.*"

Cold shivers ran down my spine again, and I folded my arms across my chest.

"That's creepy," Daphne said, reaching for her wine and taking a long sip.

Even Daniel looked a little uneasy. "So, you think Edna might have been talking about her life before she joined the church?"

"It's certainly possible," I said. "Of course, knowing the context of why she said it would help. I don't suppose that's in your notes."

Daniel flipped the pages back. "Not exactly, but I didn't jot down everything. Just a few key highlights. Or what I thought were key. I'll have to go back to the original notes from the interviews."

"Maybe we should review them as well," I said.

Daniel threw me a sharp look, and I bristled. I could practically see his brain turning with all the objections he was undoubtedly getting ready to make.

"She's right," Mia said before Daniel could figure out which objection to voice first. "We might see something you wouldn't recognize, since you weren't a part of that culture."

"And it doesn't sound like any other member is helping you," I added.

Daniel pressed his lips together in a flat line. "I'll see what I can do."

I blinked in surprise. I was sure he would find all sorts of reasons why it was a bad idea. From the beginning of our relationship, he hadn't been keen on my getting involved in any official investigations. Although, to be fair, at the end of the day, if I insisted I wanted to be part of one, he would generally keep me in the loop.

For some reason, that thought made my chest ache.

"While you're at it," Mia said. "Maybe we should look at *all* your notes, not just the ones on Edna. Just to be sure nothing was missed."

Daniel gave her a look. "I'll see about that." His tone wasn't convincing.

"Well, if you want to find out what happened to Edna, I would think you'd use every resource available to you," Mia said.

Daniel grimaced. "Noted."

Mia gave him a sweet smile that disappeared a breath later. "How did … how did she die?" She swallowed hard.

Daniel's expression turned back to stone. "She was found in the alley behind the community center. There was blunt force trauma to the back of her head and … she was strangled."

My eyes widened. "That's horrible."

Daniel's eyes shifted to mine. "I'm hoping she didn't suffer. The medical examiner's initial findings were that she was likely knocked unconscious before she was strangled."

"That would be a small blessing," I murmured, which, while true, did nothing to dislodge the terrible picture of Edna lying dead in the alley from my head.

"The back of the alley?" Aiden asked. "You didn't have any officers watching that area?"

Daniel stiffened slightly. "Believe it or not, this isn't our only case. The police department is stretched thin as it is. Which is why we had cameras installed—"

"Cameras?" Aiden's jaw dropped. "You have cameras there, but you don't know what happened to Edna?"

"There's only one in the alley," Daniel said. "The rest are installed around the perimeter and inside. We're reviewing all of them, but it seems that whoever killed Edna was either aware of the cameras, or lucky."

Of course that would be the case. Nothing could be easy.

"So you've got nothing?" Daphne asked flatly.

"Nothing helpful," Daniel said.

"What about the other cameras?" I asked. "Did they show anything?"

"We're reviewing the footage now," Daniel said. Then, he cleared his throat. "Which is also turning out to be more of a challenge than you would think. As it turns out, most of the church members are careful to avoid the cameras."

"What do you mean?" Aiden asked.

"Somehow, they found the areas that aren't covered by the cameras, and that's where they spend most of their time," Daniel said. "And if they do happen to be where the cameras are, they hide their faces … either by covering their heads or keeping their eyes down. We didn't even realize this was happening until we started going through the footage to see what happened to Edna."

Aiden was staring at Daniel in amazement. "You didn't know? Wasn't anyone monitoring the cameras? Or were you just too busy for that, too?"

Daniel's expression was neutral, but his eyes narrowed slightly. "It's not as simple as you might think. Yes, we noticed they kept their heads down, but that wasn't out of character with how they handle themselves overall. As a whole, they're quiet and reserved. They don't talk much, even to each other. They don't want television, even though we've supplied several, nor do they touch any of the computers."

"What do they do then?" I asked.

"They take walks," Daniel said. "A lot of walks. They—mostly the women—help with the cooking and cleanup. They spend a lot of time alone, in silence and in prayer." He shrugged. "I think a lot of us thought they were struggling with what happened to them. It would make sense if they were in shock or experiencing grief over what happened. Some of them have been in the Church for years and years. Facing the truth about what they were really a part of ... well, it has to be terrible, if they truly didn't know what was going on. Not to mention they've also now lost their way of life. That alone might be overwhelming to them, as they try to figure out how they're going to function in society moving forward. It's a lot to handle."

"So you've been giving them space to deal," Daphne said. She was leaning forward slightly, like she was trying to cut the tension between the two men who were staring at each other like predators sizing each other up. I wondered where the hostility was coming from. As far as I knew, Daniel and Aiden hadn't had much to do with each other, so why were they acting like nemeses?

Daniel was the one who moved first, shifting his gaze to Daphne. He smiled a little, but there was no warmth to it. "I wouldn't call it that, exactly. Yes, the upshot was we were giving them time to think things through, but that wasn't out of the kindness of our hearts. We *are* trying to solve a case, and I think we were all hoping that the ones who had a conscience, who maybe were uncomfortable with what was going on whether they fully realized it at the time or not, would finally come around and tell us what they knew."

"It sounds like it might have worked," I said. "At least with Edna."

Daniel muttered something that sounded like a curse under his breath. "Yeah. Too bad it turned into an even bigger mess than it was. If anyone was considering talking to us, they definitely won't now. Everyone is avoiding us." His fingers tightened on his pen.

"Which is why you need us," Mia said.

"And we're happy to help," I added.

Daniel looked like he was doing everything he possibly could to keep from rolling his eyes.

What Wasn't Forgotten

Chapter 5

That night, I couldn't sleep.

The darkness seemed to press against me, like a living, breathing entity, pulsing with unnatural life.

My mind perpetually whirled with images of Edna. I could practically see her broken body in the alley, arms and legs bent at unnatural angles, her eyes glazed and lifeless ... staring at nothing but shadows that seemed to coalesce behind me, gathering together to leap upon me ...

I jerked in bed, clawing at my throat. I couldn't think, couldn't breathe. It was like the darkness had turned thick and muddy, and I was trying to breathe water, or maybe the earth itself, as tendrils slowly worked its way around my neck like a noose, tightening, tightening ...

The panic threatened to overcome me. The urge to run pulsed through my veins. Whatever was haunting the Hoffman Farm had clearly followed me home, and now it was here, in my bedroom, just biding its time until I lowered my guard so it could pounce ...

With a strangled cry, I rolled out of bed and scrambled to the door. I had to get out. Before it was too late.

My fingers clawed helplessly at the doorknob, unable to grasp it, to turn it, and I could feel my heart stop in my chest. I was locked in.

I was going to die.

I could feel the darkness approaching, whispering against my bare skin. I wanted to scream; I *tried* to scream, but managed nothing more than a pathetic whimper. I attacked the door like I was trying to tear it from its hinges. Suddenly, it flung open, and finally, I was out.

I didn't think, just ran down the hallway. I needed to get as far away from the darkness hiding in my room as possible, though I could feel it patiently waiting for my return.

I practically threw myself down the stairs, somehow managing to stay on my feet. From there, I skidded into the kitchen, my hand reaching desperately for the light switch.

Except there was no switch, only smoothness beneath my hand where the light switch should be.

Wildly, I glanced around the room. Was I remembering it wrong? Had I come in the wrong door? Was I losing my mind?

I couldn't see a thing. The kitchen was shrouded in darkness, illuminated only by the pale-gray from slip of moonlight filtering through the window.

It only served to highlight the shadows.

Shadows.

My eyes flickered across the kitchen as an icy cold tendril trailed down my spine. I tried to tell myself that shadows were normal. There were large appliances in the kitchen, along with furniture and the kitchen island; of course they would cast shadows.

There was nothing strange about that.

Nothing at all.

Except ... one of the kitchen chairs didn't seem right. It was bigger than it should have been. Or maybe it was just the back of the chair that made it look like someone (or something) was sitting in it, hunched over, like they were trying to hide ...

"Hello, Becca."

I let out a little scream at the sound of the male voice. The shadow had started to unfold itself, to straighten up and face me. I could only watch in horror, my legs frozen in place, my feet glued to the floor, like I was trapped in a dream and couldn't move.

But I wasn't in a dream. I had been awake in my bedroom before the entity chased me out.

Hadn't I?

The shadow extended an arm. "Why don't you come sit down?" The voice was gravely, as if it were speaking through a mouth full of sand.

I had no intention of sitting anywhere near that ... that *thing*, but my body seemed to have other ideas. My legs carried me forward on their own accord, and I found myself settling down into a chair.

This had to be a dream. Because if it wasn't ... no, I wasn't even going there.

"Who are you, and what are you doing in my house?" My voice was thin and reedy, the exact opposite of how I intended to sound.

The shadow tilted its head. At least, I thought that's what it was doing. "I live here. Same as you."

My mouth dropped open, and I stifled another scream.

Dear lord, my biggest fear had come true. I *did* drag that evil entity home with me, and now, I was going to have to figure out how to get rid of it.

I tried to wet my dry lips with my tongue, but every drop of moisture seemed to have evaporated from my mouth. "You are not welcome in my house."

There was a low rumble from the shadow that sounded like a chuckle. "Alas, I'm not a vampire, but nice try." There was a note of amusement in the voice.

"You're still not welcome," I insisted. "I wish you would leave."

"Unfortunately, that's not up to you. Or me. Someone else made that choice for both of us." There was no trace of humor in the voice anymore. Just bitterness.

"Who?"

The shadow didn't immediately answer. Instead, it just cocked its head again, staring at me. I could almost make out a pair of eyes in the smoky haze that appeared to be its face.

"A storm is coming."

It felt like the air had been punched out of my lungs. "What did you say?"

"You heard me."

The longer I sat there, the more the wisps of smoke came together to form the shape of a man. I could see the faint lines of high cheekbones and a firm jaw. "But that can't be. The Church of the Forgotten is dismantled."

I was sure I could see lips stretch across the shadow's face. "You sure about that?"

I tried to suck in air, but my lungs refused to cooperate. Even though I was freezing, a bead of sweat had gathered near my hairline. "What are you saying?" My voice was barely above a whisper.

"I think you know."

"But how do you know?"

"I know lots of things, Becca. You could, too. If you were willing to pay the price."

The sweat started to drip down my face, leaving a trail of ice in its wake. There was something dark in the voice, though I couldn't tell if it was a threat or a promise.

The shadow tilted its head yet again. "What? No questions? Wouldn't you like to know the truth, Becca? Wouldn't you like to have all the secrets finally revealed?"

That darkness in the voice ... there was something wrong with it. Something ... evil. Just hearing it made my skin crawl.

And yet ... it was strangely seductive, as well.

I knew I had to get away. But I couldn't move. I couldn't breathe.

"Who *are* you?" I finally managed.

The shadow lifted its arms and placed its hands flat on the table. It leaned forward, closer to me, so close I could smell ... something. Something dry and dusty, like ashes. It opened its mouth, and I glimpsed a hint of pointed teeth as it hissed at me. "Your worst nightmare."

I awoke with a gasp, the sheet wrapped around my chest so tight, it felt like a steel band.

A storm is coming.

No! I squeezed my eyes shut as tightly as I could. There was no storm coming. We had headed it off. Zelda was safe, and the Church of the Forgotten was disbanded. Never mind there was another murder of a member. That had nothing to do with what Aunt Charlie and Louise and Daphne's mother Claire had called into existence.

Lily could not be reborn. It was over.

In my mind's eye, I saw the shadow sitting in front of me, the wisps of smoke knitting into the shape of a man.

You sure about that?

Enough. I was being ridiculous. I had a bad dream. That was it. It didn't mean anything. And if the dream seemed different from my other dreams—more intense, more *real*—that didn't mean anything either. I was recovering from a concussion, for goodness' sake, not to mention all the stress I had been under. No wonder I was having terrible dreams.

But that's all it was. A dream.

It was almost morning. I could see the edges of the sun on the horizon and a bit of clear blue sky. Not a cloud in sight.

It was only a dream.

Oscar was lying next to me on the pillow, his green eyes blinking as he watched me unwrap the sheet and shakily get to my feet.

Coffee. Coffee would make it better. Coffee makes everything better.

I plucked my robe off the floor. It must have fallen off the chair at some point in the night. Even though it was still technically fall, it was cold in the early mornings and late at night. Oscar stretched and hopped off the bed, padding his way to the door. He sat down and gave me an expectant look.

I stood corrected. Apparently, coffee and feeding the cat would make everything better.

As soon as I opened my bedroom door, I could smell coffee, which either meant Chrissy or Mia was already up, or I *really* wanted coffee. Oscar prowled next to me as I headed down the hall and toward the kitchen, the scent growing stronger.

Someone had to be up. There was no way this was in my head.

Sure enough, it was Mia. She was sitting at the table, her head bent over what looked like an untouched cup of coffee in front of her. Her black hair fell forward, covering her face but revealing the back of her slender neck, which seemed paler than normal. The first rays of the morning sun were starting to stream through the window, filling the kitchen with a warm, golden light, completely opposite from the darkness and shadows of my dream …

Stop it. Right now, I told myself. *I'm not dreaming anymore. I'm awake, and everything is fine.*

Still, a lump was forming in my throat.

"Good morning," I said briskly, determined to stop thinking about anything unpleasant and focus on the brand-new day in front of me instead.

Mia raised her head, blinking several times. "Hey. Sleep well?"

"As well as could be expected," I said, breezing past her and into the kitchen. Oscar kept a sharp eye on me, no doubt making sure my priorities were straight as to who got taken care of first. "You?"

"Same." The way she said it made me think she'd slept about as well as I had. She also didn't sound like she wanted to talk about it any more than I did.

A storm is coming.

I pushed that thought aside again and turned my attention to Oscar's breakfast.

"I still can't get my head around Edna being murdered," Mia said, one hand creeping forward to play with the edge of her cup. With her head up, her hair had fallen more or less back in her customary short bob, but I could see that it was starting to get a little shaggy as it lost its shape. I unconsciously reached up to touch my own mane of messy, brownish-blondish, curly frizz and thought I perhaps needed to make my own appointment with a hair stylist.

"I know. It's especially odd to think she was killed for something she knew." I plucked a mug out of the cupboard and filled it with coffee before fetching the cream and sugar.

"*If* that's what she was killed for," Mia said, her voice dark.

I eyed her as I doctored my coffee, but Mia was staring at the table with glazed and unfocused eyes. "What else would it be?"

She didn't answer until I had finished with my coffee and was seated in front of her. She was still playing with her mug, and as it was full of coffee, I hoped she didn't end up spilling it on herself. "She wasn't … liked."

I raised my brows over my own mug. "You think someone killed her because they didn't *like* her?"

Mia's eyes flicked up at me. "Stranger things have happened."

"That would be *really* strange."

"Not if ..." her voice trailed off. "Forget it."

I put my mug down. "No, I want to know what you're thinking."

"It's stupid." She gave her head a quick shake.

"I doubt it's stupid. We both know how screwed up that place was, and you were in there longer than me. Whatever you think is happening should be taken seriously."

Her lips quirked up in a tiny smile that didn't reach her eyes. "Yeah, but this is really stretching it."

"We're talking about a cult who thought they could resurrect a child who was killed over a hundred years ago."

She let out a small noise that might have been a chuckle. "Well, when you put it like that." Her fingers drummed against the mug for a moment. "I keep thinking about what Daniel asked us about ... whether Edna was in Eleanor's inner circle or not."

I looked at her in surprise. "You think she was?"

Mia twisted her mouth. "Not exactly. I suspect Eleanor's inner circle was pretty small, and Edna wouldn't have made the cut. But I do wonder if Eleanor wasn't ... protecting Edna somehow. And with Eleanor gone, Edna lost that protection."

"You think Edna needed protection?" An image of Edna asking me why I didn't want to wear clean clothes popped into my head. "Why? Did someone have a stain on her favorite muslin dress that Edna couldn't get out?"

Mia shot me a look. "I doubt it had anything to do with laundry."

"But that makes even less sense. Who would want to hurt Edna?" The image of Edna was replaced by one of Eleanor staring at me with her icy-blue eyes, and I shivered. "Not to mention, I don't see Eleanor as a big protector of anyone. She seems more likely to either throw someone to the wolves or simply let the wolves do what they want without interfering."

"Unless they have something she wants. Or needs," Mia said.

My eyes widened. "What are you talking about? She needed the cult members, and she treated them horribly. Not feeding them enough, or letting them sleep enough."

"That was so she could control them easier," Mia said. "And she never let it get bad enough for them to end up in the hospital."

I rolled my eyes. "That's hardly protecting them. That's just making sure they don't die."

Mia squared her shoulders. "All right then. What about Zelda? Or you?"

"Zelda? Me?" I wondered if I had heard her correctly. "How did she protect either of us?" I thought about Zelda, locked in a room under the barn. While it was true she had been physically taken care of, more or less, I wouldn't consider that "protecting." As for me, well …

"Did you forget she was going to take my house?" I asked.

"I didn't forget," Mia said. Her gaze was steady. "Did you forget all the things she did for you? Like taking you off weeding duty and putting you on sewing duty when you looked like you were about to keel over?"

"They needed someone to fill in," I argued. "Margot hurt herself."

"Are you sure about that?" Mia asked. "I heard some rumblings that it was all fake."

"Fake? You think Margot hurt her hand on purpose?"

"Why are you so convinced she hurt herself at all?" Mia asked. "Anyone can wrap a bandage on their hand and say they injured it."

I thought about the quiet afternoons sitting in the room sewing while Maude supervised me. Or organizing the room. Or in the kitchen talking to people. Was it possible she had been faking it? "But why would she pretend to be injured?"

"As I said, probably because you looked like you were about two seconds away from collapsing. If you had, Eleanor might have felt like she would have to let you leave, and she wasn't going to do that."

"But …" I still couldn't get my head around it. "How would she have known I could sew?"

"That was just luck. If you hadn't said anything, she still could have told Maude to train you, which was likely what she was about to do when you jumped in to volunteer."

I couldn't stop staring at Mia. "Even if that's true, it still doesn't prove she was protecting me."

"She gave you her name," Mia said. "Why would she possibly do that, except to protect you?"

I pursed my lips. All Church of the Forgotten members changed their names when they joined, but since the list of approved names wasn't very long, many had to choose variations of the approved names. However, that required special permission from whichever member had the name first. Eleanor had never allowed anyone to take any rendition of her name ... until me. "I agree it was ... weird. But I don't think it had anything to do with protecting me."

"Then why do you think she did it?"

I raised my hands. "Probably for the same reason she switched my chores. She wanted to keep me at the church and in her good graces, so she could get her hands on my house." As my house was on the land that had once belonged to Lily's family, Eleanor was desperate to acquire it.

Mia sat back in her chair and tapped her coffee mug thoughtfully. "Maybe 'protecting' is the wrong word. I'm sure all she was really protecting was her own best interest. She did what she could to keep you at the church and feeling indebted to her, so you would sign over your house without too much fuss. She took care of Zelda, at least physically, to get her through the Harvest. I'm thinking she might have been ... 'taking care' of Edna the same way."

"I'll buy that Eleanor *took care* of people she needed one way or another," I said. "But that still doesn't explain Edna. What would Edna have that Eleanor needed?"

Mia kept tapping her mug. "That's what I can't quite figure out. Other than Edna being some sort of spy for Eleanor, I don't know. But if that were the case, it makes a lot of sense. Eleanor is gone ... maybe Edna's conscience was prickling at her, and she was ready to talk."

An uneasy feeling settled around me like an old, worn cloak. "But if that's what happened, Edna was clearly a threat to someone other than Eleanor."

Mia continued to stare at me. "Can you think of another reason why Edna would be targeted?"

I shifted uncomfortably in my chair. "No. But you realize what this means, right?" I paused for a moment as the horrible thought sunk in. "It's not over."

Mia's eyes darkened, the expression inscrutable. "Did you really think it would be that easy?"

Chapter 6

For a moment, I couldn't move. Or even breathe.

A storm is coming.

Did this mean that the shadowy figure from my dream was right, and the Church of the Forgotten *wasn't* dead yet?

No, I refused to go there. It had to be over. All the members were being investigated, after all.

And yet ... Edna was murdered.

"Do you think ..." The words seemed to stick in my throat, so I downed some coffee and tried again. "Do you think someone is trying to revive it?"

Mia looked at me in horror. "Revive the Church of the Forgotten? No! Where did you get that idea from?"

I certainly didn't think now was the time to share my dream with her. "You just agreed it isn't over."

"Well, yeah, but I was talking about the members who were part of the kidnapping and murder." Mia's face looked even paler as she tightened her fingers around her mug. "They certainly seem willing to continue their criminal ways."

I was wondering if it was more than that. "Well, at least in order to protect their identity and secrets. And it might just be one or two members. You were the one who said you didn't think Eleanor's inner circle was that big, right?"

Mia didn't immediately answer. Instead, she got up again and headed to the sink with her still full mug. She dumped half of the coffee out, likely because it was cold. Then, she brought it and the coffeepot to the table, where she offered to refill my cup before fetching the cream and sugar.

"Right?" I asked again as I watched her busy herself.

She finally sat back down in front of me, focused on doctoring her coffee. Her eyes looked huge in her face. Finally, she spoke. "Do you remember that last night ... how shocked everyone was by the things you said?"

I blinked at the change of subject. "What does that have to do with Eleanor's inner circle?"

Her eyes finally flickered up to mine. "Even the men she was ordering to take you were surprised. I could tell they were blindsided."

"Well, it was pretty shocking, what she was planning," I said. "She was going to have her ten-year-old niece kill another ten-year-old. I suspect most of the members would object to that, so it made sense for her to not tell anyone until it was ... well, too late."

"But that's the point. What did she think would happen after this 'Harvest,' or whatever it was? All those people were going to witness this horrible thing. Did she really think everyone would just accept it? Simply say, 'Oh, okay ... that's what the Harvest is,' and go right back to their chores like nothing happened?"

Eleanor's plans for after the Harvest hadn't even occurred to me. I was far more concerned with stopping the Harvest and getting Zelda out of there.

But now that Mia had brought it up, I could see the discrepancy. Eleanor appeared to have been a meticulous planner, having controlled a number of people for many years. Why hadn't she thought through how most of her members would view the horror she was planning?

Unless ...

Mia was watching me, and she slowly nodded. "You see it now, don't you?"

"Maybe," I said, my voice hollow. "I can think of two possibilities, actually."

She sat back and cocked her head. "Go on."

"One is that she figured she would be successful resurrecting Lily." My mouth was still so dry. I picked up my mug to take a sip. "And that would give her access to all kinds of power ... in which case, it wouldn't even matter if the other members freaked out. She would have enough power to control and brainwash them."

Mia nodded again. "And the second?"

I wrapped my fingers around my mug, trying to ward off the deep chill I felt settling into my bones. "She knew they wouldn't care. Once they got over the initial shock, they simply wouldn't care."

Mia's mouth flattened. "Exactly."

As if flipping through a pile of photographs, images of the members flashed through my mind. Winnie. Margot. Trudy. I couldn't imagine they would have signed on for such horror.

But then, my brain shifted to Gertrude ... and Beatrice ... and Edward, the man who had shuttled me to and from the front gate. I could totally see them accepting whatever insanity Eleanor brought. Heck, I could even see them participating. Enthusiastically.

The question then became how many members were in the former group versus the latter. Before learning about Edna's death, I would have assumed the Gertrudes and Beatrices and Edwards were in the minority.

But now? I wasn't so sure.

"What do you think we should do?" I asked.

Mia picked up her coffee. "Why do you think I pushed for us to see the transcripts? Why do you think I wanted us to be a part of the case, even though I know Daniel is ... less than excited, to say the least, about having us involved?"

I slunk down a little in my chair. "You mean *me* involved."

Her eyes crinkled, but her mouth stayed flat. "I think you've managed to redeem yourself."

I wasn't so sure. While it was true I ended up being right, well mostly right, about the Church of the Forgotten, the fact that I put myself in danger to do it didn't sit right with many of the officers.

Including Daniel. Even if he hadn't actually said anything to me about it.

Not that he could. We weren't together anymore.

"I think a lot of folks may have wished I handled things a little differently," I admitted.

Mia wrinkled her nose. "You saved Zelda. And you did it without killing anyone else, including yourself. I would say that's a win, no matter how you look at it."

I couldn't argue with that.

She took a sip of coffee, still watching me over the top of the mug. "Speaking of Daniel …"

"I didn't realize we were speaking of Daniel," I said. Actually, it may have been closer to a snap. Which wasn't exactly necessary. I winced and picked up my cup. "Sorry. Probably just need more caffeine."

Mia didn't seem all that perturbed. In fact, she looked almost … amused. "Well, he is a part of this investigation, and if he gets permission for us to review the transcripts, that probably means we're going to be spending more time with him."

My heart did a strange flutter in my chest, which made no sense. He had made his feelings known. I made a point out of shrugging—so much so, I nearly spilled my coffee. "So?"

Mia hadn't stopped watching me, that amused glint still in her eyes. "Well, it just might get a little … awkward, don't you think?"

"Why would it be awkward?"

Mia's expression shifted, and she looked at me like I was an idiot. Or pretending to be one. "Because of Aiden."

Rather than skipping a beat, my heart seemed to sink in my chest. "Aiden? What does he have to do with anything?" I tried to be flippant, but I could feel a weight settling over me.

Mia stared at me. "Oh, come on! Becca, you can't be that obtuse. You must have seen how he looks at you."

I played with my coffee cup. "We're friends. Nothing more."

She snorted. "That may be what you are now, but I'm sure he wants something more."

"Maybe. But he hasn't said anything."

"Well, he's trying to," Mia said. "He basically said he was going to leave Redemption … unless you stop him."

I looked away, my mouth tasting like it was full of ashes. I didn't want Aiden to move. He was my friend. He was one of the few people who supported me and believed in me over the past couple of months. I didn't think I would be here today if it wasn't for him.

But dating him? Especially with my track record? I didn't want to chance it. I'd already lost so many people. I didn't want to lose him, as well.

At the same time, I had a terrible feeling I would lose him no matter what I did.

"I'm not ready," I said. "I just broke up with Daniel. I don't need a rebound relationship."

Mia's expression was unreadable as she took another sip of coffee. "I know breaking up is painful," she said carefully. "Especially when you are the one who is ... well, dumped."

I huffed a breath through my nose. "Thanks for being so understanding."

"It's not that I'm not understanding ... it's the truth. Right?"

I glowered at her as an answer.

"Well," she continued, looking like she was trying to hide a smile. "What I'm trying to say is, I get it. I know it can take a while. But ... it has been over a couple of months since you two broke up ..."

"You just said it could take a while," I said.

She held up a hand. "I did. But Becca, Aiden is living in a hotel room. And he's only still there because he doesn't want to push you into making a decision, what with your concussion and everything that's been going on. But you and I both know that's not fair to him. If he doesn't have a chance with you, you need to tell him, so he can move on."

I slumped in my chair, suddenly completely exhausted. "I don't know what I want. Well, that's not true. I want him to stay. I know that."

Mia looked at me with knowing eyes. "But do you want to date him?"

I didn't have an answer.

In my mind, I could see us standing in front of the gate of the Church of the Forgotten. I had just finished talking to Jeb in the car and was preparing to go back inside to find Zelda. Aiden hadn't wanted me to; he thought it was too dangerous. He stood so close to me, I could smell the woodsy scent of his soap and shampoo. His gray eyes were *so* intense.

A part of me had thought he might kiss me.

And a part of me wanted him to.

But I had to go. Time was running out, and I had to get back inside.

And now I wondered, would things be different if he *had* kissed me?

"You know you're going to have to make a decision soon," Mia said, still watching me over her cup. "Maybe as soon as tonight."

Tonight. I closed my eyes. Of course. Aiden would be back for dinner, just like always, and he would want to finish the conversation that Daniel so rudely interrupted yesterday. I sighed and rubbed my forehead. "I guess I have lots to think about while I'm cooking today."

Mia looked at me in surprise. "Cooking? Why are you cooking?"

"Who else is going to? You?"

Her expression was still surprised, but now, it was also tinged with worry. "Becca, we're going out tonight. Don't you remember? We're all meeting up at The Tipsy Cow."

My mouth went slack as I stared at her, feeling a dull ache start to creep across my temple. "I ..." I couldn't form any words. Instead, I wracked my brain, trying desperately to find a shred of the memory.

Mia was still staring at me. "We talked about it a few days ago. It was Daphne's idea. She thought it would be good for us to get out of the house for a bit and see our other friends." She paused as she furrowed her brows. "You even put it in your phone."

My phone. I reached over to grab it off the kitchen counter and unlocked it. The first thing I noticed was another missed call from my mother. Actually, it appeared she also left a voicemail and a text. I cleared the notifications without looking at the messages and felt my usual pang of guilt. I was far too worried about that wary look in Mia's eyes. I promised myself I would deal with my mother later.

I opened up the calendar app, and there it was, just like Mia said. *Meet up at The Tipsy Cow.*

I couldn't be losing my mind. Just couldn't be.

"Becca?" Mia's voice was soft. "Are you okay?"

My right eye twitched as a thread of pain seemed to wind its way across my temple. I turned off my phone and placed it face down on the table. "The doctor said this isn't unusual. Memory loss is common with concussions. It's just temporary." Even to my own ears, I didn't sound believable.

Mia's gaze was steady. "Have you told the doctor you're still experiencing ... issues?"

"Of course." And that was true. Mostly. He thought I was being more forgetful than usual ... misplacing my phone and car keys. Not that I was finding them in the fridge or next to the laundry detergent, which was where my phone had been the other day.

I didn't correct his false impression. I still wasn't sure why. If there was really a problem with my brain, I should be open and honest with him.

"And he wasn't concerned?" Mia asked.

"Not at all." I forced myself to smile as I repeated the doctor's words. "The brain can sometimes take a while to heal, and as it does, strange things can happen. But it's nothing to be alarmed about. Plus, in my case, my healing is more complex, because I'm also trying to work through a lot of trauma related to what happened. So, he said I shouldn't be surprised if it takes longer than normal."

Mia leaned back in her chair, her expression softening. "Well, that makes sense. I know I'm still working through a ton of crap, and I don't even have a concussion, so I can imagine how it would further complicate things." She paused as she picked up her coffee cup, almost like she was contemplating her next words. "You know, you don't have to be a part of the investigation if you don't want to."

Now it was my turn to look at her in confusion. "Why wouldn't I want to be a part of the investigation?"

She toyed with her cup. "Well, I know you're supposed to rest your brain to help it heal, and helping with the investigation isn't going to be very restful."

I waved a hand at her. "I'm fine. Honestly. All I do all day is rest. Heavens, I'm sure I could use a little mental stimulation. Maybe that's why it's taking me so long to heal."

She eyed me. "If you're sure …"

"I'm sure." There was no way I was going to let Mia read those transcripts without me. I needed Edna's killer to be found and for this nightmare to be over. ASAP.

A storm is coming.

I pushed that thought away and reached for my coffee cup. My hands trembled slightly as I picked it up to take a drink, spilling the coffee over the side.

Mia noticed and gave me a twisted smile that looked more like a grimace. "We can do it. We'll get to the bottom of what's going on with the Church of the Forgotten. I know it."

I met her eyes as I took a sip of coffee. "I do, too."

I didn't add what I was really thinking.

We must.

Because the alternative was unthinkable.

Chapter 7

The Tipsy Cow was packed, which I wasn't expecting. It was Thursday, not the weekend, but apparently, a lot of people were interested in kicking it off early.

"Oh look! Barry's sitting at our old table," Mia said as she threw him a quick wave. Together, we wove our way through the crowd, and I tried not to cringe at the sight of his wife, Celia.

Celia had never liked me much.

The Tipsy Cow was a favorite hangout in Redemption, for both locals and tourists. It was all polished wood, from the floors to the tables, and it perpetually smelled like a combination of beer, whisky, and fried food, though it also featured the best Cobb salad in town.

"You guys really are alive," Barry said, sliding out of the booth to give us both a hug. Celia stayed where she was, a cosmopolitan in front of her. She gave me a brittle smile and Mia a warmer one.

"Of course we're alive," Mia said, hitting him lightly on the chest. "You don't think you could get rid of us that easily, do you?"

Barry laughed. He was a big guy with dark-red hair and a smattering of freckles across his nose and cheeks. He slung an arm around me, and I caught a whiff of his soap and shampoo, which for some reason reminded me of Daniel. I quickly pulled away.

"Take a seat. I'll go grab the waitress." Barry didn't seem to have noticed my reaction as he waved us toward the large circular booth.

"You don't have to do that," Mia said. "I'm sure the waitress will be here in a bit."

"It's no problem. I need to use the restroom anyway. I'll be right back." Barry flashed us a grin before disappearing into the crowd.

I slid into the booth after Mia, who smiled as she greeted Celia. "It's been a minute since I've seen you."

"Definitely too long," Celia said. She even seemed sincere, although she kept her eyes firmly on Mia. She looked exactly the way I remembered her—thick black hair pulled into a ponytail that emphasized her sharp, heart-shaped, heavily made-up face that reminded me of a fox. She wore a black turtleneck sweater that dripped with silver jewelry. "I think the last time we went out was over a year ago."

Mia's face fell slightly. "Yeah. That's my fault. Just way too busy with work and school. Moving forward, I'm going to be better."

"Hey guys, sorry we're late," Daphne said cheerily as she joined us. She nodded to Celia and slid into the booth next to me followed by Aiden. "Where's Barry?"

"Gone to find the waitress and the restroom," Mia said. "Although probably not in that order."

"I would hope not," Daphne said before introducing Aiden to Celia.

"Aiden?" Celia asked. Her eyes glinted as she gave him an appraising look. "The same Aiden who helped with the investigation?"

Aiden looked startled. "How did you know that?"

She shrugged. "It's a small town. Or haven't you figured that out yet?"

Daphne nudged him with her shoulder. "Don't mind Celia. She probably knows because Barry knows *everyone* in town. He's also good friends with Daniel."

"Speaking of Daniel," Barry said, appearing by our table as if by magic. The waitress was not far behind him. "Look who I ran into as he was picking up dinner." He stepped to the side with a flourish, revealing Daniel.

I froze. This was the last thing I wanted. Last night was bad enough. I certainly didn't want a repeat of it.

"I thought you were working," Celia said. "And that's why you couldn't meet us."

"I thought so too," Daphne said quickly, glancing over her shoulder to make eye contact with me, a worried expression on her face. I could practically hear her voice in my head telling me she had no idea this was going to happen.

"I am working," Daniel said, despite being dressed in a pair of jeans and button-down shirt. "I'm just on dinner break."

"Which is why I told him to join us," Barry said, clapping him on the shoulder. "Come. Sit."

Daniel hesitated, his eyes briefly finding mine before glancing away. "I shouldn't."

"Of course you should. Don't be silly," Barry said, sliding into the booth. "You have to eat, right? I know you've been putting in tons of overtime, so taking a half-hour break is probably not going to cause the Redemption Police Department to combust into spontaneous flames." He smirked at Daniel. "Although, come to think about it, you probably should get back there ASAP. The other officers are surely wandering around the station as we speak, unable to focus without their fearless leader ..."

"Alright, alright," Daniel said, giving Barry a shove so he could sit down. "You don't have to be such an ass."

Barry's grin widened.

The waitress sidled up to the table, tablet in hand, to take our orders. I was barely listening as I wondered how bad it would be if I simply just left. I had the car keys, so that wouldn't be a problem, although I would have to come back for Mia if she couldn't get a ride home from someone else. But I could do that. The bigger problem was how I could get out of the booth, as I was jammed in the middle with people on both sides of me. Unless I was prepared to crawl under the table, I was going to have to make people move. Maybe I could say I had to use the restroom and simply not come back ...

"Becca," Mia said, nudging me with her shoulder. "Do you know what you want to drink?"

I blinked and saw the waitress staring at me. Actually, the whole table was.

I could feel myself flushing. Ugh. Really not a great start for the night.

"Red wine," I said. "A cab or merlot."

"We have both," she said.

"Either is fine." Just as long as it was alcohol.

I could feel Mia's eyes on me, but I ignored her. I knew what she was thinking—that with my lapses in memory, the last thing I needed was alcohol. But one night wouldn't hurt.

Probably.

"So," Barry started, leaning back in his seat as he held up his glass toward me. "A toast to the conquering hero. Taking down the Church of the Forgotten all by herself."

"Honestly, that's not necessary," I said quickly, trying to deflect as much attention away from me as possible, even as I felt Daniel and Aiden turn their disapproving gazes toward me. Stupid Barry. He always did this. Find the one thing that would cause the most drama and make a big deal about it. In this case, it was reminding Daniel and Aiden how much they disliked me putting myself in danger by joining the Church. "I think that's overstating my role a bit."

Barry frowned. "That's not what I heard. You were the one who rescued that girl. What's her name? Zoey or Zora or …"

"Zelda," Celia said.

Barry snapped his fingers. "That's right."

I briefly closed my eyes, wishing the black upholstered seat would swallow me whole. "Well, it wasn't just me," I said, trying to keep my voice light. "Mia was there, too." I nudged her with my shoulder. "I couldn't have done it without her."

Barry's eyes flickered between her and me. "Ah yes. Of course, how could I forget about Mia? You joined first, didn't you?" He grinned at her as I gritted my teeth. Great. I traded one dangerous topic of conversation for another. Yes, Mia and I had a fight, which led to her joining the Church of the Forgotten, and part of why I had joined was to look for her. But based on how Mia was shifting uncomfortably next to me, I had a feeling she didn't want to talk about it anymore than I did it.

Luckily, we were both saved by the waitress choosing to appear at that moment with our drinks. Thank goodness for small favors.

As soon as the waitress handed me my wine, I guzzled down a long swallow. I could feel the burn as it slid down my throat. The effects hit me just as quickly, the warm fuzziness seeming to expand throughout my body. I reminded myself to take it easy. I hadn't had a drink in weeks, since before I left for the Church of the Forgotten, which felt like a lifetime ago. I also reminded myself it would be a very bad idea to get drunk while sitting at a table with Aiden and Daniel. Not to mention Celia. And Barry the Flamethrower.

Ugh. I again entertained the thought of just going home and opening a bottle of wine instead.

"So, what was it like?" Celia asked as soon as the waitress left. "The Church of the Forgotten, I mean."

"Was it as crazy as everyone says it was?" Barry asked, wagging his eyebrows up and down.

"It was pretty intense," Mia said. "A lot of working and very little sleeping. And not much to eat."

"What *did* you eat?" Celia asked.

Mia made a face. "Boiled vegetables. Bread. A little cheese."

"No meat?" Barry asked, his expression horrified.

"Nope," Mia said, picking up her glass of wine. Apparently, I wasn't the only one who decided to splurge and have a drink tonight. "Nor any of this." She tilted her glass.

"The horror!" Barry joked.

"What kind of work were you doing?" Celia asked.

"Typical farm chores," Mia said. "A lot of weeding and planting and harvesting. There was always something that needed to be done, whether outdoors or inside. Like some women had kitchen duty, which meant doing all the cooking and cleaning."

"And if you weren't working, you were praying," I added.

"Praying?" Barry asked. "Who were you praying to?"

"They called it 'The One,'" Mia said, rolling her eyes. "It was a trip, let me tell you."

"What about those ugly dresses?" Celia asked, her mouth puckered, like she had eaten something sour. "Did you have to wear them?"

"Unfortunately, yes," Mia said. "Although you get used to them."

"I don't see how you could stand it," Celia said with a shiver.

"It wasn't all bad," I said. "We didn't have to do our laundry, so there was that."

"True," Mia said.

Celia looked as horrified as her husband had at the mention of the lack of booze. "Who washed your clothes?"

Edna's face flashed through my mind as she argued with me about wearing dirty clothes. I squeezed my eyes shut as I gulped down a mouthful of wine, hoping to wash away the memory.

"There was ..." Mia said, her voice flat as she too had a memory she wanted to wash away with wine. "One of the members. Her job was to wash everyone's clothes."

"Seriously?" Celia couldn't have looked more shocked if Mia had said the Church of the Forgotten was actually a sex cult. "Everyone's clothes mixed together? Gross."

Mia's smile was bitter. "Trust me. How my clothes were being washed was the least of my worries. The whole experience was a beat down. Literally. We barely slept, barely ate, and were constantly pushed to do more physical activity. And like Becca said, if we weren't doing something, then we were reciting weird 'prayers' that seemed to be more about brainwashing than anything else. Especially when you combine those so-called prayers with being so worn down, you feel like you're sleepwalking through your day. It was awful."

Celia pursed her lips. "And you didn't leave?"

Mia raised her hands, palms up. "How could I? The whole reason I joined was because I was sure they were hiding something, and the longer I stayed, the more convinced I was that I was right. Why else would they drive you to such mental and physical exhaustion? They *were* hiding something. I was sure of it."

Celia didn't look convinced. "But isn't that what cults do? Brainwash people? Jim Jones made all his followers drink poisoned Kool Aid, for goodness' sake. How could you be so sure they were actually hiding something, versus ... well, just acting like a cult?"

"I just knew," Mia said. Her voice was even, but underneath the table, I could see her hands clenched into tight knots. "You can't tell me you didn't think there was something off with the Church of the Forgotten? They show up here, and then Penny dies ..."

"Penny was old and sick," Celia said.

"No, she wasn't," Mia said. "They killed her."

"Yes, we know that now," Celia said. "But we didn't then. More importantly, *you* didn't. Yet you stayed."

"But that wasn't the only death," Mia said. "Pamela was clearly murdered. And her daughter was missing. Do you really think it was a coincidence that some nutty cult shows up and people almost immediately start dying and disappearing?"

"This is Redemption," Celia said. "There's always something horrible going on here. And while there's no question the Church of the Forgotten was creepy—all you have to do is look at those dresses to see that—it's hardly the creepiest thing to have ever been associated with Redemption." She shivered again and picked up her drink, her eyes cutting toward Barry. "This town really isn't safe. We should seriously consider moving."

Barry ignored his wife. "That's why you joined the Church of the Forgotten? Because you really thought it had something to do with that woman's death?" His gaze was going back and forth between Mia and Daniel, and there was something unhappy in his eyes. Daniel, for his part, had an impassive, almost bored expression on his face, like we were talking about the weather rather than a huge misstep he was part of. "I mean ..." He picked up his beer and took a quick swallow, his eyes darting back to Daniel. "You're saying you saw a connection that the police missed?"

"We're human. We make mistakes," Daniel said quietly, his eyes flickering up toward me.

My jaw dropped. "You admit you made a mistake?"

Daniel nodded, his eyes never leaving mine. "The Church of the Forgotten was always on our radar. There was something fishy about it, but Celia is right-"

"Of course I'm right," Celia interrupted, muttering into her drink. "Why I ever agreed to move to this horrid place ..."

"About cults," Daniel said smoothly as Barry rolled his eyes and took another swallow of beer. Celia's hatred for Redemption was well known, but for better or for worse, she was stuck in it. Not only because Barry had taken over his father's car dealerships, but because Redemption had a reputation for deciding who was able to stay and who was able to go. It always seemed a little far-fetched to me ... this idea that a town could decide that. But there were a lot of strange things about Redemption, so why not add one more to the list?

As much as I wouldn't have minded seeing Celia leave, I suspected both Celia and I were doomed for disappointment, as Redemption had no plan to let her go.

"Yes, cults are known for brainwashing their members," Daniel continued. "But that doesn't mean they're in the business of kidnapping and murder. So, to assume that the Church of the Forgotten was behind everything that happened without hard evidence is a stretch." He paused and grimaced. "That said, we probably should have been more thorough in our initial investigations."

I wondered if he was thinking about when I first told him about hearing a noise in the barn on the Church's property. It was coming from the other side of a door with a brand-new padlock. Nothing about it made any sense, and I wondered now if Daniel was regretting not doing a more thorough search of the farm then.

"Wow," Aiden said, his voice thick with sarcasm. "A cop who admits he's wrong. That's got to be a first."

My stomach began twisting itself into knots as everyone's head swiveled toward Aiden, their expressions ranging from surprise to suspicion.

Except for Daniel. His remained impassive as his gaze slid over Aiden. "Like I said ... cops are human, too."

Aiden's eyebrows went up. "That's very true. Does that mean moving forward, you've learned your lesson?"

Daphne's eyes were wide, and I saw her put a hand on Aiden's arm, but before she could say anything, the waitress appeared again. "Another round?"

"Yes," I blurted out, seizing my wine glass to down the rest of it. Mia eyed me, faint concern in her eyes, but I ignored her, turning all my focus to my glass.

"I heard you were a big help with the investigation, too," Barry said as he focused in on Aiden. He was still leaning back in the booth, his body relaxed, but his eyes were tense.

Aiden's eyes flickered between him and Daniel. "I did what I could."

"You're some sort of professional investigator, right?" Barry asked.

"Insurance investigator," Aiden said.

"Oh, that's right. Are you still doing that, or something else now?" Barry lazily twisted his stein on the polished table, his eyes hard.

Aiden narrowed his eyes. "Why does that matter?"

Barry shrugged. "I was just curious if you're going to stick around Redemption or not?"

Even though Barry's manner was relaxed, almost friendly, there was an edge to his tone that was anything but. No one spoke, and an awkward silence fell over us, finally broken by the waitress returning with our drinks. It was all I could do to not leap on my wine.

"I'm still weighing my options," Aiden said stiffly. "Especially with this new murder. I think I might extend my stay …"

"Murder?" Celia broke in. "There's been another murder?"

"One of the Church of the Forgotten members," Daniel said.

She frowned and reached for her cosmo. "I'm going to need a checklist to keep track of them soon."

"How is that investigation going?" Aiden asked.

Daniel's eyes were hooded. "Slower than we would like."

"Are we going to be able to see the transcripts?" Mia asked.

"Transcripts?" Celia asked.

"Of the interviews," Mia explained.

Celia's face was still blank. "What interviews?"

"With the Church of the Forgotten members," Mia said.

"They're not being very … forthcoming," I said, as Celia's expression was still mystified. "Some of them have been a part of the Church of the Forgotten for years, and I think they, well, forgot what it was like to be a part of regular society."

"So, we thought we might be able to fill in the blanks," Mia said. "See if we can shed some light on what they're saying or not saying."

"That makes sense," Barry said. "The sooner we can move on from this cult, the better."

"Here, here," Celia said, lifting her glass. "When are you going to see the transcripts?"

"That's a question for Daniel," Mia said.

Daniel had busied himself with his water glass. "I was going to call you tomorrow."

"Oh, well, as we're here, we just saved you a call," Mia said.

Daniel still wasn't looking at us. "Yes ... and, as it turns out, the chief does think it's a good idea. He'd like you to come in tomorrow afternoon."

"Tomorrow afternoon?" Mia's brow furrowed. "I think I might be working. I'll have to check my schedule and see if I can switch." She started digging into her pocket for her phone.

I was studying Daniel, who was fidgeting with his water glass. "Why would you call us tomorrow morning to come in tomorrow afternoon? Why not give us a little more notice?"

"What does that matter?" Daniel asked. "If you couldn't do it tomorrow, we would find another time."

"Yes, but isn't time of the essence? Why would you want us to wait?"

Mia had fished her phone out, but she hadn't unlocked it, as she was watching our exchange.

Finally, Daniel looked up and met my eyes. "You're making a big deal out of nothing."

I could feel the ball of anger start to form in the pit of my stomach. "Am I?"

"Maybe you didn't learn anything after all," Aiden murmured. Daniel and I both ignored him.

"Becca, believe it or not, I'm busy," Daniel said. "I have a lot going on. Just because I didn't drop everything to call you and Mia to ask you to come in doesn't mean anything."

I narrowed my eyes at him. "You sure about that?"

Daniel raised his hands in exasperation. "Becca, what are you implying? Just spit it out."

I clenched my hands around my glass, fighting the urge to throw my wine at him. Nothing had changed. He was doing exactly what he always did—trying to get me to back off and stay out of it.

I was so sick of it. So sick of everyone thinking I was weak and needed to be protected and taken care of. I was done. DONE.

I tossed back the rest of my wine in one swallow, coughing slightly as it went down. "Nothing. Absolutely nothing. Can you let me out? I need to use the restroom." That was a lie, but I had to get out of there, or I was going to start screaming. The small lie felt like the fastest way to get people to move.

Daphne shot me a surprised look, but both her and Aiden started shuffling out. I unobtrusively grabbed my purse as I slid out behind them, just in case I decided to head for home.

Daniel had gone very still as he watched me walk off. Aiden was also studying me carefully.

I ignored both of them.

This night was such a bad idea. I knew I should have listened to my gut and stayed home.

Chapter 8

The bathroom was empty, which was a relief. I locked myself in a stall and sat on the toilet, focusing on my breathing. It was cool and quiet, especially compared to the overheated and crowded bar. I pressed my hands against my temples, trying to force back the headache that was starting to curl around my forehead. I was feeling a little lightheaded as well, presumably from the wine. Even though I'd only had two glasses, the alcohol hit me harder than I'd anticipated. In retrospect, I should have expected it.

I massaged my temples and wondered how long I could sit there before someone, probably Mia, came looking for me. Or, better yet, could I slip out the back?

No, that wouldn't be right. Not to mention I was Mia's ride home. I had to at least give her the option of coming with me.

Unfortunately, I was going to have to go back out there and face everyone. I didn't really see any way around it.

Exhaling a long sigh, I let myself out of the stall and headed to the sinks to wash my hands and check my appearance. It wasn't pretty. My hair was a wild mess, and my lipstick was merely a stain where it had worn off. I had even managed to smear my mascara, at some point.

Geez ... you really couldn't take me anywhere, could you?

I spent a few minutes repairing the worst of the damage. It wasn't great, but the results were mostly acceptable. Mostly. Especially if I ignored the black circles under my eyes.

I tucked my lipstick and brush back into my purse and left the bathroom.

The hallway was empty, and I breathed a sigh of relief. Or was it disappointment? I had half expected to find Daniel waiting for me, as it seemed like he was always waiting for me when we found ourselves at odds at The Tipsy Cow.

But it was good he wasn't. I didn't want to see him anyway. I wanted to go home and take a bath, or maybe just lie down with a warm washcloth over my face to help my headache go away.

The last thing I wanted was to argue with him anymore. Especially if I was going to see him tomorrow.

I turned to head back toward the bar when I nearly smacked right into Daniel. I was so startled, I dropped my purse, and half the contents spilled out.

"Sorry," Daniel said, but he didn't sound it. I shot him the evil eye before crouching down to gather my belongings.

"You don't have to help," I said as he knelt down next to me, reaching for my lipstick that had rolled a few feet away.

"It was my fault you dropped your purse. The least I can do is help," he said mildly. He was so close, I could smell him—that distinct scent that was all him and soap and shampoo. I shivered despite myself.

He glanced up and narrowed his eyes. "Cold?"

"I'm fine," I said, my voice clipped as I plucked my lipstick from his hand. Even though I tried to be careful, my fingers grazed his skin, and I could feel my stomach twist in a knot.

Ugh. Was this the way it was always going to be now?

I was going to have to do a better job avoiding him in the future.

"What are you doing here anyway?" I asked, scooping up my cell phone and keys and shoving them into my purse. "Aren't you supposed to be waiting for your food?"

"I wanted to talk to you." His voice was mild.

I glanced at him in surprise. Usually, I didn't get such honesty from him. His dark-blue eyes were so close … closer than I expected.

I sucked in my breath and leaned back, nearly falling over in the process. His hand snaked out to grab my upper arm. "Careful."

We always had great chemistry, but this was another level. It was like a live wire had touched me. Electrical sparks sizzled across my nerve endings, and it was all I could do to keep my expression neutral. "I'm fine," I said again, jerking away as I struggled to get to my feet. A woman with painted-on jeans, a tight red sweater, and very high heels tottered by us as she headed for the bathroom. She shot me a dirty look as she passed, nearly tripping over herself in the process. I moved a couple of steps closer to the wall to get out of the way.

Daniel rose to his feet far more gracefully than I had, which made me grit my teeth even harder. Wordlessly, he came toward me and held out my brush. I took it from him, with probably more force than necessary, and jammed it in my purse. "What do you want to talk about?"

He took a step back and stuffed his hands in his pockets. For the first time, he seemed uncertain. "I ... I wanted to see how you're doing."

I blinked. "Are you serious? You want to know how I'm *doing*?"

"Your health, I mean." He rocked backward, taking another step away from me. If I didn't know better, I would think he was flustered.

"My health? What are you talking about? Did I imagine it, or were we not just all sitting in a booth talking just a few minutes ago? And didn't I just tell you I'm fine? Not once, but a couple of times?"

"That's not what I'm asking about." His eyes flickered over my face, as if that would reveal whatever answer he was looking for. "I can see you're doing *fine*, or at least fine enough to spend an evening at a local bar with some old friends. I'm talking about how you're *actually* doing. Like, how is your concussion healing? How are you healing mentally and emotionally from what you went through at the Church of the Forgotten? Are you still having nightmares? *That's* what I'm asking."

For a moment, I could only stare at him. No one had asked me that. Not Daphne, not Chrissy, not Aiden, not even Mia. Although, to be fair to Mia, she seemed to be struggling as much as I was and probably didn't want to talk about it anymore than I did. As for Daphne and Aiden, my guess was they wanted to give me space and let me decide when or if I wanted to talk about it.

And, until that second, I would have assumed the answer would have been no ... I didn't want to talk about it. Ever I wanted to forget and move on.

But that wasn't actually true.

I *did* want to talk about it.

The words were on the tip of my tongue. *No, I'm not sleeping. I'm convinced that whatever dark entity was living at the Church of the Forgotten has followed me home and won't leave me alone. I'm constantly forgetting and misplacing things and have started to think I might be losing my mind. I still have headaches and feel like I'm popping ibuprofen like candy.*

And none of that was even the worst part. The worst part was the image of that shadowy figure in my kitchen.

A storm is coming.

The reality was, even after everything that had happened, it still might not have been enough to save Redemption.

I could practically feel the words fluttering in my mouth, begging to be released, but I refused to let them go. Because once I said them, there was no taking them back.

Nor had I any way to know what the repercussions might be.

He must have seen something in my face, some glimpse of my internal struggle, because his eyes softened, and he lifted a hand like he was about to stroke my cheek. "You can trust me." He was so close, his warm breath grazed my lips, and shivers ran down my spine.

Part of me wanted nothing more than to lean into his warmth and feel his touch again. But another part—the part that got stuck on the word "trust"—resisted.

Because that was the kicker. I had no idea if I could trust him or not.

I tilted my head to meet his eyes. "Can I?"

He leaned in a shade closer. "Of course. You know that."

You know that. It was like being doused with cold water. I took a step back and folded my arms across my chest. "I do? How?"

His eyes widened in surprise at my abrupt tone. "What do you mean, 'how'?"

"Exactly what I said. How do I know I can trust you?"

He stared at me like I had suddenly grown a second head. "We dated for almost a year. You didn't trust me?"

"I didn't say that," I said.

"You just did."

"Well, I wasn't talking about while we were dating," I said. I was starting to feel flustered, and I wished I hadn't had that second glass of wine. Or maybe I just needed a third. "I was talking about these past few months. How you didn't believe me when I said there was someone following me and watching the house …"

"That's not true," he interrupted. "I did check it out. I just didn't find any evidence."

"How you thought I actually burned down The Jack Saloon …" I continued as if he hadn't said anything.

"Again, not true," he said. "Do you not remember how I was calling you and Mia and Daphne trying to find you? How I came over and told you what was going on?"

I glared at him. "You thought I did it."

"I was trying to protect you," he snapped.

"By not believing me?"

"By not arresting you!"

I stared at him, a sharp pain of betrayal shooting through me. "You were going to arrest me?" I couldn't keep the hurt out of my voice.

He stared right back at me, his eyes simmering with something that looked suspiciously like betrayal. Which made no sense … HE was the one who had betrayed me, not the other way around. "What is wrong with you? Why pretend to be so dense? That's not what I said, and you know it." He took a step back again, raking his hands through his hair. "You know the evidence I had against you. You must also know that there was some pressure for me to at least bring you in for questioning, if not outright arrest you. But I didn't."

His eyes glinted in the low light, and all of a sudden, things didn't feel as clear-cut as they had a just few minutes before. Of course I had known I was in trouble, just as I knew how bad the evidence was against me. That is, until I was cleared. But I didn't realize Daniel was *still* protecting me, even while planning to break up with me.

He could have thrown me to the wolves, but he didn't.

Did that excuse the times he didn't trust me? Or the times he'd let me down? I wasn't sure anymore, especially since I had an uncomfortable feeling I wasn't entirely innocent in all of it, either.

I wished life wasn't so complicated.

"What about Mia?" My voice cracked, as if the words had been so deeply buried inside me, they had to be dragged to the surface.

"What about her?" Daniel's voice was tense, but some of the anger had drained from his voice.

"You didn't believe me when I told you she was in trouble." As soon as the words were out of my mouth, the realization hit me—*this* was the source of so much of my anger and heartache and betrayal. And suddenly, I couldn't stop. "You didn't even look for her. You just assumed she was mad at me because YOU were mad at me. So, you just left me to go into the Church of the Forgotten all alone, with no backup other than Aiden and Daphne, and I had no idea if you would believe them either, if they came to you for help getting me out. You didn't believe me, and you didn't trust me, and because of that, things could have gone even more horribly wrong than they did."

Something that resembled shame flickered across Daniel's face. But it disappeared so fast, I couldn't be sure what I had seen for sure, if anything at all. He turned away then, swallowing hard. "You're right. I should have trusted you and believed you. That was a mistake … one I'll regret for the rest of my life." His voice was rough, and he scrubbed at his face before turning back to me. His cop face was back, and even his eyes were shuttered. Still, I could see a glimpse of pain in their depths. "I'm sorry."

I was so surprised, I nearly dropped my purse again. Of all the things I expected him to say, an apology wasn't one of them. Even more unexpected was how it made me feel. I had thought I would feel vindicated, but instead, I felt ashamed. "Well, I know I didn't always make things easy for you." I shifted from one foot to the other. "And I know you did check out the Church of the Forgotten once before and didn't find anything."

"I remember," he said softly, his eyes still on mine. "But just because we didn't find anything then didn't mean there wasn't something to find. We all knew there was something off about them, the whole department did … and we should have paid attention. *I should have paid attention.*"

I shifted my weight again. The conversation had taken such a strange turn, I wasn't sure where to go next. "If that's the case, why didn't you bring Mia and me in to look at the transcripts already? Why did you wait to tell us?"

He looked away again, and I saw a muscle jump in his jaw. "You're reading too much into it. I told you, I'm busy." His voice had flattened, and he wasn't looking at me anymore.

"Am I? I know you said you should have believed me about Mia sooner, but it doesn't feel like anything has changed. It still feels like you don't trust me to be involved in the investigation, even though I may be able to help."

"It's not about trust," he began. But he stopped short, clamping his lips together as if he'd said too much.

"What do you mean, 'it's not about trust'?"

He gave his head a quick shake before letting out a long sigh. "You've been through a lot." His voice was quiet, and his eyes were intense as he stared at me. "Not just the trauma, but also the concussion and lack of decent food and sleep and who knows what else. I just don't want to set you back."

I could feel my chest tighten as I straightened up. I was such a fool. Nothing had changed. "So, you *were* trying to keep me from helping."

Daniel's jaw worked as he stared at me. "Why do you always assume the worst about me? I just …" he took a step back and shook his head in frustration. "Forget it."

My head jerked back as if I had been slapped. "What are you talking about? I don't think the worst about you. I'm just stating facts."

His eyebrows went up. "Oh, facts. That's what you're calling it. Good to know." His tone was heavy with sarcasm.

"There you are, Daniel."

Both of our heads whipped around to see Aiden standing a few feet away, his arms crossed. His eyes swept between us. "I just came to tell you that your food is here. I know you said you don't have a lot of time, since you need to get back to the station."

Daniel straightened. "Right. Thanks for letting me know. I'm actually going to get it to go." He glanced at me. His eyes were hooded, but his expression had smoothed over, leaving no sign of the fight we were having. "I'll see you tomorrow."

"Right," I said tightly.

Aiden stayed where he was as Daniel strode away toward the table. "Are you okay?"

My fingers clenched together. I was so sick of people asking me if I was okay, but I forced myself to breathe. None of this was Aiden's fault. "I'm fine." I forced a smile, then glanced over to the booth to see if Daniel had left with his food. Instead, he appeared to have sat back down. Crap. Now what? Maybe it was a sign for me to leave. Immediately.

Aiden cocked his head as he studied me. "You know, we don't have to go back to your friends if you don't want to. We could grab a drink at the bar."

The last thing I needed was another drink. "No, I should probably go home."

"You sure? I'm a good listener."

My lips quirked up in a real smile. "I appreciate the offer, but I'm pretty tired. I guess I'm not used to being out."

"Makes sense."

I expected him to turn and go back to the booth, but he stayed where he was, his gray eyes almost piercing as he studied me.

Self-consciously, I ran a hand through my hair. I must look worse than I thought. Aiden was looking at me like he was waiting for me to keel over. "Really, I'm fine. I just need to tell Mia that I'm going, in case she wants to leave too." Even though I didn't want to have anything to do with anyone in that booth, my eyes had drifted back to Daniel again.

It was just so infuriating. How could he possibly think I only thought the worst of him? He was the one who broke up with me. He was the one who didn't believe me.

I had to get a grip on myself.

"I can take Mia home," Aiden said, his voice low. I jerked my head toward him. He was still in the same place, but he had uncrossed his arms and stuffed his hands in his pockets. He flashed me one of his charming grins, but there was something missing ... like it was a pale, faded imitation of the real thing. "It's really no problem. Especially if you'd rather sneak out the back."

My own smile was rueful. "Is it that obvious?"

"Well ... kind of." His smile seemed more genuine, but his eyes continued searching my face. "I know breakups can be ... complicated."

There was a hesitation in his voice I couldn't figure out. "Yeah, they can be. But I'm fine." How many times was I going to repeat those two words? I was getting sick of myself. I straightened my shoulders. "Redemption is a small town, and we have a lot of the same friends. We're just going to have to get used to running into each other and be grown-ups about it. That's all."

"Oh, that's all." He rolled his eyes. "Like that's so easy to do."

I laughed, an actual real one. It reminded me of how long it had been since I had laughed. "Okay, maybe it's not that easy. But we'll get there."

"I'm sure you will."

There was an intensity in his eyes I wasn't sure what to do with. I suddenly felt very exposed and very awkward. "Well ... um ..." I cleared my throat. "I should probably get back. I appreciate your offer to tell Mia, but like I said, Daniel and I are going to have to learn to deal with each other in public. Like grown-ups." I started toward the booth.

"Becca?" His voice was so quiet, I almost missed it. I turned toward him, feeling my heart begin to thunder in my chest.

His eyes still had that intense look. "The offer to have a drink stands. Maybe tomorrow or this weekend? Or, if you don't have to have a drink, we could meet for coffee."

My mouth had gone dry. I wasn't sure what to say. Did I want to have a drink with him? Alone? We had always spent time together as a group. Mia, Daphne, Aiden, and me. All of us as friends.

But if it was just him and me … I swallowed hard. A part of me wanted to say no—to keep everything the same as it was. Aiden was my friend. I didn't want to lose that.

Especially since I seemed to have such crap luck with boyfriends and husbands. The last thing I wanted was another ex in my life.

On the other hand, Aiden had been one of the few people I could count on. When I was trapped in the Church of the Forgotten, knowing he was out there doing whatever he could to keep me safe kept me going.

I remembered the look in his eyes as we stood on the side of the road just outside the Church of the Forgotten, when he tried to convince me not to go back. I remembered the spark I felt between us.

Maybe I wasn't being fair to Aiden. Maybe I should give him a chance. Maybe we could eventually work something out, even if it now wasn't the right time.

"Okay," I said, and his face lit up. "I think tomorrow will work, but let me text you when I get home from the police station."

"Of course," he said quickly. "Just let me know. And if you decide the weekend will be better, that's fine, too."

"Will do," I said, trying to ignore how my stomach seemed to be twisting itself into knots. Was that a good thing or bad? I no longer knew.

I turned around and headed for the booth, only to see that Daniel was still there, and he was staring right at me, his face grim. I forced myself to turn away, even as my steps faltered and my heart felt like it had lodged in my throat.

What a disaster of a night. I definitely should have stayed home.

Chapter 9

I slept fitfully, tossing and turning, convinced I was being watched. I could feel its presence, hiding in the shadows, biding its time until I was at my most vulnerable. Then it would attack, tearing into me with rows and rows of sharp, pointed teeth, crushing me, devouring me, until there was nothing left ...

"Becca? Are you down here?"

The voice seemed to slice through my thoughts as easily as those teeth would carve into my flesh. I shuddered and tried to look around, but everything seemed gray and murky, like I was trapped under a lake, fighting to swim. Maybe drowning was a more accurate description ...

"Becca? Where did you ... oh, there you are. What are you doing in here?"

I blinked, my eyes slowly focusing. I was staring at a bookcase full of old books and knickknacks. Where was I?

"Becca? Are you okay?"

The voice was louder now, and behind me. A cool hand touched my arm, and it was like I had just been dashed with cold water. I turned to face Chrissy, who was staring at me.

"What's going on?" she said, her eyes searching my face. She was wearing jeans and a black sweater, and with her black hair slicked back in a ponytail, she reminded me of a young Audrey Hepburn.

"I ... I ..." I swallowed and tried to think of something, anything, to say. The truth was, I had no idea what was going on. The last thing I remembered was tossing and turning in my bed, and for the life of me, I couldn't figure out how I even got in the family room ...

The bookshelf.

I whirled back around, my chest so tight, I could barely breathe. It felt like a large hand was squeezing my heart.

This couldn't be happening. It couldn't.

"Becca, what's going on?" The worry in Chrissy's voice was unmistakable.

I was going to be sick. I could feel the bile rising from my stomach, but I forced it down. I had to pull it together. I couldn't put Chrissy through more stress.

I plastered a smile across my face and turned back to her. "Sorry, I didn't mean to scare you. I was looking for something, and you know how forgetful I've been. Not to mention I haven't had my coffee yet."

Chrissy was eyeing me, not the slightest bit convinced. "What were you looking for?"

"Oh …" I flapped my hands. "Just a book. I'll find it later. What do you need?"

Chrissy craned her neck to peer over my shoulder. "Which one? I can help you look."

"Nonsense." I began steering her back toward the kitchen. "I need my coffee anyway. Why were you looking for me? Shouldn't you be getting ready for school?" I was babbling, trying to distract her from asking any more questions, and then I practically had another heart attack as I realized I was so flustered, I had no idea what day it was. What if it wasn't a school day?

"You weren't in your bedroom," Chrissy said, allowing me to herd her into the kitchen as I quickly headed for the coffeemaker to start a pot. My hands were shaking, and I tried to angle my back so she wouldn't see them. "And you're usually up by now anyway."

"Yes, I usually am." I kept my tone light as I scooped grounds into the filter. A dark shadow caught my eye, causing me to jerk and spill the grounds. Just Oscar, prowling into the kitchen. "What did you need?" I repeated my question yet again.

There was a long, awkward pause. I filled the carafe with water, trying to simultaneously tell myself to calm down while also wracking my brain for some answer as to what I could have possibly been doing in the family room that was so important, I didn't even get the coffee brewing first. I was terrified to look at Chrissy, sure I was going to see all sorts of accusations in her face as she assumed there was something horribly wrong with me.

I turned the coffeemaker on, and having no other excuse for keeping my back to Chrissy, I forced myself to turn around.

She was looking at the ground, a faint red circle high on each cheekbone. If I didn't know any better, I would have guessed she was embarrassed. "Chrissy? Is everything alright?"

She scuffed the toe of her sneaker against the tile floor. "It's just …" she hesitated.

Alarm bells starting going off in my head. Was something going on with her? Snippets of my dream flashed before my eyes, the dark entity hiding in the shadows … had it gotten Chrissy? I took a step toward her. "What? What is it?"

Her eyes flickered toward me. "It's … well, can I borrow some money?"

For a moment, I didn't think I heard her properly. It couldn't be that simple. Nothing in my life was that simple. "You … you want to borrow some money?"

She flushed even more. "Forget it." She turned away and started fiddling with her phone.

"No, no, it's fine. Of course you can borrow some money. How much do you need?"

"You know I wouldn't normally ask," she said, her words rushed. "I know we agreed that maintaining the car was my responsibility, and I promise I'll pay you back. It's just the repairs cost more than I thought, and I just need some money to tide me over until my next paycheck. And I'm so sorry for asking, especially now, with everything you have to deal with …"

"Chrissy, it's fine," I said, heading over to my purse. Sometimes, I forgot how afraid she was of becoming like her father, and how she tried so hard to never ask anyone for anything, especially when it came to money. It was as if the simple act of asking would turn her into a sociopathic con man, like her dad. Not to mention how hard she tried to not be a burden on me, no matter how much I told her that for all practical purposes, she was my daughter now. I wasn't sure if it was because she was afraid I might kick her out, or if she was trying to make up for how bitchy she was toward me in the beginning. Maybe it was a little of both. "How much?"

She rattled off a number, her voice nearly breathless, as I dug through my purse for my wallet. My phone tumbled out, and I saw that my mother had called. Again. And left a voicemail. Again.

I really needed to return her call one of these days.

Chrissy kept talking, explaining the situation in great detail, but I was only half-listening. A part of me was relieved, as she was so busy promising me how she was going to pay me back and apologizing, she seemed to have forgotten about finding me in the family room. Which worked out well for me, as I had no idea what to say to her about it.

I had no idea how to explain it to *myself*.

It wasn't until Chrissy left for school (after promising me yet one more time she would pay me back) that I allowed myself to collapse. I slumped into a chair, my cup of coffee on the table in front of me, and concentrated on keeping myself from hyperventilating.

What happened this morning? How did I end up in the family room? In the exact same spot I had found both Mia and Chrissy when they were sleepwalking?

I couldn't be sleepwalking. I *couldn't* be. I had never in my life sleepwalked.

But … I also had no memory of coming down the stairs. I remembered going to bed, trying to sleep, and then … Chrissy talking to me while I was standing in the family room.

This couldn't be happening. It just couldn't.

I rubbed my temples, trying to shove down the raw panic that felt like a dozen mice skittering around my chest. In my mind, I could see the images of Mia and Chrissy as they stood in the family room, talking to me in voices that didn't sound like theirs and telling me things that made no sense.

It was almost like they were possessed.

Of course, that couldn't be right. They were fine! They were both fine! They couldn't have been possessed.

Again, I saw Mia standing in the moonlight, her eyes open but not seeing, telling me to stop calling her Mia.

She was dreaming. That's all it was. Just a bad dream. Same as Chrissy. And in this house, it wasn't at all unusual.

I must have been dreaming, too. Simple as that. Even if I couldn't remember dreaming. Even if I couldn't remember coming down the stairs in the middle of the night. Even if I couldn't remember whether I was saying words that made no sense as I stood in the family room facing a shelf of books, too.

Maybe it was the concussion. It could have changed my sleep habits. That and the wine I drank. Ugh. Another reason not to indulge. I rubbed my face and tried not to think of my blowup with Daniel, or how I had agreed to a date with Aiden. That was actually the last thing I needed ... another complicated relationship.

The more I thought about it, the more I decided that must have been what happened. A toxic combination of my concussion, the stress of the night before, and wine. No wonder I ended up sleepwalking.

It didn't mean I was possessed.

It didn't mean I was crazy.

It didn't mean a dark entity had followed me home from the Church of the Forgotten.

A storm is coming.

I squeezed my eyes tightly. No, I wasn't going to think about that shadowy figure sitting across from me at the table. That was just another symptom of my healing brain. That was all.

"Morning, Becca."

I turned to see Mia yawning as she shuffled into the kitchen. Her hair was bunched up on one side of her head, and her eyes were barely open. She hardly looked at me as she headed straight for the coffeepot.

Thank goodness. It gave me a few minutes to compose my expression. *Everything is fine*, I told myself. *I am fine. Everything is fine.*

"Did Daniel tell you when we're supposed to be at the station?" she asked, pouring herself a cup of coffee.

"I thought he said sometime this afternoon, but let me check my texts." I rose from the chair to grab my phone, grateful for something else to focus on.

"I thought so, too," Mia said, holding her cup as she leaned against the counter. "Although I did manage to switch my shift, so I'm not working today at all. I can go any time. Maybe we could go earlier."

I located my phone and started flicking through my texts. "That's fine with me. I'd rather have more time to go through those transcripts and not feel rushed."

"Yeah, it doesn't make sense to me why we would need to wait until this afternoon," Mia mused. "Wouldn't they want us to start working on the case sooner?"

I sucked in my breath, my anger at Daniel sweeping through my body, its cleansing fire burning away the last of the panic from my sleepwalking episode. I welcomed the anger; it was so much better than the helpless fear of something being a lot more wrong with me than the stress and concussion …

The doorbell rang.

Mia looked at me, an eyebrow raised. "Are you expecting anyone?"

I shook my head. "I guess that means you're not either?"

Mia frowned. "Could it be Chrissy? Or one of her friends?"

"I doubt it. They should all be at school."

Mia's frown deepened. "Daphne maybe?"

"She usually texts before she comes over, especially if it's this early. Same with Aiden, and there are no texts." I put my phone down and ran a hand through my wild, tangled hair. I was still wearing what I normally slept in, which was an oversized tee shirt and sweatpants. I didn't look great, but I was probably decent enough to answer the door. "I'll get it."

The only person I could think of who would stop by in the morning without texting would be Daniel. But there was no reason for him to do that anymore … unless he wanted to finish the fight we'd started at The Tipsy Cow. Ugh. That was the last thing I needed.

I strode over to the door, trying to think of an excuse to send Daniel on his way. Maybe I should tell him I wasn't feeling well. No, then he would tell me not to come to the station to review the transcripts. Maybe I should tell him I had some work to do, although I hadn't done any work for weeks now …

I didn't even look through the peephole. I flung open the door, more than ready to tell Daniel I wasn't in any mood to talk to him.

The words never left my mouth.

"Rebecca. So you are alive, after all."

Actually, I had no words at all. I couldn't think of a single thing to say. All I could do was stare at the person standing on the porch, who I never in a million years thought I would see in Redemption.

My mother.

Chapter 10

"Close your mouth, Rebecca, before you catch flies," my mother said.

I hadn't realized it was still hanging open, and I quickly snapped it shut. "What ... why ... how ..."

My mother stared at me, her hazel eyes cool. As always, she was dressed impeccably in gray wool pants, short gray boots, a cream cashmere sweater, and a long, gray wool coat. Her hair was pulled back in a sleek, smooth bun—the kind I could never replicate with my own wild locks—and her makeup was expertly applied. The look was complete with a simple string of pearls. "If you would have taken a minute to answer my texts or call me back, you would know the answer to that."

Inwardly, I winced. It was true ... I had been ignoring her. But never in a million years did I expect her to show up on my doorstep.

"I ... I've been busy," I said and immediately cringed. I sounded pathetic.

My mother's look narrowed. "Too busy to answer a text? To spend ten minutes talking to your own mother, who has been worried sick about you?"

Worried sick? As far back as I could remember, my mother had never been worried sick about me. "You were worried sick because I didn't answer a text?"

Her eyes hardened. "I was worried sick because of this whole Church of the Forgotten business. Why wouldn't you think we would be, after hearing about it?"

For the second time, my mouth fell open. "The Church of the Forgotten? How did you ..." my voice trailed off. The media. Of course.

"You think we don't read the newspaper?" She asked as if reading my mind. "Now, are you going to invite me in, or just stand here with the door open, letting all the heat out of your house?"

I immediately took a step back, gesturing for her to come in. My mother shot me one of her looks as she swept inside, bringing with her the scents of fall—crisp air with a bite of cold laced with decaying leaves—and her expensive Giorgio Armani perfume.

"Oh, my luggage," she said as I began to close the door. "Would you be a dear and bring it in for me?" The underlying steel note in her voice made it clear it wasn't a request.

Luggage? My heart stuttered in my chest, and I numbly opened the door to find a matching pair of silver Tumi suitcases, one large and one small. Oh no, this couldn't be good. If she was bringing luggage to my home, that meant she was probably going to want to stay with me. Which would be bad enough if I had a spare bedroom for her, which I didn't, as Mia was sleeping in what used to be my office. So what were my options? Have her sleep on one of the couches? In the attic, which was also now my office and painting studio? Or maybe give her my room, and I could take a couch or the attic …

Then there was the fact that she had brought not one, but two suitcases …

Ugh. This was going to be a nightmare, even if I hadn't woken up to find myself in the family room.

No, I wasn't going there. That was a strange one-off, brought on by alcohol, a brain injury, and stress. It meant nothing.

Feeling like I might throw up the coffee I'd just finished drinking, I reached out to roll both pieces of luggage inside. Maybe at the very least, I could talk her into getting a hotel room.

"Becca, who was … oh." Mia was standing by the staircase, clasping her coffee mug and blinking owlishly at my mother, who was looking back at her with a faintly disapproving expression in her eyes. I was suddenly very self-conscious of what we were both wearing—my old sweatpants and tee shirt and Mia in old, faded pajamas with a huge coffee stain across the front. All I wanted to do was yank Mia up the stairs so we could both put on proper clothes. Maybe I could maybe spend a few minutes trying to tame my hair, too … although I already knew from experience that it would never be as smooth and sleek as my mother's.

I had to stop. All my old insecurities were flooding back. I was an adult who carved out a nice life for myself in Redemption, Wisconsin. Never mind that things were a little ... wonky, at the moment. That didn't mean I wasn't a capable grownup who could handle life without looking like I had just stepped out of the pages of a magazine.

Still, I couldn't help but run a hand through my hair in an attempt to smooth it down as I left the suitcases by the door and hurried forward to introduce them.

"Uh, Mia, this is my mom. Mom, this is Mia, my roommate."

My mother's head snapped around to me. "Your ... *roommate*? Is she the reason you won't move back home?"

It took me a moment to parse together what she was implying. "What? No, Mia is a friend who also happens to live here."

"In her own room," Mia added, her eyes sparkling. I shot her a look.

My mom didn't look convinced. "What about Chrissy?"

"Chrissy also has her own room."

My mom's eyes flickered around the house. "So the three of you live here? Together?"

"We make it work," I said, swallowing hard and running a hand through my hair again. "Would you like to sit down? Maybe have some coffee?"

She was still studying the room, slowly turning around and pausing at certain points, likely when her eyes caught something. She stopped altogether in front of one of the end tables that held a lamp and a framed photograph of Aunt Charlie and me. I was maybe five years old, and we were both grinning like lunatics at the camera. She picked it up, running a finger down the glass.

Mia and I glanced at each other. "Mom?"

She seemed lost in thought as she stared at the photo, and it suddenly occurred to me this might be the first time in years that she had seen her sister. There were no photos of Aunt Charlie at my mom's penthouse—at least, not as of the last time I had been there.

The thought wedged itself in my chest, and my own grief over the loss of my aunt swamped over me.

I took a step toward my mom. I wasn't sure what to do, as we were never a touchy-feely family, but just the movement toward her must have been enough to jerk her out of her thoughts, because she abruptly straightened and placed the photo back down.

"Sure ... coffee would be lovely." Her tone was brisk, like she had not just spent several minutes staring at a photo of her little sister.

Sister. It was always difficult to get my head around the fact that my mother and my aunt were siblings. They were so completely opposite.

I led my mom into the kitchen as Mia trailed behind us. I collected my own mug from the table to refill it and fetched a clean one for my mother. "Go ahead and have a seat," I called over my shoulder as I doctored my coffee with cream and sugar, then brought both mugs to the table. "I can make breakfast, as well. We've got eggs and toast ..."

"Coffee is fine. I had something at the hotel. As you know, I never like to eat much for breakfast." Her back was straight as she sat in her chair, eying Oscar, who was curled up in his usual spot next to the window. He had one green eye open, eyeing her right back. "You have a cat."

"His name is Oscar, and he came with the house." My ears had perked up at the word "hotel," and a flicker of hope surged inside me. Maybe I didn't have to worry about her staying with me after all. Although if she had already booked a hotel room, bringing her suitcases with her was a little ... odd. I put her coffee down in front of her and sat down next to her, while Mia chose to sit on my other side. "Which hotel are you staying at?"

She picked up her coffee, her eyes settling on me. "I'm not staying at a hotel. That was just for last night, because my flight was delayed, and it was late by the time I flew into Riverview. I found a room by the airport and drove here this morning." She shot me another disapproving look. "I didn't want to come all the way out here in the middle of the night only to discover you weren't home, so I thought it would be best to wait until this morning."

I winced. Yet another dig. "I'm sorry I didn't get back to you. Truly."

She put her cup down, her lips pursed. "Rebecca, how could you not know how worried we would be? When we saw your name in the paper and couldn't get a hold of you, we assumed the worst."

"I know. I'm sorry." I was babbling, but even worse than babbling was sounding like a broken record. I hated how simply being in my mother's presence immediately reduced me to a self-conscious ten-year-old. "If I had known you knew about the Church of the Forgotten, I would have called back."

My mother's eyes went very wide. "So, in other words, you have no *intention* of calling me back unless it's an emergency?"

Too late, I saw the trap and tried to backpedal without babbling, although that seemed a bit out of reach, at this point. "No, of course it doesn't require an emergency for me to call you back."

"But you just said if you had known we knew you were hospitalized because of that horrid cult, then you would have found the time in your *busy* schedule to reach out to us."

"I … uh … that's not what I meant …" Although, in truth, it *was* what I meant. It just sounded horrid when my mother said it out loud.

"Mrs. Kingsley, you have to understand that …" Mia began.

My mother's head snapped toward her. "My name is NOT Kingsley. It's *Livingston*."

Two spots of faint color bloomed on Mia's cheeks. "Oh, apologies, uh, Mrs. Livingston."

But my mother wasn't done. She swiveled her head back toward me. "Rebecca, I had assumed you went back to your maiden name. That's what you did after your first marriage."

There was a pause as I contemplated how to answer a question that wasn't exactly a question. Nor did I particularly want to answer it, as I had a feeling she wasn't going to approve of me taking my aunt's name, which was also her maiden name.

Her face softened slightly. "Was it because of Chrissy, then?"

Now, she had completely lost me. "Was what because of Chrissy?"

"That you kept Stefan's name. As her stepmother, you wanted to remain connected. I can respect that."

It was on the tip of my tongue to correct her. I could practically taste the words rolling around in my mouth. *Actually, I took the name Kingsley. It just seemed to make sense. Aunt Charlie willed me her house, and as everyone in town knew her, it felt like the right thing to do.*

But I couldn't do it. I couldn't force the words out of my mouth. Instead, I gave her a tight smile and took a long drink of coffee, scalding the roof of my mouth in the process.

Somehow, that felt justified.

Mia glanced at me, her brow furrowed in confusion, before turning back to my mother. "Um, well, Mrs. Livingston, what I was going to say is that it isn't all Becca's fault. Not completely, at least. She was diagnosed with a bad concussion …"

"What?" My mother's head swiveled back to me, a shocked expression on her face. "Are you okay?"

"Yes, I'm healing nicely, according to my doctor," I said.

My mother's eyes continued to search my face, as if she would somehow be able to see my concussion. "Oh, Rebecca … you should have told us."

"But that's the thing about concussions," Mia continued, plowing on before I could apologize again. "You're not supposed to use your phone. Like, at all. Nor a computer. You have to give your brain a rest. So, Becca didn't even see you had called or left messages until just a few days ago. And yes, she probably should have responded sooner. But it's difficult, when you're recovering from a brain injury, to balance all the things you need to do for the short amount of time you're on your electronic devices."

Mia was giving me a little too much credit. I certainly could have reached out sooner. But I chose not to, mostly because I rarely felt like talking to my mother.

Although if I had known she would eventually show up on my doorstep, I definitely would have called her back. Probably immediately.

"Plus, the concussion isn't the only thing she's been dealing with," Mia continued. "It was … well … grueling, living at the Church. Not to mention exhausting, with the constant stress of being found out. They didn't feed us nearly enough or let us drink enough water or allow us more than a few hours of sleep at night, so physically, she needed a lot of rest and healthy food to build her strength back. And that's on top of all the … well … processing all the mental trauma, which was more challenging because she was also dealing with a brain injury. So, it was a lot."

My mother's lips pursed as she turned back to me, but I could see the worry in her eyes. "Are you sure you're okay?"

"Yes, I'm doing much better." At least, I hoped that was true. "It has been a challenge these past few weeks, but I agree—I should have called."

My mother studied me, and inwardly, I braced myself, sure she wasn't going to drop it. Instead, she picked up her mug. "Well, it's a good thing I'm here now. It sounds like you could use the help."

I tried to keep the panic out of my voice. "That's really not necessary. I'm so much better now …"

"Nonsense," she cut me off, her eyes narrowing. "Rebecca, don't insult me. I have eyes. You are still way too thin and way too pale. It can take people months or even years to get over a traumatic experience, and you're trying to do it with a brain injury. I'm sure you're improving, but if someone was here taking care of you, you could probably heal even faster."

"Honestly, I'm fine. We're fine," I said. There it was again … that word. *Fine*. I really needed to come up with something else. "Besides, you shouldn't leave dad alone …"

"Your father will be fine for a few weeks," she said firmly, taking a sip of her coffee.

My jaw dropped. "A few weeks?" I pictured the two suitcases still standing by the doorway and wanted to pull my hair out. "You can't stay here for a few weeks."

She put her coffee cup down with a clink. "Why on Earth not? I am your mother. I should be able to spend a few weeks with my daughter."

"Well, we don't have a room for you, for one thing," I said.

My mother stiffened. "You can't find room for your mother?"

"I … ah …" my voice failed me, and I felt myself start to curl up. Crap, I was going to end up on the couch after all.

Luckily, Mia came to my rescue again. "Unfortunately, all the bedrooms are taken. But we could set up the attic for you."

Now, it was my mother's turn to look shocked. "The attic? You would put your mother in the attic?"

I finally found my voice again. "It's a very nice attic. It's large and airy. My office is up there, along with a daybed. You would have a lot of privacy. Or there are a couple of couches on this floor, one in the living room and one in the family room. I can show you if you want. But you might be more comfortable in a hotel …"

"The whole point of me staying here is it helps you out. I will not be staying in a hotel." My mother's voice was firm as she placed both hands on the table and pushed herself to her feet. She took a few steps toward the doorway before turning back to Mia and me. Neither of us had moved. She raised an eyebrow. "Well? Aren't you going to show me around?"

Swallowing hard, I shot Mia an apologetic look before getting to my feet and facing my mother. I forced a smile and said, "Let me give you the grand tour."

Chapter 11

Mom wasn't impressed with the house.

I could practically see the wheels turning in her head as she compared my hundred-year-old farmhouse with her penthouse in New York. Even though she didn't say it, I could almost feel her judgment. Why would I possibly stay here, in a small town in the Midwest, when I could be living in a beautiful apartment in New York? When I could be married again, hopefully to someone more suitable than my first two husbands?

And an even deeper question—why would her sister also choose this life?

But she kept those questions to herself, and for that, I was thankful.

I started the tour with the family room, as that's where my mother was already heading, although as soon as I stepped through the doorway, my mouth went dry and my heart began to pound. I kept my face angled away from the bookshelf and told myself I would deal with it later.

"Is that one of the couches?" My mother asked, her voice wry.

My steps faltered. I had definitely not thought this through. There was no way I was letting my mother sleep in the family room. Not after what happened last night. It wasn't an option, even if I had to give her my room. "Yes, but you don't want to sleep there. It's not comfortable," I said quickly. That wasn't true. Of the two couches, it was by far the better one. Plus, the family room was more private than the living room. Although thinking it through, that couch wouldn't work either, because it was right next to the staircase.

Ugh. It was either going to be the attic or my room. Maybe I would be able to talk her into a hotel after all. Or maybe I should be the one to stay in a hotel.

My mother circled around the downstairs as I trailed after her before heading up to the second floor. I rattled off who was in each room, pointedly ignoring the room at the top of the stairs, before turning toward the steps to the attic.

Of course, my mother had other ideas.

"What about this one?" She asked from behind me.

Crap. I so didn't want to have this conversation with her. Slowly, I turned back as she remained standing next to the door, an expectant look on her face.

There was no way I was letting her anywhere near that room. As far as I was concerned, it was the very heart of the problems in the house.

"That room is for storage." I waved toward the steps to the attic. "If you want to follow me ..."

"Storage?" She shot me a funny look. "Why would you waste a perfectly good room on this floor for storage?"

"Actually, it's a perfect room for storage," I said, my voice stiff.

"Not particularly," she argued. "The attic would be better. That's what attics are for. Storage."

"Not this attic. You'll see once you walk up ..."

"But there's all these extra steps to climb," my mother interrupted. "It would be so much easier if I was on this floor like everyone else."

"Well, that's not possible," I said. "As I said, we don't have room on this floor."

"Oh, nonsense," she said, reaching for the doorknob. "I bet with a little elbow grease, we could fix it up just fine ..."

"No! Stop!" My voice was high and panicky as I slammed a hand against the door, as if that would keep her from opening it. "Don't go in there!"

My mother froze, her hand still on the doorknob. "What?"

"Just don't go in there." I wasn't sure why I didn't want my mother to open the door. It wasn't like we didn't ever go into it. For one, half of Mia's clothes were still in that closet. Although, to be fair, they were the clothes she rarely wore. But still, we did use the room. Sparingly.

But something was screaming inside me to not let my mother open the door.

She stared at me, looking completely put out, but at least she didn't turn the doorknob. "Rebecca, you're making no sense. Why can't I go into this room?"

"You just ... it's better this way." Even to myself, I sounded lame. "No one uses it."

Her eyes narrowed as she glanced between me and the door. "Is there something wrong with it?"

Why, yes. If you sleep there, you may end up sleepwalking. Or worse. "You could say that," I said. "Can I show you the ..."

But my mother wasn't done. "Is there structural damage?" She squinted at the door, as if that would help her see inside. "I didn't see anything from the outside, but that doesn't mean anything. Or ..." her eyes widened. "Is it mold? Is that the problem? Maybe we need to get the whole house checked out ..."

"It's not a mold problem," I said, thinking the last thing I needed was a parade of contractors tromping through my house, poking in all the corners and generally making a mess. And my mother would be right behind them, her eagle eyes checking out every little nook and cranny. "But the room isn't safe. Trust me on this. Please."

She opened her mouth but must have seen something in my expression... or maybe it was the "please," because she closed it without saying a word and dropped her hand away from the doorknob. "Fine." Her voice dripped with disapproval. "If you want to show me the attic that badly, then show me the attic. Let's go."

My stomach twisted in an old, familiar knot, and I desperately wanted to say something to smooth things over with her. But what? I absolutely did NOT want her staying in that room, which was completely the opposite from what she wanted. And my mother was not used to hearing the word no, especially from her daughter. It was already bad enough I had stayed in Redemption and didn't take her calls. Now, I was denying her the small convenience of staying in a room that wouldn't require her to climb stairs?

But what else could I do? Tell her the truth? That the room is haunted, and I don't want her exposed to whatever is in there? Yeah, that would go over well. I didn't even want to consider that conversation.

Instead, I turned and trudged up the stairs, my mother following behind.

The attic was a huge space filled with sunlight, thanks to the multiple windows and high ceiling. The whole room seemed very light and airy. During the summer months, it could get oppressively warm, but with the weather getting cooler, it would be perfect. Most of the room was set up for the tea business, with a desk, filing cabinets, and a couple of shelves filled with dried herbs and flowers. There were also rows of racks where I dried the herbs, and tucked away in the corner was my painting studio.

Oh no. I had forgotten about that. Maybe my mother wouldn't notice it.

Like that would ever happen.

"Here's the daybed," I said brightly. It was pushed against the wall between the filing cabinets. "It's quite comfortable. I've taken many naps here."

I turned to look at my mother, who was standing in the middle of the room, surveying everything around her, a faint frown on her lips. "There are a lot of windows here without shades," she said.

"As you've probably noticed, we don't have any neighbors," I said. "Don't worry; it will be dark at night. And we can always get you an eye mask if you need one."

She put her hands on her hips and gave me *the look*—the one that made me shrink into myself as a child. "I just don't understand why you want me to stay up here, when there is a perfectly good room on the second floor."

My heart sank. "But that's not a perfectly good room. This is much better."

"If you would let me see it ..."

"I told you, we don't go into that room. It's better that way."

"But why? It makes no sense."

"It's just ..." *You see, it's haunted, mom. That's the room CB slept in, and we all know how he turned out. Chrissy and Mia slept in there, too, and both of them experienced terrible nightmares and sleepwalking. I don't want you to go through any of that.* I tugged a hand through my hair, wishing I was anywhere else. "You just have to trust me," I finally said, my voice cracking a little at the end. "Can you do that?"

She narrowed her eyes as she surveyed the room. "I don't like this, Rebecca."

Join the club, I thought sourly. *And maybe get a hotel room, if it's so bad here.* But I kept the words inside. I had a feeling if I said them out loud, I would sound exactly like the child I had regressed into. "You'll have a lot of privacy up here. If you give it a try, you may find you really like it."

She raised an eyebrow. "Oh? And where are *you* going to work?"

"I'm not working much right now anyway," I said truthfully. "And if I need to, I'm sure we can figure out how to keep out of each other's way."

She didn't look convinced.

"Well, the Redemption Inn is only a few minutes away from here …" I started to say, but she interrupted me.

"I'm not getting a hotel room," she said abruptly.

I closed my mouth and nodded.

She looked around again, seeming more upset than she was when she first walked in, before giving her head a quick shake and striding across the room where my painting supplies were. "What's this?"

"Oh, that's … that's nothing," I stuttered before hurrying over to her, my heart in my throat. This was turning into an even bigger disaster that I had imagined. Maybe I should have just let her stay in the room at the top of the stairs after all and just kept my fingers crossed that whatever was in there would leave her alone. "Really, you shouldn't pay any attention to any of those …"

But she had already started turning around some of the paintings I had lined up against the wall and was flipping through them.

"You really shouldn't …" my voice broke as I suddenly lost the words. My mother had never wanted me to paint. She considered it a waste of time. When I'd hesitantly brought up attending art school instead of college, she stared at me with such a horrified look, you'd think I'd told her I wanted to leave civilization behind and move to a forest to live with a pack of wolves. I never brought it up again.

"Who did these? Was it Chrissy?" She flipped past another one and paused for a moment. Her eyes flicked toward me. "Was it Charlotte?"

I looked at her in confusion. "Charlotte?"

She pressed her lips together in a flat line and flipped to another painting. "My sister. *Charlie.*" She spat the name out. "I always hated that nickname."

Oh. Of course. I should have known. She hated that Aunt Charlie called me Becca, too. "No, the paintings aren't Aunt Charli ... Aunt Charlotte's. Or Chrissy's."

Her hands stilled. She met my gaze. "Are they yours?"

My mouth was so dry, I didn't think I could speak, so I forced myself to nod.

She glanced back down at the painting in her hand. "They're good."

My mother complimenting my paintings? I almost fell over in shock. Almost ... because it didn't sound much like a compliment. Her voice was emotionless, like she was simply being polite. The knot in my stomach twisted tighter. "Thanks, but I know they're pretty rough." My words came out in a rush. "I did them back in high school, mostly as a lark ..."

She leaned the paintings back against the wall. "Rebecca, I mean it. They're good." She turned and looked me in the eye. "You obviously have talent. I'm sorry I didn't see it sooner."

Now I really thought I might fall over. I had no idea what to do with her words, especially because they still didn't sound like a compliment. If anything, she sounded ... angry.

She brushed her hands together as if dusting them ... though it could have been the imaginary dirt she assumed must cling to my art. "I guess this will have to do." Her tone implied she wasn't the slightest bit happy about it, but if she must suffer, then suffer she would. She walked over to the daybed and started examining the quilt. "I'm assuming the sheets are clean?"

"I'll get some fresh ones," I murmured as I began moving toward the stairs. I hadn't yet decided if I was relieved or not that she had agreed to stay in the attic.

She prodded one of the pillows. "I'll need my suitcases as well."

I tried not to sigh. "Of course."

I could hear footsteps creaking on the steps, and Mia's head poked around the corner. She had washed her face, combed her hair, and changed into a pair of jeans and a hooded, red sweatshirt. Her eyes shifted between me and my mother. "Not to interrupt, but we should get going."

I could have kissed her. "Yes, of course. Let me finish getting my mother settled, and I'll get dressed."

"You have to go somewhere?" my mother called out from behind us. "I just got here."

Mia crossed her eyes at me, and it was all I could do not to burst out laughing. "Yeah, I know, but it's important."

I could hear the creak of the floorboards as my mother approached us. "Surely not as important as spending a little time with your mother."

I tried not to sigh as I turned back around to face her. "I shouldn't be long, and besides, I'm sure you want a little time to get settled and freshen up."

She stopped a few feet in front of me and tilted her head. "Where are you going? Maybe I could come with you."

I blanched. I couldn't help it. The idea of my mother in the police station hovering behind me as Mia and I read transcripts and Daniel watching everything with his cop eyes … ugh. Not going to happen.

Her eyes went wide, and she took a half step back, folding her arms across her chest. "Is it really that terrible to spend time with me, Rebecca?"

Her voice was quiet, but if anything, it made the impact even more powerful. It cut through me like butter, leaving me feeling wretched, guilty. Why oh why didn't I just respond to her messages? This was turning into a complete nightmare.

"It's not like that," I said, rubbing my temple. I was going to have to tell her the truth. If I didn't, I was never going to hear the end of it, and just the thought of listening to her never-ending passive-aggressive jabs made me want to crawl back into bed. "Mia and I are going to the police station."

Her jaw dropped. "The police station? Rebecca, what did you …"

"Nothing," I cut in hastily. "Nothing like that. We're helping with an investigation. Actually, we're helping with the investigation into the Church of the Forgotten."

Her brows furrowed. "Why do you need to help with that?" Her voice dripped with disgust, like I was about to pick up something nasty.

"Because Mia and I were there. We know the members, know what it was like, know some of the language. We might be able to spot something that the police would never notice."

"But why can't they just ask the actual Church of the Forgotten members?"

"Because they aren't being very helpful. They're refusing to say much, so Mia and I offered to help. Hopefully, we'll find something that can help them crack the case." I decided to avoid mentioning Edna's murder. If my mother was already concerned about us, or at least me, getting involved, knowing there was a murderer still at large wouldn't help.

My mother was studying my face, and I braced myself for more objections, or even worse, another offer to come with us to the police station. But when she finally spoke, it was not what I expected. "Are you sure you're okay doing this? Your … concussion …" her words were unsure, and her voice was halting. "Mia made it sound like you're still healing. Do you think you're up for this?"

Despite everything—including the annoyed, nervous wreck she had turned me into since the moment she walked through the door—her concern touched something deep inside me. "I'll be fine. It's important for me to do this. To help. I want this to be over, for everyone involved, and if I can make that happen any faster, I'm happy to do it."

She was still watching me closely, and she must have seen something that convinced her, because she nodded once and turned away. "I'll get myself settled while you're gone, so when you're back, we can get caught up."

I sagged, feeling a strange mixture of relief that she was agreeing to staying home and apprehension of the fallout. But I would cross that bridge when I came to it. "That sounds good," I said as I started down the stairs.

She didn't turn around. "Don't forget the sheets. Or my suitcases," she called out.

I could feel my shoulders tense. "I won't."

What Wasn't Forgotten

Chapter 12

"You're early," Daniel grumbled as he led us through the station to the interrogation and conference rooms in the back. "I told you to come this afternoon."

"Our plans changed," Mia said shortly. Mentally, I sent her yet another "thank you." The last thing I wanted was for Daniel to know about my mother's unexpected visit.

Daniel eyed her but didn't answer. He didn't look great. In fact, if I didn't know better, I would have thought he was hung over. His face was pale, and there were dark circles under his eyes. I suspected it was probably the result of a lot of late nights and too much bad coffee.

After our fight at the bar, I hadn't rejoined my friends. Instead, I stopped by the booth just long enough to tell everyone I was getting a headache and felt like I had enough for one night. Mia did want to leave with me, and it was a quiet ride home. Once there, I immediately went up to take a bath and go to bed.

I didn't want to think about how the rest of my night had gone.

"It's going to take me a bit to gather the files and bring them to you," Daniel said, opening the door to one of the rooms and gesturing us inside.

"That's fine. We can wait," Mia said.

Daniel shot her another look, but left without responding.

"Well, he's in a cheery mood," Mia said sarcastically, settling down in one of the straight wooden chairs in front of a long, scarred table. "You'd think it was *his* mother who paid him an unexpected visit this morning." Her eyes gleamed at me.

I sat down heavily next to her, rubbing my face. "I'll try and get her to leave as soon as possible."

"There's no rush," Mia said, sitting back like we were getting ready to enjoy a nice relaxing meal rather than reading transcripts of discussions with potential killers. "It's your house. If you want your mother to stay for six months, that's your business."

"Oh, don't even say that," I groaned. "This is such a disaster."

Her lips curled up in a commiserating half-smile. "Has she ever done this before? Dropped in unexpectedly?"

I shook my head. "Although I've never ignored her like I have since moving out here, either. When I was living in New York, I guess you could say I was … a more attentive daughter."

"Ah, that makes sense. She seemed a little … put out."

I barked a laugh that didn't have much humor in it. "Yeah, you could say that. She is definitely not used to anyone else being in charge. She's in uncharted territory."

Mia chuckled under her breath. "I can see that." The humor quickly faded from her voice, though. "But it's weird. I don't ever remember seeing her in Redemption before. Not even when Charlie was alive. Did she ever visit?"

"Not to my knowledge. When we were younger, she would accompany CB and me on the plane, but she would never come to Redemption with us. Aunt Charlie would always meet us at the airport and bring us here. And then, of course, when we got older, she would have the flight attendant keep an eye on us."

"Huh." Mia's face was thoughtful. "It's kind of … something, that she would come out now, after all this time. I guess she must have been really worried about you."

I hadn't thought about it like that. Why would she decide to visit Redemption now, after all these years, when she never had before? Not even those last few months of Aunt Charlie's life when she was sick and dying?

What did it mean that she was here now?

A storm is coming.

An uneasy feeling seemed to wind its way from my stomach to my chest, and I struggled to push it down. It had to be a coincidence. I couldn't see how my mother would have anything to do with whatever was going on with the town. Especially since this all could have been avoided if I had just done what any other daughter would have and called her back.

"Also, sorry I almost let it slip that you had changed your name to Kingsley," Mia said. "I didn't realize your mother didn't know. Although it's possible you told me, and I don't remember."

"You have nothing to be sorry about," I said, raking my hand through my hair. "I can't remember if I told you or not, but it doesn't matter." I stared at the dingy cinder-block walls. They were painted white and gray, but the paint was starting to fade, and it appeared to be chipped in places. "There's a lot I didn't tell my mother, mostly because I didn't want to have any more uncomfortable conversations than I was already having with her. I figured since she was likely never going to come here, I was safe." My lips twisted in a sarcastic smile. "Joke's on me."

Mia's smile was sympathetic. "Don't be too hard on yourself. Now that I've met her, I can say I would probably have done the same."

My smile became a little more natural at that, but before I could say anything more, the door flew back open, and Daniel came in, arms so full of file folders, I could barely see his face. He set them down on the table, and the ones on top immediately started sliding every which way.

"Oh." Mia said, leaning forward to catch one before its contents spilled out onto the floor. "This is … um … a lot of files."

"This is about half," Daniel said grimly as another officer came into the room with his arms full, too.

I reached out to help straighten out Daniel's pile in order to make room for the rest. "I guess it's a good thing we came early."

Daniel didn't respond, but I could see his jaw tighten. He was clearly not happy, but I wasn't entirely sure why … unless he was still upset about us being involved in the case at all.

Or maybe it was just me he was upset with.

Argh. I had to stop this. I was already out of sorts with my mother here—I didn't need to keep rehashing how irritated I was with Daniel in my mind. Especially when it was more important that I focus on helping solve the case.

"You're going to find a lot of repetition here," he warned once we had organized the folders into two piles, once for each of us. "So, it might feel like a slog as you go through it."

"Are people saying things verbatim?" I asked, flipping open the first folder with the name "Clementine" on it. I searched my mind but couldn't remember meeting anyone by that name.

"Pretty close," Daniel said. He had seated himself in the chair across from us, a yellow notebook and pen in front of him. "But you'll see when you go through them."

There was a photograph stapled to the first page in the file, which was something of an information sheet, containing details like the person's name, age, eye color, and other physical details. I squinted at the picture, which looked about as flattering as a driver's license photo. Her face was puffy and wrinkly, and her hair was straggly, but she seemed vaguely familiar.

"Do you remember a Clementine?" I asked Mia.

Mia frowned. "Wasn't she the one who took care of the chickens?"

The chickens. Ugh. I shuddered, remembering one in particular that seemed to have it in for me. No wonder I couldn't remember the person who took care of those beady-eyed little monsters.

I flipped the page over and started reading the transcript.

After going through several of them, I could see where Daniel was coming from. They were all eerily similar.

Do you remember a Pamela?

Pamela...? I'm sorry, but that sounds like a Temporary Name.

Do you recognize this picture?

Oh. That looks like Iris. Is she...

Dead? Yes.

Oh. I'm sorry to hear that. She was a lovely woman. Very devout to The One. That's very sad.

So, you're saying you didn't know she was dead?

No, of course not. I thought she left.

Left? Without her daughter?

No, I thought her daughter went with her.

You didn't know that Eleanor had kidnapped her daughter?

No, of course not. We're a peaceful religion. We don't kidnap people.

But you kidnapped Zelda.

Zelda? Who is Zelda?

You may have known her as Lily.

Oh yes. Of course. Lily. She was a sweet girl. Very quiet. Very obedient.

So you're saying you didn't know your church had kidnapped her?

Surely there has been some mistake. We don't kidnap people. We're a peaceful religion.

Yet, Iris was murdered. And Lily was kidnapped…

Which is very unfortunate. But it has nothing to do with us.

How can you say that? Lily was found on your property, chained up in a barn.

I'm sure there's been some misunderstanding. None of us would kidnap a child. We are a peaceful religion.

And it just went on and on. No matter what the officers said to them, they denied it. No, Pamela—or Iris, as was apparently her name—couldn't have been killed by the Church of the Forgotten, as they were *a peaceful religion*. Someone else must have killed her. No, they couldn't explain why they had Zelda or Lily on their property. It must be some sort of misunderstanding.

The more I read, the more ill I became.

When they were asked to describe their religion, their answers were also uncannily similar. It was all about taking care of those who had fallen through the cracks. The "forgotten" ones. But they weren't forgotten, because The One was watching out for them.

Surely, you've heard that the meek shall inherit the Earth? The Bible tells us that is the truth. Well, we are the meek, and The One is there to make sure we do inherit the Earth. That is why we worship The One.

Just reading those words made my skin crawl.

"Did you know they were quoting the Bible?" I asked Mia at one point.

Mia shook her head. "I never heard anyone talk about the Bible. Maybe that was something they told people when they were recruiting them from the streets."

Maybe. Or maybe it was something they trotted out now, during a police investigation, to try and make it sound like they were less crazy than they actually were.

"Anything jump out at you?" Daniel asked at one point. He had been bouncing in and out of the room, never leaving us alone for very long.

Mia sighed. "Nothing yet. At least nothing that we haven't told you before. I see what you mean about them all sounding the same."

Daniel flashed her a slanted smile as he rubbed his chin, where I could see a faint shadow of stubble. He was normally clean-shaven, but it seemed he may have skipped that particular task this morning. "It sure seems like it was coordinated, doesn't it?"

It did. Although some of the transcripts—like Edward's, the silent man who met me at the gate, and Gertrude's—seemed even more creepy than the rest. I could almost see their smugness dripping off the page. Even their photographs seemed to laugh at us.

Although ... there was something off about Gertrude's photo. I couldn't quite put my finger on it, but something didn't seem right. Maybe it was that her head was tilted down and her hair was more in her face than I was used to seeing. Not to mention her entire world has just turned upside down.

Daniel scratched his neck. "But when would this coordination have happened? They couldn't have known Becca was going to blow things up as spectacularly as she did that night. So at what point would they have managed to get all of those people on the same page? When could they have memorized the lines?"

A cold sense of dread crept its way up my spine. When indeed? This case was getting stranger and stranger.

"Did anything like this happen to you? Or did you witness anyone else being coached?" Daniel asked.

"I was never asked to do anything like this," I said. "Nor do I remember groups getting pulled aside. But to be fair, I wasn't in the best mental shape when I was there, and most of my focus was on searching for Zelda. So it's possible I didn't notice."

"I was never asked either," Mia said, but her face was contemplative. "I will say, though, there were ... times when I was sent away, usually to complete some chore. I didn't think too much of it, as it was explained to me that it was because I was the newest member, and the newest members were always assigned those chores. They said I would eventually 'graduate' out of it."

"That never happened, I presume," Daniel said.

Mia shook her head. "Becca showed up, so you would think she would have been assigned those duties, but ... " she paused and tilted her head as she thought. "Now that I think about it, they just ... stopped, after Becca arrived."

Those icy fingers of dread trailed up my back again.

"Do you think Becca's arrival changed something?" Daniel asked.

"It's possible," Mia said. "Eleanor sure seemed intent on getting Becca's house. Plus, it was so close to the Harvest. Maybe she thought she was safe and didn't have to worry about cops or investigations after all."

"Yeah, I guess that didn't work out too well for her," I said under my breath. Mia huffed a laugh. Daniel's expression remained impassive.

I picked up the next file from my pile. Margot. The image of an older woman with a gaunt face but kind eyes flashed in my mind. Her job was the sewing and mending. Until she hurt her hand, that is. Then, her job became supervising me while I did all the sewing and mending.

I flipped open the folder, and the first thing that hit me was her photo. Unlike the others, who were either expressionless and emotionless, or like Edward and Gertrude, slightly smug as if they knew no one could touch them, Margot seemed … distressed. There was a tightness in her jaw that I didn't remember, and her eyes were bleak. I wondered about the cause—was it learning that the Church had been involved with a murder and kidnapping? Or was it something more selfish … like now that the Church was gone, she was worried about her future?

Or maybe it was grief over Eleanor's death. I remembered her speaking privately to Eleanor a few times. It was possible they were friends. If they were, did that mean that Margot knew the truth all along?

I thought of being in her quiet, comforting presence, and I wanted to vomit. I considered Margot one of the good guys, and if it turned out I had misread yet another person …

Swallowing my uneasy feeling, I turned the page and started to read Margot's transcript.

It began like all the rest, parroting the same words and phrases. But then, it shifted.

Do you remember a Pamela?

You mean Iris.

So, you do remember her?

Yes. She was a lovely woman, very devoted to The One. It's very sad what happened to her.

How do you know what happened to her?

Do you think no one is talking about their interviews, detective?

But you're the first one to admit you know her.

<Pause> This has been a very difficult time for everyone. People deal with their grief in different ways.

What do you mean by that?

Exactly what I said. None of this was supposed to happen.

What wasn't supposed to happen?

Iris. Lily. All of it. <Pause> We are a peaceful religion. It's unfortunate what happened to Iris and Lily, but it has nothing to do with us.

Yet, Iris was murdered, and Lily was kidnapped...

Which is very unfortunate. But it has nothing to do with us.

How can you say that? Lily was found on your property, chained up in a barn.

I'm sure there's been some misunderstanding. No one would kidnap a child. We are a peaceful religion.

I stopped breathing as I stared at the transcript.
None of this was supposed to happen.
"Becca, did you find something?" Daniel asked. I glanced up to find him watching me, and my breath snagged in my throat a second time. His entire body was still, like a predator poised to attack its prey.

"You found something?" Mia craned her neck over my shoulder. "What is it?"

I turned toward Mia, trying to shake off Daniel's intense stare. I never could hide anything from him. "I'm not sure." I cleared my throat as I shoved the transcript toward Mia. "Remember Margot? The seamstress?"

"How could I forget?" she grumbled. "Especially seeing as how you got to be her backup, as Eleanor's *favorite*."

"I was only Eleanor's favorite because she wanted my house," I said, tapping the paper. "Read it."

Mia bent over and skimmed the transcript. I didn't look at Daniel, but I could sense the tension in his body, as if he was ready to leap over the table and snatch it away from us.

It didn't take long for her to see it, too. I watched as her eyes widened before she raised her head. "It's not the same."

"What isn't?" Daniel asked between clenched teeth.

I pushed the paper toward him. "Right here."

He practically snatched the paper from me, his eyes skimming it. "She knew Pamela's real name?"

"Not that," I said. "Well, maybe that, too. But I believe her when she said people were talking."

His eyes continued to move down the page. "Do you see it yet?" I asked. "The differences?"

His eyes flicked toward me from over the page. "I do. What does it mean to you?"

I glanced at Mia. "I'm not sure, but I think she might know something."

Daniel put down the transcript and picked up his pen. "What makes you think that?"

I looked at Mia again. "I don't know this for a fact, but it's possible Margot and Eleanor were friends."

He started to take notes. "What makes you think that?"

"I saw them talking together privately. A few times."

"I did too," Mia said.

Daniel eyed her. "So, you have the same impression. That they were friends?"

"I never thought about it one way or another, but ... it wouldn't surprise me."

He jotted down a few more notes. "Is that the only reason you think she might know something?"

"No. It's because of what she said." I leaned over to tap the manuscript. "*None of this was supposed to happen.*"

Daniel stopped writing to stare at the transcript before looking at me. "You think she thought something else was going to happen." It wasn't exactly a question.

I threw him a half-smile. "I think we need to ask."

Chapter 13

It took a bit to convince Daniel to let us interview Margot.

"We'll take it from here," he'd said, making a few final notes on his pad.

"What, and get the same results you got before?" Mia asked. "Isn't that the definition of insanity? Doing the same thing over and over and expecting a different result?"

His eyes narrowed. "It won't be exactly the same. We have a new direction to go in now, thanks to you."

"Not exactly new," I said. "Whoever questioned her did pick up on it during the initial interview, but then Margot switched back to her 'approved' talking points."

"We can revisit what she said in light of Edna's murder," Daniel said. He reached over the table to start gathering up the folders.

Mia and I glanced at each other. "I don't know, Daniel. I think if she was willing to talk with the police, she would have said something more at the time," I said.

"Or, at the very least, she would have approached you after Edna's death," Mia chimed in. "But she hasn't, sooo ..."

Daniel made a face at her. "I'm sure she's scared. I think they all are. It's not surprising no one has approached us yet. But just because she hasn't talked yet doesn't mean she won't."

"Or, that's exactly what it means," I said. He was still fiddling with the folders, so I leaned forward, trying to catch his eye. "Daniel, you know it makes sense for us to try and talk to her. She knows us. Or at least she knows me. Remember, we worked together for a while. I think we'd have better luck than you."

Daniel finally paused his paper shuffling and looked at me. "You do understand there is likely a killer hiding amongst those members, right? And if you show up and start asking a bunch of questions, you'll reveal yourself to them. Do you really want to do that?"

In my mind's eye, I was back on the Hoffman Farm, surrounded by all the members, with only the rusty hand rake to protect Zelda.

Their faces were a blur, but I could still sense their animosity toward me.

Was one of them Edna's killer?

A shiver went through me, but I forced myself to push it down. I couldn't afford to let Daniel see my apprehension, because I knew if he did, he would use it against me. Besides, too much had already happened. There was no way I could just go back home without doing everything I could to solve this. "I wouldn't be revealing anything. They already know who I am. You and I both know that. Just like they already know we were working with the police. Our showing up isn't going to change any of that."

Daniel's lips were pressed together in a thin line. "Having them know something and shoving it in their face are two different things."

"We'll be careful," Mia said, glancing between us. There was a worried look in her eyes, and I wondered if she felt the same cold shock of fear as I had. "But you bring up a good point. Maybe we should go alone. Just the two of us, without any police. Like we just want to talk."

It didn't seem possible, but Daniel looked even more unhappy. "I don't think that's a good idea. We don't know what we're dealing it."

I squeezed my fingers into fists so tightly, I could feel my nails digging into my palms. "Look, I get it. But the reality is, until we get to the bottom of what's going on and you have the real culprit behind bars, we truly aren't safe. Because they're going to be watching for any loose ends, and I imagine that could include us."

"She's right," Mia said. Her face was pale, but her mouth was resolute. "We need to do this, Daniel. Not just to help you solve the case, but … for ourselves, too."

Daniel glanced between us before releasing a long sigh and dragging a hand through his hair. "Would you be willing to wear a wire?"

A wire. I hadn't actually considered that. I glanced at Mia and saw her nod slightly. "Of course. Whatever we need to do to make this happen."

"And keep us safe," Mia added, shooting a quick, worried look in Daniel's direction. "The sooner we get whoever is responsible behind bars, the better for all of us."

Daniel raked his hand through this hair again before giving us both a curt nod. "I'll get it set up," he said as he stood up. "I need a few minutes. You can wait here."

"Of course," I murmured, but it didn't matter, as he strode out of the room without waiting for an answer.

There was a long moment of silence as Mia and I looked at each other.

"I can't believe it," she finally said, her eyebrows going up. "It's like an episode of *Law and Order*."

I let out a laugh that sounded on the verge of hysteria. "Yeah, and we're undercover."

"Totally." Mia laughed as well, but like mine, it sounded more nervous than anything else. I found myself wondering again ... what were the nightmares that kept her up at night?

And were they anything like mine?

***

"Remember, we'll be close by listening in the van," Daniel told us for the hundredth time.

"Got it," I said, adjusting my green hoodie sweatshirt. The mic was hidden underneath it next to my bra, and even though I knew it was tucked away and unable to be seen, I was still self-conscious about it.

After some discussion, we had decided that I would drive Mia and I to the community center. That way, if anyone happened to be standing outside or otherwise watching the street, they wouldn't see us come out of a police van.

"We'll be parked somewhere on the street, close to the community center," he told us again. "The van is dark blue, but if you look in the parking lot as you're leaving ..."

"Daniel," Mia interrupted while finger-combing her hair. "We'll be fine. Honest. It's not like we're infiltrating a drug gang."

"Most of the Church of the Forgotten members just want a quiet life, away from the stress and overwhelm of modern living," I said. "They aren't violent at all."

Daniel's eyes were like hard chips of blue ice. "I'm not worried about most of them. I'm worried about the one or ones who don't seem to mind kidnapping and killing people."

"We'll be fine," I said, echoing Mia. "It's the middle of the afternoon, and we're going to be surrounded by people. I seriously doubt anyone is going to attack us under those circumstances."

Daniel's jaw tightened. "Don't indulge in a false sense of security. Stranger things have happened."

"I know. We won't let our guard down." Impulsively, I reached out and gently touched his arm. A jolt ran through my senses at the contact, making my nerves tingle, and I quickly snatched my hand back. He looked at me then, an unreadable expression in his eyes.

"I, uh …" I could feel myself blush, and I had no idea what to say. Why would I touch him like that? It wasn't like we were dating anymore.

Luckily, Mia came to my rescue. "Becca is right. We'll be very aware of our surroundings, and we won't let anyone sneak up on us. If we're uncomfortable at any time, we'll leave. And if we're feeling threatened and need you to come rescue us, we'll say …" she paused and squished up her face. "What will we say? We need a code phrase … something like, 'The eagle has landed.'"

"'The eagle has landed?'" I repeated, feeling the heat on my cheeks finally start to dissipate. "What kind of code is that?"

"Well, it's sure better than 'Daniel, can you come save us?'" she retorted.

"Not much," I said.

"This is such a bad idea," Daniel grumbled. "I can't believe I let you talk me into it."

"Maybe we should say something about the weather," I said. "Like, 'It's getting really hot in here'?"

"Oh, I like that," Mia said. "Let's do that."

Daniel shook his head. "Just don't get yourself killed. Be safe, and remember ..."

"You'll be right outside," Mia and I said at the same time.

***

The community center was a squat, red, brick building a few blocks away from what was considered downtown Redemption. It was on a quiet street across from duplexes and small, neat apartment buildings. Surrounded by towering oak and maple trees vivid in autumn splendor, the grass was starting to yellow as winter approached. I wondered how the neighbors felt, having a bunch of cult members living right next door to them. Hopefully, the uniformed cops slowly patrolling the area provided them some comfort.

There were only a handful of cars in the parking lot, which wasn't a big surprise considering how the community center was currently being used, so finding a place to park wasn't much of an issue.

"Ready?" I asked as soon as I shut off the engine.

"As ready as I'll ever be," Mia answered, but she didn't move. Neither did I. We both just sat in the car staring out at the fiery red leaves of the maples and the bright-gold leaves of the oaks.

We hadn't spoken at all on the way over. I wasn't sure if it was because we were both thinking about the task ahead of us, or the fact we were both wearing mics. We knew the transmitters were turned off, so we could save the batteries until everyone was in place and we were ready to go. Still, it felt strange to speak.

I assumed Mia felt the same. Eying her now, I could see how pale she was, and a vein near her temple had started to throb. "You okay?"

Her mouth worked for a moment, but nothing came out. "It's just ... it feels stranger than I thought. Seeing them again. You know?"

I did know, but Mia didn't wait for a response. "I always had a feeling there was something off with them. From the moment they moved to the Hoffman Farm, it just didn't feel like they were up to any good. The way they would walk around town in those long muslin dresses ..." she shivered. "So, it's not like it was a huge surprise to learn what they had been doing. It was a realizing you were right about it. But I didn't know for sure when I was living there. I suspected, but I didn't know. Not like now. Now, I know for sure. And I'm just trying to get my head around what it's going to be like to walk in there and face all of them knowing that they truly were a part of a murderous, child-kidnapping cult."

"Not everyone knew," I said.

Mia rolled her eyes. "Oh, come on, Becca. They had to know. Maybe not all the particulars, but they knew."

I tilted my head as I studied her. "You really think so? Even Winnie? Trudy?" As I said her name, a flash of something hit me ... something that felt a lot like grief. I owed my life to Trudy, twice—first for helping me when I almost fainted out in the fields with her, and again when she called the cops at the end.

The cops never did find her, though Daniel said they were still looking. Had she gotten away? Or did something happen to her?

Mia pursed her lips. "Okay, probably not Winnie. But I don't know about Trudy."

"She called the cops though," I reminded her.

"True. But that could have been her guilty conscience."

Again, I saw Trudy in my mind's eye as we walked through the fields together ... her curly black hair bouncing on her shoulders and mischievous brown eyes as she answered my questions about the Church of the Forgotten. I just couldn't believe she knew. But it wasn't worth arguing about.

Instead, I thought about the other members. Especially the quiet ones—the ones who kept their head down and did their work without complaining. Could they really have known? "I don't know. I find it hard to believe they all would stay if they had known."

Mia shrugged. "People hide all sorts of inconvenient truths from themselves all the time. Especially if acknowledging those truths means they'll need to make some changes in their own life. Change is hard under the best of circumstances. In their case, we already know that most of the members were having trouble living a normal life—having a job, paying bills, cooking meals, taking care of a house, etc. — so they traded all of that stress in, letting Eleanor handle it. They just had to show up and do what they were told, and they were taken care of. Life suddenly got really simple for them, and if that meant they had to turn a blind eye to some ... unsavory things, well, there's always a price to be paid."

She paused and noticed me staring at her. "What?" A faint flush rose in her cheeks.

I shook my head. "I'm just ... that's horribly cynical."

She shrugged again. "You weren't with them as long as I was. But regardless, why else would anyone choose that life? You and I both know it wasn't easy, so why stay? Unless the alternative is worse."

"They were also deliberately broken down," I reminded her. "Lack of protein and sleep. It doesn't take long before you can no longer think straight. And you don't know what they left. Gertrude told me she was abused and on the streets when Eleanor found her, so yeah, living on the farm was probably preferable. We didn't hear all of their stories, but I suspect a lot of them are like Gertrude's. What they were leaving behind was even worse than what they experienced at the Church of the Forgotten."

Mia's eyes crinkled. "You do know you're arguing my side now, right?"

I made a face at her. "My point is, I don't think they were ever thinking straight. They were plucked out of a bad place from the start and immediately brainwashed. They were in no shape, physically or mentally, to question anything. Even if they had a few intuitive hits that something was off or wrong, it wouldn't have mattered. They would have told themselves they were better off now than before, and for some of them, they would have been right. So, I honestly don't think they knew. I think they were just trying to survive."

Mia chewed on her bottom lip. "Maybe. What you say makes sense, but ... I still feel like they must have known something wasn't right, brainwashing or not. That whole place felt ... wrong." She shivered, even though the car was still warm, and I had parked in the sun.

Suddenly, my mind shifted to the dark entity that I had felt watching me, and it was on the tip of my tongue to ask Mia if she had felt it, too. I wanted to confess how afraid I was that it had followed me home. But now wasn't the time. We had a job to do, and that's what we needed to focus on—not on the shadowy being that may or may not still be haunting us and how we were about to walk back into the belly of that beast. "I know what you mean. But you should never underestimate how much people can lie to themselves."

"I suppose not," Mia said with a sigh. She glanced out the passenger window toward the community center. "I guess we'll find out which one of us is right. The cat's out of the bag now. So, if they were hiding the truth from themselves, they can't anymore."

"Hey you two," a tinny voice spoke in my ear, making me jump. Actually, both Mia and I jumped. "Where are you? Are you ready to do this?" Daniel's voice grew tense. "Please don't tell me you're already in and forgot to turn on your mics."

I locked eyes with Mia, and she nodded. I fumbled with the receiver, which was taped right above my belly button, and flipped it on. "No, we're still in the parking lot, going over some last-minute strategy. But we're ready."

Chapter 14

There was a sign on the front door explaining how the community center was closed to the public for the foreseeable future. A police officer spotted us through the glass, or he had been watching for us, and let us in.

The first thing I noticed was the temperature, which was overly warm. I could already tell that I was going to be uncomfortable in my sweatshirt. The second was the smell. I wrinkled my nose and noticed Mia doing the same. Too many unwashed bodies in too small of a space. I wondered if they were unable to bathe or choosing not to. What made it even more pungent was the strong odor of garlic and onions mixed in. I decided to try breathing out of my mouth for a bit.

We were directed toward the gym, which had been set up with cots for the members. It had also been sectioned off, so the men were on one side and the women on the other. Two multi-purpose rooms had also been taken over by the members—one was set up with clusters of couches and chairs, two television sets, and a couple of computers in the corners. None of that was being used. The other room appeared to be some sort of makeshift dining hall with rows of tables and folding chairs.

Most of the members were milling about near the edges of the rooms, although there was one fairly large group of women sitting in the corner in the TV room crocheting. They still wore the same long, muslin dresses, and even though I expected it, it felt a little creepy. They looked up at us as we approached, but there was no recognition in their glances, only a faint wariness. I was sure Margot would be with them, but she wasn't.

I wondered why.

While the gym was crowded with cots and trunks and small tables, there weren't as many people as I'd expected. The bleachers were tucked tight against the wall, and other than the basketball nets still hanging limply under the baskets, there was no sign of any other gym equipment. Such a difference from the one and only other time I had visited the community center. It was nearly a year ago, during Mia's winter break between semesters. She had gotten it in her head to do a ton of working out to make up for all the exercising she hadn't been doing during classes. She didn't want to join a gym, and the community center offered pay-as-you-attend workout sessions. She had dragged me to one of the Zumba classes. Neither of us enjoyed it very much—there was something off with how the speakers were set up, and the music echoed strangely. I left in the middle to find the women's locker room, which was down a long hallway. Not wanting to rush my return, I ended up wandering around back there and poking into rooms and doors I really had no business being in. Luckily, no one had caught me.

Just then, we spotted Margot sitting next to a pale, thin woman whose name escaped me in the middle of the sea of cots. Bertha, maybe? Bernice? Something with a B, I thought. I was also pretty sure she had worked in the kitchen, but now, she was concentrating on her sewing. A pile of flowered, muslin material spilled out from her lap, and Margot was looking over her shoulder as she stitched.

"Hi Margot," I called.

Maybe-Bertha jerked at the sound of my voice, stabbing her finger with a needle. She let out a little yelp and stuck her finger in her mouth.

Margot also turned to face us, her expression darkening when she recognized us. "Oh. You."

Oh boy. This was going to be fun. Not even five minutes in, and it was already unraveling.

I plastered a smile across my face. "Yes, me. I was hoping we could chat for a few minutes."

Margot turned her back to us. "I've got nothing to say to you." Maybe-Bertha was staring at us with a panicked look on her face, reminding me of a cornered rabbit.

"Great," I heard Daniel mutter in my ear. I ignored him.

Mia gave me a sideways look, which I also ignored while I circled around to stand in front of Margot. "I don't understand. We were friends, weren't we?"

Maybe-Bertha threw one last frightened look at me before leaping to her feet and hurrying away. Margot opened her mouth like she was going to tell her to stay, but then closed it and shot me a dirty look. "Happy now?"

I looked at her in exasperation. "Why would I possibly be happy? I came here because I was hoping we could talk, and you're treating me like an enemy."

She folded her arms across her chest and glared at me. "Why wouldn't I? You are one."

"I'm not ..." I closed my mouth and took a breath. This was going nowhere fast. I had to figure out another way. "Look, I know I ... wasn't completely truthful when I joined the Church of the Forgotten ..."

"You lied," she snapped.

The venom in her voice was so strong, I almost took a step backward, but I forced myself to hold my ground. "You're right. I lied. But it was only because I was trying to find Zelda. None of this was about you. It was about Eleanor ..."

"But that's the thing. You didn't just lie to Eleanor," she said. "You lied to all of us. And now look at us." She stretched out her arms, gesturing around the room. "You've taken away our home, our land, our life. We're trapped here in this ... gym, watched by cops all day and all night. But ..." she leaned closer to me, her eyes glittering. "As bad as that is, it's going to get worse. Way worse. Once they decide they're done with us, then where do we go? We have no money, no job, no family. What are we supposed to do?"

"I ..." I wasn't sure what to say. She wasn't completely wrong. If I hadn't shown up, she would still be back on the Hoffman Farm, spending her days sewing in that cozy, if not slightly claustrophobic, room. She certainly wouldn't be worrying about where she was going to sleep that night, how she was going to pay the bills, or what she was going to have for dinner.

But Zelda would still be there too, chained up under that barn, or worse ... being forced to kill another child.

"It doesn't bother you, what Eleanor did?" Mia asked, and I stiffened. Oh no. I tried to nudge her, but it was too late. "That she killed a woman and kidnapped her child?"

I gritted my teeth and nudged her again. She looked at me as she raised an eyebrow. I could almost hear her thoughts. *What? We tried it your way, and she wasn't talking. Maybe she needs to be shocked. And it's not like that wasn't what she was doing.*

All true. But challenging Margot felt like it could easily backfire. Our job was to help police crack the case by making Margot feel like she could trust us with the truth. I wasn't sure if Mia's approach would accomplish that, either.

Margot looked away, and I could see her throat working as she swallowed. "It wasn't supposed to be like that." Her voice was so low, I could barely hear it.

I took a step closer. "Then what was it supposed to be like?" I kept my own voice soft and compassionate. Maybe this would work after all. Maybe we could do the good cop/bad cop routine.

She shook her head. "You don't understand. We're a peaceful religion. No one was supposed to get hurt."

I could feel Mia tense next to me. I took another step closer. "But someone did get hurt, Margot. More than one person. You know this."

Margot squeezed her eyes together tightly. "But it wasn't supposed to be like that."

"Then what was it supposed to be like? What was supposed to happen?"

She hesitated. I could almost feel her gathering herself, like she was steeling herself to finally share the truth. She took a deep breath and opened her eyes.

It was so subtle, I almost missed it. Something like a filter slid over her eyes, dampening them. At the same time, I could feel the hairs on the back of my neck stand on end.

Like someone was watching us.

I wanted to turn around, but I also didn't want to lose the moment. If Margot was getting ready to trust us, me turning around could break the connection. I had to stay focused.

But those eyes. I could practically feel them burning a hole through my skin. Who could possibly be so interested in us? Could it be whoever killed Edna? A cold pit of fear lodged itself in my stomach as Daniel's warnings rang in my ears.

I had to pull myself together. I had a job to do. And it was possible Margot was finally going to say something useful. The quicker we solved this case, the sooner we would all be safe.

Margot was still not meeting my eyes. The film that seemed to have covered hers had snapped over her entire face, flattening her expression. There was something about it that was starting to make me uneasy, but before I could figure it out, she blinked once, twice, then slowly focused on me. "I'm done with this conversation." Her tone was flat.

I did a double take, feeling like I had just been slapped. "But why?"

She lifted her head. "I'm just done. Please leave."

"I don't understand..." I started to say, but then I realized I DID understand. Of course. The feeling of eyes boring into the back of my neck. I jerked my head around, but there was nothing. A few people walked past, heads down. Another woman I didn't recognize disappeared down the dark hallway that led to the locker rooms. Two people were lying on their cots, staring at the ceiling. No one seemed to be paying the slightest bit of attention to us. I turned back to Margot and took a step closer. "Are you in danger?" I kept my voice low.

Her expression didn't change, but I was sure I saw it. A flicker in her eyes. It was gone so fast, I couldn't be completely sure. "I already told you, I don't trust you."

Seriously? This again? I tried to tamp down my irritation, especially since I thought it was probably likely she was just throwing something out to get us to leave. "Like I said, I wasn't trying to fool you. If anything, Eleanor was doing that, as she was the one who was behind what happened to Zelda and Pamela."

Margot's eyes narrowed. "Fool me once, shame on you. Fool me twice, shame on me."

"I didn't …" I started.

"Just go," she interrupted as she stood up. "I'm serious, *Elle*." I winced at the sound of my Church of the Forgotten name. She took a step closer to me, and her voice dropped. "I know you're smart … smart enough to get away from here and stay away. Got it?"

My head snapped toward her. Was she saying what I thought she was? I kept my voice equally low. "Margot, if you're in trouble, I can help you. But you have to give me something …"

"I mean it, Elle." Her voice was loud as she took a step back. "I have nothing to say to you. Don't come back." She turned and strode away, her dress flapping behind her.

"Well, that sucks," the tinny voice said in my ear, startling me. I hoped no one was watching me closely enough to notice.

"Should we go after her?" Mia asked in a low voice.

I was about to say yes when I felt it again.

The feeling of being watched.

I whirled around, sure that this time, I would see something. But no. There weren't even any people walking by.

I rubbed the back of my neck. What was going on with me?

"I don't think we're going to get anything more out of Margot," I said. "At least, not today. Let's just go."

Mia nodded as we headed out of the gym. While we walked, I continuously swiveled my head around, trying to see who had been watching us. But everyone still seemed to be ignoring us.

"What are you doing?" Mia whispered. "Is something wrong?"

"Not sure," I said just as softly as we entered the hallway that led to the front door. I peeked into the rooms as we passed, but I couldn't see anything other than shadows near the door where the light didn't reach.

Shadows …

I whirled around again, and that's when I saw it—the pools of darkness where the lights didn't quite hit, especially in the corners. They weren't dark enough to hide a person, but that didn't mean there wasn't something else there … maybe something even more evil …

"Becca, what is going on with you?" Mia hissed.

"Is there something wrong in there?" The tinny voice in my ear asked.

I forced myself to face forward and quickened my steps. "Nothing," I said. "Nothing is wrong. I just thought I might have seen something is all."

Mia raised an eyebrow, but she didn't say anything. We strode across the floor, our shoes making squeaking noises against the linoleum, and pushed open the door to the parking lot.

The cool air was like a shock against my flushed face, but a good one. I hadn't realized how hot and stale the air inside the building was. I breathed deeply, inhaling the clean, crisp, fresh air, noticing but ignoring the slight odor of decay.

"We'll meet you back at the station," the voice in my ear said.

"Why?" I asked, fumbling for my keys.

"Well, we need the mics back," the voice was faintly amused. "Plus, we should debrief."

Oh. The mics. Yeah, that made sense. "Fine," I said, reaching under my sweatshirt to turn off my transmitter. "Ugh."

Mia rolled her eyes as she snapped hers off, too. "I'm not sure what there is to debrief. But whatever. I suppose we should give back the mics. The last thing we need is to be arrested for stealing."

***

The debrief was minimal, as there wasn't much to say. Margot hadn't said anything, but both Mia and I agreed she was hiding something—what, exactly, was a different story. Mia still thought Margot knew more about what was going on than she'd let on. I wasn't as convinced.

After removing my mic, I headed for the parking lot, intending to wait outside for Mia. I was feeling grungy and sticky—like the stench in the community center was still clinging to me—and I was hoping if I stayed outside long enough, it would disappear. I was basically airing myself out. I stared at the few trees dotting the edge of the parking lot and focused on taking long, deep, cleansing breaths.

"Becca? You got a minute?"

I turned to see Daniel standing next to me, although I wasn't sure when or how he'd appeared. His hair was tousled, like he had run his hands through it more than once, and his shirt was unbuttoned at the top.

I was going to say no. I didn't really want to talk to him. I didn't want to talk to anyone. But there was something about his eyes … he looked almost … unsure. And that was a look I didn't remember ever seeing on him before. "What's up?"

He hesitated. "I just … I guess I just wanted you to know that you weren't entirely wrong."

I blinked, trying to recalibrate. That was definitely not what I'd expected. "I wasn't entirely wrong about what?"

He slid his hands into his pockets, looking a bit sheepish. "About today. You being involved in the case …"

I tilted my head. "I'm still not following."

He scuffed his foot against the ground and looked up at the sky. "You're going to make me say it, huh?"

I almost laughed. "I'm not trying to make you say anything. I'm just not sure where you're going with this."

He sighed and finally met my eyes. "When you accused me of not wanting you involved with this case, and I told you it wasn't true? I was lying. I didn't want you involved."

I sucked in my breath. I wanted to yell at him, but his eyes were so intense, all my anger melted away just as quickly. "Why didn't you want me involved?"

His eyes clouded over. "Because I was worried about you. I know," he held up a hand. "I know we aren't dating anymore, so it's not my business. But I also know you're still recovering. And not just from the concussion, but from everything else you went through. And I was afraid this might set you back."

My mouth was dry, although I wasn't sure why. I forced myself to swallow. "You don't need to be worried about me ..."

"I know that," he cut in, taking a step closer to me. "Trust me, I know that. But that doesn't change how I feel."

"Becca, you out here?" Mia's voice floated toward us, and I glanced over Daniel's shoulder to see her coming out of the station. Her voice shifted. "Oh, there you are. I can wait for you by the car."

"No need," Daniel said, taking a step back as he flashed me a lopsided smile that made my heart flip. "We're done here. I'll see you guys later."

Chapter 15

The first thing I noticed when I turned onto my street was that there were too many cars in front of my house.

Chrissy was home; I recognized her car parked on the street, along with the rental that I knew was my mother's. Ugh. It was like an instant punch to the gut. I had completely forgotten to tell Chrissy about my mother showing up, and here she was home alone with her. I could only imagine the third-degree Chrissy was being subjected to. I was going to owe her big time.

But there was also a car I didn't recognize, which somehow made me feel even more alarmed. I supposed it could be one of Chrissy's friends, although again, that meant that Chrissy and her friend were in the house with my mother.

I would think my mother would have the sense to leave them alone, if that were the case, but I also never dreamed she would arrive unannounced on my doorstep.

"Are you expecting anyone?" Mia asked, unbuckling her seatbelt as I parked along the side of the road.

"Nope. But maybe it's one of Chrissy's friends." I turned the car off.

Mia's brows had furrowed. "Maybe. But she doesn't bring her friends over very much."

That was true. She was far more likely to be the one visiting others. I suspected some of that had to do with my house's haunted reputation, but maybe she now had a braver friend.

"Well, there's always a first time," I said as I opened the car door.

Mia shot me a sympathetic look as we crossed the driveway and headed up the porch. "Hopefully, they're having a nice chat with your mom."

Another knot twisted in my stomach. "I can hope," I said as I opened the front door.

Immediately, I knew that wasn't the case.

Oscar was sitting on the stairs, where he never sits. He almost always hangs out in the kitchen, or if not there, in the family room. His tail was twitching dangerously as he fixed his green eyes on us. I could almost hear him say, "About time you got home."

And based on the commotion coming from the kitchen, I didn't blame him for retreating to the stairs. There was the clanging of pots and pans and at least three voices talking very loudly, two of which I recognized.

"What the ..." Mia muttered as I practically ran into the kitchen only to be greeted by a scene I couldn't make any sense of.

Chrissy was standing in one corner, her arms crossed, her cheeks bright red. My mother was in the other corner, looking equally agitated as she faced her. But in the main part of the kitchen was a woman I had never seen before. She was in her forties, maybe early fifties, with light-brown hair pulled back in a ponytail and large, purple-framed glasses. There was a variety of chopped vegetables on the counter in front of her and she was stirring something in a pan on the stove.

"Becca," Chrissy said the moment she saw me, straightening up.

"Her name is *Rebecca*," my mother corrected.

Chrissy gave my mother a withering glance. "*Becca*, thank goodness you're home. You have to do something."

"Rebecca doesn't need to do anything," my mother said. "I have everything under control."

"You have what under control, exactly?" I asked, taking a step forward. "And who is this in my kitchen?"

"This is Tammy, and she may be our new personal chef," my mother said proudly.

Personal chef? My head jerked toward my mother. "Wait. What?"

Mia poked her head around me. "Did your mother just say we have a personal chef?"

"Well, you have to eat, right?" my mother asked.

"I keep telling her you don't need a personal chef," Chrissy said. "I can cook."

My mother's head snapped around to Chrissy. "You're a high school teenager. You shouldn't be expected to cook meals for your stepmother. You should be focused on school."

"But I LIKE cooking," Chrissy spit out. "I want to be a chef."

There was a clatter from the kitchen as Tammy dropped the chef knife on the floor. "Sorry," she said as she bent to pick it up, a nervous smile twitching on her lips. "Look, as I said before, I'm happy to come back another day, and we can do the test then ..."

"There is no reason for you to come back," my mother interrupted, her voice firm. "You're here now, and I'd like to make a decision today, as we'll need you to start immediately."

"Hold on," I said, holding a hand up. I could see Chrissy's head was about to explode. I turned to my mother. "What are you talking about? Why do we need a personal chef immediately?"

My mother huffed. "Well, *someone* has to do the cooking, right? And as you well know, it absolutely can't be me. You don't want me anywhere near a stove."

"Yes, but we've been doing just fine on our own. We don't need a personal chef," I said, offering Tammy an apologetic smile.

"Of course you do," she said, her voice impatient. "Tammy comes with excellent references. She'll come in every week—maybe twice a week, we'll have to see how it goes—and prep and cook enough meals for the entire week. We have one in New York, and I honestly don't know what I would do without her."

"I'm sure Tammy is wonderful," I cut in. "And I can imagine, if you don't like to cook, that having a personal chef is great. But that's not the case here. As Chrissy keeps telling you, she loves to cook, and she's very talented at it ..."

"But who is in charge of the cooking?" my mother interrupted.

"Well ... we all do-" I started, but my mother interrupted again, shaking her head firmly.

"No. Someone is in charge. Someone here is the one who makes sure dinner is ready every time. I don't see any task list anywhere, so I know you're not taking turns. Which means it's one person. Who is it?"

"Um …" I found myself fumbling for words and inwardly cursed myself. Again, I felt like I had traveled back in time to my childhood. "I guess it's mostly me …"

"Precisely my point," she said triumphantly. "You're the one with the concussion. You're the one who should be resting, not cooking meals for everyone." She made a point of gazing around the room, fixing a pointed stare on Mia, who looked a little chagrined.

"But I'm not doing all the cooking. It's more like… pulling the meals together," I said quickly, trying to diffuse the uncomfortable energy that was steadily building. "Chrissy is a great help. She makes a lot of food in advance. All I have to do is heat it up."

"And you're the only one who can heat things up?" my mother asked.

I could feel a flush creeping up my neck. "Mia helps out, too, if that's what you're implying. And she would help out more if I asked, but I don't mind cooking. Especially since that's one of the few activities I can do."

"You should be resting, not cooking." My mother's voice was unyielding. "I'm sure Chrissy helps when she can, but she's got school and a job and a social life to focus on. She doesn't need to be worried about all the planning and shopping and cooking for the week. Did I mention Tammy does all the shopping too? Who normally shops here?"

My neck was burning. "We take turns." Which we did, but again, it was really mostly me. Both Mia and Chrissy had been consumed with work and school over the past year, and while yes, I did have a business to run, my schedule was a lot more flexible than theirs. Plus, Mia always left more than enough cash to cover the groceries, along with the rest of the utilities, so it felt like a fair trade to me.

My mother's stare didn't waver. "Uh huh." It was clear she didn't believe me, and my flush deepened. "Rebecca, you must see this is part of the issue." Her voice had softened. "This is why you're not healing as fast as you should be. You're doing too much. You really need to rest."

"Becca is fine!" Chrissy shouted. Her hands were clenched, and her face was a mottled red. "You weren't here! You don't know! We've been taking good care of her. *We!*" She pounded her chest and pointed at Mia. "Mia and me. We've made sure she's had healthy food to eat and plenty of time to rest-"

"You are a child. Taking care of your stepmother is not your job," my mother interrupted. I noticed two red spots high on my mother's cheekbones. "I'm sure you did the best you could, and I commend you for it. But it's high time we get Rebecca some real help."

There was another loud bang from the kitchen as Tammy dropped something else. "I'm so sorry," she mumbled. "Honestly, I don't mind coming back another time."

"You never have to come back," Chrissy snapped. "No one needs or wants your help."

"Young lady, that is uncalled for," my mother said.

This whole thing had started out bad and was getting worse. I could feel a dull headache starting to form at the back of my right temple. "Chrissy, let's just take a breath ..." I started to say.

Chrissy whirled her head toward me, her eyes full of betrayal. "You're siding with her? After all we've been through?"

I held up my hands. "I'm not siding with anyone. I'm just trying to calm things down so we can discuss this rationally ..."

"There's nothing to discuss," Chrissy said. "Or at least there shouldn't be. But, if you're going to take *her* side, then I guess I'm not needed. Or wanted."

"Chrissy, don't do this," I said, but she flounced past me and out of the kitchen. After a moment, I heard the pounding of her feet on the stairs, and a moment after that, the slamming of her bedroom door.

I closed my eyes. Now, along with feeling like I had regressed to a child when talking to my mother, I also felt like my relationship with Chrissy had just regressed to when we had first moved to Redemption.

Could this day get any worse?

I heard the buzz of my cell phone indicating a text. Ugh. That was the very last thing I needed. Especially if it was Daniel. My stomach flipped around thinking of that lopsided grin. Oh no. I'm not going there. This was absolutely not the time.

Instead, I turned to my mother. "Did you have to do that? You know what Chrissy has been through. Did you have to just ... dismiss her like that?"

My mother waved her hands. "She'll be fine. She's a teenager. That's what teenagers do ... have fits."

"Not this teenager," I said. "She's normally fine."

My mother rolled her eyes. "Oh, come now. I remember you complaining about her after you married Stefan. Said she couldn't stand being in the same room as you."

"That was then." My voice was stiff. "Our relationship has come a long way since then. Chrissy has come a long way since then. Finding out your father is a dangerous sociopath can really make you grow up fast."

"Well." For a moment, my mother seemed a little taken aback, but she quickly recovered. "She's still a child, and she shouldn't have to grow up so fast. Isn't she a senior? She should be enjoying her last year in high school, not worrying about making meals for her stepmother."

I opened my mouth, then closed it. Guilt swamped me. My mother wasn't wrong. Chrissy *should* be enjoying her final year of high school. She shouldn't have to worry about me and make sure I eat properly.

My phone buzzed again, causing my stomach to clench even tighter.

My mother's eyes hadn't left my face, and she must have seen something in my expression. "Really, I'm doing her a favor by hiring the housework out. I know she doesn't see that now, but she will."

My head was pounding. I reached up to rub my temple, wondering if I should just excuse myself to take some ibuprofen when my mother's words finally sunk in. I eyed her. "Housework?"

My mother shrugged. "Well, obviously. Cooking and grocery shopping aren't the only household chores."

My phone buzzed again. Oh my gosh, I was going to throw it against the wall. I finally snatched it out of my purse, fully intending to tell Daniel this was not a good time, and that I'd deal with him later.

Except it wasn't Daniel. It was Aiden.

Hi. Still on for tonight?

?

Becca, are you there?

I started typing furiously. *So sorry, something has come up. Raincheck?*

In the back of my head, I knew it was lame. I knew Aiden deserved better. But at that moment, I just couldn't deal with even one more thing. I would just have to hope I could explain it all properly to him later.

"Who's that?" my mother asked as I dropped my phone back into my purse.

"No one. It was nothing. What other household chores are you talking about?"

My mother's eyes narrowed. "Did you have other plans for tonight? The first night I was here?"

Now, I wanted to throw my mother across the room. "No! I told you it was nothing. What else did you hire out?"

She looked at me like I was being incredibly slow. "What do you think? I hired a housecleaner, of course. Frankly, I'm surprised you haven't already done that. It's not like they're that expensive."

My jaw dropped. "You did what?"

My mother pressed her lips together. "Rebecca, I fail to see why you're being so dense. This is a big house, and someone needs to stay on top of the cleaning." She shot Mia a look full of reproach. "Again, *you* need to be resting."

"But ..." My head was pounding so hard, I couldn't even sort my thoughts out. The idea of someone else, a stranger, going through my house, with all of its history and issues ... I couldn't let that happen. "You can't do that."

My mother straightened. "I can, and I will. Rebecca, how many times do I have to say it? You need to be resting. The last thing you should be doing is cleaning. And if other people aren't stepping up, well, then we need to bring in outside help."

"We all help with the housework. We have a system." I turned to Mia. "I'm so sorry about this."

Mia gave me a twisted smile as she squeezed my hand. "Don't worry about it. I'm going to go up to my room." She let go just as my phone buzzed again. Ugh.

"Well, whatever your *system* is, it isn't working," my mother said. "Have you seen the dust everywhere? And that shower—when was the last time it was cleaned?"

I whirled around to face my mother. "I can't believe how rude you're being. Mia is my roommate, and she *pays* to live here."

My mother raised her eyebrows. "Oh, so you're saying the rent she pays is more than enough to compensate you for your time cleaning and cooking?"

Crap. My mother knew me too well. "We have a system," I said again through gritted teeth. "It was working just fine. Everyone was happy."

My mother cocked her head, her gaze knowing. "Maybe it was *working* when you were healthy. Or maybe I should say it didn't matter when you were healthy. But you're not right now. You need time to heal, Rebecca. You can't be doing all the things. Other people can and should step up. At least ..." she amended, "other *adults* should be stepping up. Not necessarily children."

"But ..." My head was hurting so badly, I just wanted the conversation to be over. But I also knew I had to stand up to her, not just for myself, but for Mia and Chrissy, too. Together, we had created a lovely life for ourselves, and she was making it seem ... wrong. Like I was a bad stepmother for letting Chrissy take on too much adult responsibility, even though it was what she wanted, or at least what she told me she wanted. Suddenly, a different thought hit me—what if she was only telling me that because she didn't want me to kick her out? I felt myself grow cold at the thought, especially since I knew she sometimes worried that it was her against the world, and no one else was going to fend for her. Her father was in jail, and her mother, for all intents and purposes, had abandoned her.

And Mia. Maybe she could have done more to help around the house, especially since despite paying utilities and for groceries, she wasn't paying rent. But the reality was, I hadn't minded doing the lion's share of the housework. Mia was my friend, and I was happy to be in a position where I could help her out as she worked toward getting her law degree.

But trying to explain all of this to my mother would be exhausting. Even when I had my wits about me, she was a master at twisting my words, so I inevitably ended up on the wrong side of the issue. And I absolutely wasn't at my best right then. Maybe I could put off the whole conversation until morning. Then, I could work on convincing her that we didn't need the help ... that we were perfectly fine taking care of the house ourselves ...

I heard footsteps behind me, and I quickly turned, hoping it was Chrissy. But it was Mia with a strange look on her face. "Didn't you say your mother was staying in the attic?"

I felt my heart stop. Oh no. I didn't think I wanted to hear whatever she was about to say. "Yes, that was the plan. Why?"

Mia swallowed, her eyes flickering behind me to where my mother stood. "Well, I think there might have been a change of plans."

"What?" I whirled around to face my mother. "What is she talking about? What did you do?"

My mother just looked at me, an innocent expression on her face. "I got myself settled in, exactly like we talked about."

A surge of fury ignited inside me. "We talked about you staying in the attic."

"Which we both know is silly, when there's a perfectly good room on the second floor," my mother said smoothly.

It was all I could do to keep from screaming in frustration. "But it's not a perfectly good room," I said, my jaw clenched so tightly, I could feel the muscles jumping. "There's not even a bed in it." We had moved it to my old office, so Mia could still sleep on it.

"Yes, that was a bit ... inconvenient," my mother said. "I don't know why you didn't replace the bed in that room. You have plenty of room for one."

"It's because it's not meant to be used as a bedroom," I said.

"Which, again, is silly and a waste of a perfectly good room," my mother said.

I threw my hands up in the air. "This is ridiculous. You would rather sleep on the floor in a bedroom I told you not to go in rather than on a daybed in a very nice and spacious attic?"

"Actually," Mia said, rubbing the back of her neck. "There is a bed in there now."

I snapped my head around to Mia. "There's a bed in where? What bed?"

Mia's eyes flickered toward my mother again. "The ... uh ... daybed from the attic. Although I'm not sure how she got it down the stairs."

"How do you think? I hired someone," my mother said. "Actually, two someones, from a moving company. They were very nice and got it taken care of right away."

"Excuse me."

All of us turned to look at Tammy, who had been edging away from the kitchen but faltered when we all turned toward her. She was clutching her purse in a death grip, and her expression was strained. "I'm so sorry, but I have to go. Normally, I would finish cleaning up first, but I didn't expect to be cooking for you today, so I have somewhere else I have to be." She was talking so fast, she was nearly babbling as her eyes shifted frantically between us. "But everything is washed and air drying." She waved a hand toward the sink, and I noticed all the dishes were neatly stacked next to the sink. "There's a chicken and wild rice casserole in the oven; it will be ready in about twenty more minutes. I set the timer, so you'll know. I also made a salad, and on the stove is my navy bean and sausage soup, which is one of my clients' favorite dishes." She resumed edging toward the door. "There's no rush, just let me know what you decide if you'd like me to ... ah ... start cooking for you."

"Thank you, Tammy. I appreciate that," my mother said. "It all smells delicious."

Tammy's lips stretched into what I think was supposed to be a smile as her pace toward the door sped up.

My mother was still talking, telling her that she would definitely be in touch and if the food tasted as good as it smelled, how soon could she start? I suddenly couldn't stand it anymore. Standing in the kitchen, listening to my mother play lady of the house while completely ignoring what I wanted—hell, she was completely ignoring what I explicitly told her not to do—and I couldn't deal anymore. My head was pounding so hard, my right eye was twitching, and the anger had built up inside to the level of a fireball. I was starting to really think if I didn't let it out, I was going to self-combust.

I opened my mouth. I wasn't sure what I was going to say or if was just going to be a primal scream, but nothing came out.

Instead, everything went black.

What Wasn't Forgotten

Chapter 16

I'm not sure which I became aware of first—how cold and hard the kitchen floor was, how much my head ached, or the voices arguing above me.

"We need to call 9-1-1."

"I don't think that's necessary. She just fainted."

"*Just* fainted? People don't 'just' faint for no reason. She needs a doctor."

"Let's see how she is when she comes to. Then, we can decide."

"No, we shouldn't wait …"

"Becca!"

I blinked. Both Mia and my mother were crouched down, one on either side of me, matching worried expressions on their faces. They could have been twins, despite looking nothing alike.

I was really starting to lose it. Maybe I needed to call it a day and head up to my room, where I could crawl into bed and never come out again. I struggled to sit up, and Mia grabbed my arm. "Easy there. You took a bit of a tumble."

"Rebecca, I think you should lie back down," my mother said. She also had a hand on my arm, but in her case, it was to gently push me back to the floor.

I ignored her, and with Mia's help, managed to pull myself up into a seated position. "What happened?" I croaked. My head was still pounding, and everything seemed to be swimming before my eyes.

"You fainted," Mia said. She handed me a glass of water, and I took a long drink, hoping the cool liquid would help clear my head. It didn't, but I still felt a tiny bit better.

"We should probably take you to the hospital and let them check you out," my mother said. "Or at the very least, call your doctor."

"I'm fine," I said, pressing the glass against my sweaty cheek before taking another sip.

"You are NOT fine," my mother retorted. "People who are fine don't faint for no reason." Her eyes went wide. "Wait ... are you *pregnant*?"

I nearly choked on my water as Mia hid a smile. "No, I'm not pregnant." I wanted to add that pregnancy requires sex, and it'd been quite some time since there was any of that. But that was surely TMI for my mother.

"It's probably because she didn't eat much today," Mia said. "Did you?"

I thought back over my day and realized Mia was right. Other than a couple pieces of toast for breakfast, I hadn't had anything. We were so caught up with the investigation, I didn't even realize we had skipped lunch. Between that and my mother, I had completely forgotten about food. Although now that Mia mentioned it, I realized I was starving, and the aromas coming from the stove were divine.

"Not much," I admitted, and is if on cue, my stomach growled.

My mother clucked her tongue in disapproval. "This is why I want to get you some help. You shouldn't be skipping meals."

"I usually don't," I said, wincing as a bolt of pain shot across my temple.

My mother's sharp eyes didn't miss a thing. "Rebecca, what's wrong? Did you hit your head?"

"No, nothing like that," I said, rubbing my temple. "It's just a headache."

"Do you want some ibuprofen?" Mia asked, her voice sympathetic.

I nodded, and she immediately stood up, far more graceful than I ever could. She disappeared, leaving me alone with my mother, who was still studying my face.

"I don't like this, Rebecca." Her voice was low.

"What's not to like?" I asked sourly, taking another drink of water and wishing it was wine, even though I knew better.

She pursed her lips. Her lipstick was still perfectly applied, as if she had touched it up throughout the day despite not leaving the house. "Obviously, something is seriously wrong with you, and the fact that the people living with you don't or can't see it, much less do anything to help you, is a problem. Not that I blame Chrissy, she's just a child, but …"

"There is nothing seriously wrong with me," I interrupted. "I told you, I'm fine."

"You fainted. You are *not* fine," she retorted. "And don't try and tell me it's because you didn't eat today. People miss meals all the time, and they don't faint."

I could feel the anger start to smolder in my chest again. "Yeah, well, if they miss meals and then have their mother show up out of the blue, they might. Especially if their mother completely ignores the *one thing* that was asked of her."

My mother pressed a perfectly manicured hand to her chest. "You're saying this is *my* fault? I travel all the way from New York because I'm worried about you, and this is the thanks I get?"

"You show up unannounced …"

"Which wasn't my fault. You're the one who didn't respond to my texts or voicemails."

I winced. "Maybe so, but you're not even here for *one day*, and you completely turn my life around. Hiring a personal chef, a house cleaner …"

She looked at me in surprise. "You're upset because you want to clean your own house? I thought you would be thrilled to have the help." She furrowed her brows. "Is it the money? Rebecca, you shouldn't be worried about that. I'm going to take care of it."

I closed my eyes. "It's not that. You didn't even ask. You just … did it."

"Probably because I assumed it would make you happy."

"Here you go," Mia said, her voice a little louder than normal to interrupt our argument. She handed me a couple of pills, which I quickly swallowed with the last of the water.

Every time I thought about what my mother had done, the anger roared back to life inside me. But now, there was fear mixed in, as well. Fear that whatever had haunted CB and Chrissy and Mia would infect my mother, too. The fear of waking to find her standing in the family room in the middle of the night, staring at the bookshelf …

I put my glass down and stared at my mother. "How could you do that? Move into that room after I told you not to?"

My mother rolled her eyes. "Why are you so fixated on that? There's nothing wrong with that room. There's no reason for me to be in the attic."

"Yes, there is—because that's where I told you to stay. No one is supposed to be in that room."

Something flitted across her face that I couldn't read. She leaned a little closer to me, so close I could smell her expensive perfume. "Rebecca, I'm worried." She kept her voice low, even though I was sure Mia could hear every word. "There is no reason why that room shouldn't be used. I checked it over thoroughly, and other than some sort of bad repair job in the closet, there is nothing wrong with it. And the fact you don't want anyone to stay in there is … troubling."

My hands were starting to shake. "But it's my house. I should be able to make the rules in my house, even if you don't like them."

"Of course you should," she said, reaching out to smooth my hair back. I jerked my head away, not wanting her to touch me. I saw a flash of hurt in her eyes as she dropped her hand, but she smothered it quickly, replacing it with the faintly reproachful look I was more familiar with. "And if there was another bedroom on the second floor I could sleep in, I would, gladly. But there isn't. And forcing me to go up an additional flight of stairs each night—and every time I need to go to the bathroom—seems unnecessary. Not to mention there are no curtains on the windows. I can't imagine getting even a wink of sleep."

"That room is haunted," I blurted out. I wasn't sure if it was going to help or hurt my cause, but I didn't think I could stand another moment of listening to her explain (like I was a child) how unreasonable I was being.

She stared at me for a moment and then burst out laughing. "Haunted? Oh, come on."

I met Mia's eyes and instantly regretted my decision. "This isn't funny."

"Of course it is," my mother said, dabbing at her eyes. "You know perfectly well there's no such thing as ghosts."

"I know no such thing," I said, desperately flipping through my memories to find some piece of evidence that my mother would believe. But everything I thought about—Lily, the sleepwalking, the nightmares—all felt like too convoluted to try and explain. "This house *is* haunted. It's the most haunted house in Redemption."

"Which means absolutely nothing, as ghosts don't exist ..."

"It's the room where Mad Martha killed herself and her maid," Mia said.

My mother's head snapped toward Mia. "What are you talking about? Who is Mad Martha?"

I could have kissed Mia. Of course! How could I have forgotten about how it all began? "Martha lived in this house back in the early 1900s. Her husband built it for her, but after the birth of her second child, she went a little crazy and ended up killing herself and her maid."

My mother's hand crept up to her throat. "And she did it in that room?"

I nodded. "And ever since then, she's haunted this house." *Along with a bunch of other ghosts, including your sister,* I thought.

"That's why they call her 'Mad Martha,'" Mia said.

My mother blanched. "Well, that's certainly a ... grisly tale. But it still doesn't change the fact that there is no such thing as ghosts."

"Honestly, even the energy is off in there," I said, a little desperately.

My mother's eyebrows went up. "Energy?"

"It's the room CB stayed in, back when we were kids," I said softly.

I watched her face shut down. "That's enough. What happened to CB has nothing to do with which room he slept in. Don't be so foolish." She turned away, but not before I saw an uneasiness in her eyes, so brief I might have imagined it.

I swallowed hard. "It would make me feel so much better if you weren't sleeping in there. It's just … it's not good. It's just not. I don't want anything bad to happen to you."

She turned back to me, and I saw her gaze soften. "Oh, Rebecca, nothing bad is going to happen to me. It's just a room! It's going to be fine. I promise."

I glanced at Mia. "You know, I could sleep in the attic, and my mom could have my room. Maybe we could just move my stuff …"

"Oh, don't be absurd, Rebecca," my mother said. "There's no reason for you to give up your room."

"Besides, it's not just about moving your stuff," Mia said. "Remember, the daybed is now in that room instead of the attic."

Ugh. I had forgotten about that. There was no way Mia and I were moving that daybed up the stairs by ourselves.

Which meant my mother would be sleeping in that room—the room at the top of the stairs.

I slumped down, all the fight draining out of me.

My mother reached out to pat my shoulder. "Rebecca, this is for the best. You'll see. I understand now that you were worried about me, and I love that you were. But there's nothing wrong with that room. Once you see that, it will be so much better for you. It will be like you have an extra room." She smiled at me just as the kitchen timer went off. "Oh!" She clapped her hands and slowly pulled herself to her feet. "Perfect timing. Dinner is ready! Once you get some food in you, I bet you'll feel so much better."

Mia gave me a half-smile as she leaned closer to my ear. "She'll probably be fine. She's only staying with us for a week or so. Right?"

Oh man … I sure hoped it was only for a week. Although the two suitcases I lugged up the stairs seemed to suggest otherwise. Still, Mia had a point—the short time my mother would be in that room likely wouldn't hurt her.

And maybe my mother was right, too, and I was overreacting. Maybe it really wouldn't matter if that room was used as a guest bedroom. Just like maybe she had a point about the housekeeper. Why was I fighting with her about that? It wasn't like I loved cleaning. I didn't mind it, but why wouldn't I want someone to help? Or a personal chef? And maybe my mother even had a point about Chrissy. She shouldn't be spending her last year in high school worried about me. And maybe I did need to rest more. After all, I did just faint for seemingly no reason.

Maybe the real problem was me and the bad decisions I was making.

"Oh, this is so wonderful," my mother said as she brought a casserole to the table. "The perfect meal for tonight. Hearty and healthy." Mia was getting plates, and I rose unsteadily to my feet to help set the table. "No, no, no!" my mother said in alarm. She pointed at one of the chairs. "Sit. Mia and I will take care of this."

"She's right, Becca. You need to take it easy," Mia said, carrying plates and silverware over. "We've got this."

Feeling out of sorts, I sat.

And wondered why it was just so difficult for me to get my act together.

Chapter 17

I sat straight up in bed.

It was still the middle of the night, and my bedroom was completely dark. But I had heard something, or someone, moving around downstairs.

Was it my mother? Was she sleepwalking after all?

Heart in my throat, I slid out of bed and headed for the door. *It's possible she isn't sleepwalking at all*, I reminded myself. *She could be downstairs getting a glass of water or a cup of tea. She could be looking for a book to read. Just because she's downstairs doesn't mean she's sleepwalking.*

Plus, it was possible it wasn't even my mother down there. It could be Mia or Chrissy getting themselves something to drink. Or it could just be the creaking and groaning of an old house.

Noises downstairs in the middle of the night didn't necessarily mean anyone was sleepwalking.

I eased the door open and crept into the hallway. The other three bedroom doors were closed, and the house itself was dark and silent, like it too was asleep.

But I was *sure* I had heard a noise downstairs. Something had awoken me, after all. Even if it was nothing but the wind, I needed to check it out.

There's another option other than the wind, Mia, Chrissy or your mother, a little voice said inside me. *It could be the darkness that followed you home from the Church of the Forgotten ... the darkness that has been watching you...*

My skin instantly prickled, like it had been drenched in ice, and I nearly stumbled on a step. Every instinct I had told me to run back to the safety of my room. I fought it, knowing if it *was* that darkness lurking in the shadows, my room wasn't safe.

Nowhere in the house was safe.

My hand tightened on the railing, but I forced myself to continue moving. If it was my mother—which made the most sense, seeing how she had always been prone to insomnia—I needed to make sure she was alright.

I continued creeping down the stairs, peering around me constantly, but as far as I could tell, there was nothing there. The living room was quiet and still, although the living room was usually empty.

The real test would be the family room.

My heart was pounding so hard, I could hear it in my ears. I silently moved through the living room toward the downstairs bathroom to check that first, but of course, it was empty.

Slowly, I started toward the family room.

My mouth was so dry, it felt like my tongue had swollen to twice its size, and there was a roaring in my ears. Cautiously, I peeked around the corner, my eyes darting around the room, searching for any sign of someone there.

But there was nothing. The room was empty.

I exhaled in relief before easing my way through it. If anyone was up, they probably *were* in the kitchen getting a drink. All I needed to do was poke my head in to check, and then I could head back up to my bedroom to see if I could salvage any more sleep out of the night. Although now that I thought about it, a cup of tea might help relax me …

"Took you long enough."

I jumped and nearly let out a shriek. A shadowy figure was sitting at the kitchen table, facing the doorway.

I pressed my hand against my chest, trying to slow my racing heart. "What are you doing here?" I whispered.

The figure tilted its head. "I told you before … I live here. Same as you."

Somehow, I found myself sitting across from the shadow, though I wasn't aware of any movement. Nor had I wanted to move. I wanted to be as far as possible from the strange, shadowy presence. Instead, I was now close enough to not just smell its foul odor, but to feel the waves of cold that seemed to emulate from it. "Then why haven't I seen you before?"

The shadow tensed, although I more sensed it than saw it. "That's not important right now."

Ugh. It was like pulling teeth. "Then what is important?"

There was a flicker of light in the distance, almost like lightning. The shadow turned its head toward the window. "A storm is coming."

The waves of cold turned to ice, so sharp I was having trouble breathing. "What storm?"

The head slowly turned back to me. Now that I was closer, I could see the faint hollows where eyes and mouth would be. "The storm that was set in motion a long time ago."

I swallowed hard. My mouth was still so dry. "What can I do to stop it?"

The hollow where its mouth would be stretched out into a parody of a grin. "There is no stopping it. There is only surviving it."

The temperate seemed to drop another ten degrees. "How do I survive it?"

The face shifted slightly, revealing a sharper cheekbone and the edge of a jaw. "By seeing what's right in front of you."

There was something ... familiar about that face. And that familiarity was both fascinating and deeply disturbing. A part of me wanted to get up, to run away, but I couldn't move. "What am I not seeing?"

There was that twisted smile again. "More than you can possibly imagine."

Argh. More pulling teeth. "I don't suppose you could give me a hint."

The face tilted to the side again. "Not all things are equal. Some things are more dangerous than others. And one may even kill you."

The air was so cold, it felt like my skin had frozen ... like my entire body was a statue of ice. "Who is going to kill me?" I tried to say, but my mouth stopped working properly. The sounds that came out didn't sound like words.

Regardless, it seemed like the shadow understood, because it leaned even closer, exhaling its cold, dank breath on me. "None of this was supposed to happen."

I blinked. Or tried to.

The figure sat back in its chair, crossing its arms over its chest. I caught a faint glimpse of an eye gleaming at me under the swirls of darkness. "This conversation is over. It's time for you to wake up."

I jerked awake.

I was in my bedroom. Actually, to be more accurate, I was standing in my bedroom, facing the wall next to the closet.

I turned around slowly, trying to piece together what had happened. The room was still dark, so it wasn't quite morning yet. It was also cold, which I couldn't figure out until I noticed the open window.

Why was my window open? I wouldn't have opened it before I went to bed. Would I? I shivered, but it went deeper than the cold air. The unsettling truth was that I still couldn't fully trust my memory.

If I didn't open it before I went to bed, then did I open it while asleep? Somehow, that seemed even worse. That meant I really was sleepwalking …

No. I wasn't going there. I must have been awake when I got out of bed. I just couldn't remember. Trying not to look at my mussed-up bed, covers thrown to one side, I crossed the room to the window to shut it.

None of it meant anything other than I was going through a stressful time. That was it.

Chilled, I dug my robe out of my closet and prepared to head downstairs. Oscar jumped off the bed and joined me. After all, it was never too early for breakfast.

The house was quiet and still as I padded my way to the kitchen. All the bedroom doors were closed, including Mia's, which I hoped meant everyone was still asleep. Of course, it might also mean that Mia was awake but hiding in her room to avoid my mother.

Ugh. Last night had been a disaster. The only thing that had somewhat redeemed it was the food. As it turned out, Tammy was a talented chef, although I should have known that—my mother had a knack for finding talent. It's how I knew whoever she found to clean the house would also be amazing. Regardless of the food, the meal itself had been uncomfortable and awkward. My mother had done most of the talking while Mia and I focused on eating. Chrissy didn't make an appearance, and I didn't blame her.

I still wasn't sure what to say to her or how to smooth things over. The easiest response would be to tell her to just suck it up until my mother left, and then we could go back to how it was. But was that the best way? As much as I detested how my mother had handled the issue, I couldn't deny her point. But would Chrissy see it like that? And was it a hill to die on?

Man, I wished I had that stepmother manual.

I stepped into the kitchen and nearly screamed. There was a figure sitting at the kitchen table—faceless and shadowy, just watching, waiting for me ...

"Rebecca. You're up early."

I blinked. It was my mother. She was dressed in what appeared to be a black silk robe, and her hair was loose and draped softly around her face. Even sitting in the dark, with the gray light of the early dawn just creeping in, she looked nothing like the shadowy figure of my nightmares. I really needed to get a grip.

She was watching me closely. "Is everything okay?"

I gave my head a quick shake. "Yeah, it's fine. Why are you sitting here in the dark?"

"I didn't want to disturb anyone."

"I'm usually up this early," I said. Which was true, although not by choice. I would definitely rather be sleeping.

"Why don't you sit down? Can I make you some tea?" She gestured at the cup in front of her.

I shook my head and headed into the kitchen, Oscar at my heels. "Thanks, but I prefer coffee in the morning. Plus, Oscar needs to be fed."

She frowned slightly. I could see the oil from her night cream glistening in the grooves of her skin. "You shouldn't be drinking coffee yet."

"Why not?" I squinted at the window. The light was starting to turn a slivery gray. "It's morning. I drink coffee every morning."

"But you need your sleep. You should be getting at least eight hours of sleep a night."

"I went to bed early." Which didn't exactly acknowledge her point. Regardless, I had no intention of heading back to bed, if that was what she was suggesting.

"Yes, but that doesn't help if you don't sleep through the whole night."

I shifted uncomfortably, feeling alarm bells at the back of my head. "I sleep through the night."

She shot me a look. "Rebecca, don't lie to me. You know how much of a light sleeper I am. I heard you walking around."

I froze, my hand holding the scoop of cat food over the empty bowl.

My mother was staring at me. "Rebecca? Are you sure you're okay?" Near my feet, Oscar let out a meow and batted my ankle with his paw.

I took a deep breath and filled his dish. "Fine." No, there was no chance I had been sleepwalking around the house. None. Zero. For heaven's sake, I had woken up in my bedroom, so obviously, I hadn't been shuffling around downstairs. All I did was get out of bed, open the window (for some unknown reason), and go to the closet, which is where I woke up. There was no way I was sleepwalking around the rest of the house. No way.

Never mind my dream where I had searched the downstairs before finding that shadow guy in the kitchen.

My mother's eyes narrowed. "You don't seem okay."

I put Oscar's food dish down and started making the coffee, trying to ignore how badly my hands were shaking. "I just woke up. I need my coffee. You know how I am without coffee." I kept my voice light.

"What you should be doing is heading back to bed." While her voice was her normal, reproachful tone, I could see faint concern on her face.

"I told you, this is when I get up."

She muttered something, but I ignored it as I filled up the coffeemaker with water, forcing myself to take deep breaths. Everything was going to be fine. I had a bad dream, and once I got some coffee into me, I would realize that I was blowing things out of proportion ...

"Rebecca, I really don't think you should be having coffee right now," my mother repeated yet again. "I know you didn't sleep well last night, and I wish you would go back to bed."

I took another deep breath before flipping on the switch for the coffee. "There's nothing for you to worry about. I slept fine last night."

"Don't tell me you slept well. Like I said, I *heard* you." Her voice was sharp.

I pulled a mug out of the cupboard. "It's an old house. It makes a lot of noise, especially at night."

"I know what footsteps sound like."

Even though the coffee hadn't finished brewing, I pulled the pot out and filled my cup, trying to do it fast enough so it wouldn't drip all over. "Okay. If that's the case, how do you know it was me? It could have been either Chrissy or Mia."

My mother watched me. "You should wait for it to finish. You're going to make a mess."

I sighed and started fixing my coffee with cream and sugar. Maybe my mother was right, and I should head back up to my bedroom. Though if I did, it would be to get away from her third degree, not to go to sleep.

"And I know it wasn't Chrissy or Mia," my mother continued, "because I heard the footsteps go up and down the hallway. Why would Chrissy or Mia be pacing the hall in the middle of the night?"

My fingers jerked as I stirred my coffee, accidentally sloshing some of it over the side. There was no way she could have heard me walking around because I hadn't been walking around. With all the sleepwalking that had gone on in this house, no one had ever left their room and returned. Hence, there was no way I had been sleepwalking.

First time for everything, said the little voice in my head. I quashed it down and took a sip of coffee, feeling the caffeine and sugar instantly work their magic throughout my body.

I plastered a smile on my face and went to the kitchen table. "Like I said, it's an old house. I don't know what you heard, but I was asleep the whole night. And ..." I held up a hand as I saw her open her mouth, "I'd really rather not argue about this anymore."

My mother was eying me suspiciously, but she closed her mouth and took a drink of tea. "Fine. Where do you want to go shopping today?"

Shopping? I stared at her, fighting to keep the horror at the thought from showing itself on my face. "Um ... what?"

"I realize the shopping options here in Redemption are ... limited." She shook her head, her mouth twisted in a manner that made me think "limited" wasn't the word she really wanted to use. "So, I thought maybe it would make sense to visit Riverview or maybe Milwaukee. Chicago would be better, of course, but that's a little too far for a day trip. Obviously, none of these options are as good as New York, but we'll have to make do." There was only the faintest edge of suffering in her voice. *If only I had the sense to have sold Aunt Charlie's house and moved back to New York, like any other civilized human would have.* I had to keep from rolling my eyes.

"I'm sorry, but what are we shopping for?" I asked.

My mother was looking at me like I had grown another head. "We talked about this last night. A mother-daughter shopping day. We're going to spend the day together, catching up."

I ... what? I tried to keep the panic from my face. There was no way I would have agreed to a day of shopping with my mother. I would rather go back to the Church of the Forgotten and spend hours weeding in a hot muslin dress in the sun than go shopping with my mother. At least I knew I could survive the farm. I had no such assurances when it came to a day of shopping with my mother. "Oh ... um ... I'm not sure today is such a good day for shopping ...."

My mother's eyes widened. "What do you mean? Last night, you agreed that it's been way too long since we went shopping together and said it was about time we did."

I couldn't even imagine a reality where those words would ever have come out of my mouth. There was a reason why it'd been "way too long" since we went shopping together. Even when I lived in New York, I tried to avoid mother-daughter shopping trips, because they inadvertently ended up with me owning a bunch of very expensive outfits that I hated but was then forced to wear at various family events. Her sense of style and mine were very, very different.

My mind desperately flipped back over the night's conversation, but there was nothing about shopping or spending the day together. She must have misunderstood me, which of course wasn't going to help me out of my current predicament.

Or, a little voice inside me said, *just like when Mia told you about The Tipsy Cow and Chrissy driving her to school, this is yet another example of you forgetting what you agreed to.*

I pushed that voice down.

"While it would be great to spend some time together, I think I may have misspoken about today," I said carefully.

She gave me a hard look. "Why? What's wrong with today?"

"Well, I'm just a little tired, and ..." As soon as the words were out of my mouth, I knew they were a mistake.

My mother slapped her hand down on the table. "I *told* you that you should go back to bed, didn't I?" She reached across the table and grabbed my mug, spilling coffee all over. "I knew you needed more sleep. Go back upstairs and lay down for a while. We can leave later this morning, after you've gotten some more rest."

"Umm, you can't take my coffee away," I said, trying to grab it back, but she moved it further out of my reach.

"You can have some later, once you've gotten more sleep." Her voice was final, like she used to sound when I was a child and wanted a cookie as an afternoon snack instead of the pile of carrot sticks in front of me.

I couldn't believe what was happening. I was a grown woman, and my mother had just taken my coffee away. "You can't do that. If I want coffee, then I'm going to drink coffee."

My mother shook her head. "As soon as you're fully healed, you can do whatever you want. But until then, you're going to have to let someone else take care of you."

"This is absurd," I said, feeling the frustration, anger, and resentment start to build inside me, just like when I was a teenager. How could this possibly be happening? "I'm a thirty-two-year-old woman. I'm perfectly capable of deciding what I can eat or drink and when I will sleep."

"Not when you keep making the wrong choices," she snapped. "Honestly, you are as bad as your aunt. She fought me, too, on her poor choices. I don't understand why both of you insist on ruining your lives rather than trusting me."

I pulled back, stung. "I'm not ruining my life. And Aunt Charlie didn't ruin hers, either." Like it was yesterday, I could practically see her in the kitchen, bustling around as she made me tea.

My mother's expression shifted, and I could have sworn I saw a glimpse of tears in her eyes. "Oh, honey. I know you think that, but it's simply not true."

I was feeling the familiar pressure in my chest—the kind I remembered feeling so often when I was growing up, surrounded and suffocated by secrets. "Why not?"

She shook her head. "It's not important now. What's important is you and your health." She patted my hand. "You need to focus on getting better. That's all."

"But …"

"No 'buts.'" Her voice was brisk. "I know you think you're fine, but you're not. You have a head injury. You're not yourself. It's obvious to anyone with eyes. You're clearly not thinking straight. I know it's difficult, but you need to trust that I have your best interest at heart. I want you to have a full recovery, and that's not going to happen unless you rest. So, go. Get some more rest. You can have more coffee later, and then, we'll go shopping."

It hadn't even been twenty-four hours, and my mother had completely taken over my life. I felt helpless and out of control, just like when I was a child, and unable to stand up to her. It was easier to just let her take over, and I could feel myself wanting to slip back into my old role … the one where I didn't rock the boat. The one where I went along with the flow. Besides, why I was making such a big deal about her taking away my coffee? Maybe I did need to go back to bed. Would that be so bad, to try and get a little more sleep?

Especially since … she might be right.

That was what scared me the most.

I knew I should be better by this point. I shouldn't be forgetting conversations or where I left my keys. I shouldn't be sleepwalking. I certainly shouldn't be dreaming about some shadowy figure sitting at my kitchen table delivering cryptic messages.

I should be well.

"Fine," I said, rising to my feet. If nothing else, by going to my room, I wouldn't have to deal with her while I tried to figure out a way to get out of the pending shopping disaster.

My mother nodded her head in approval, one hand still clutching my coffee cup. "I knew you'd come to your senses. Trust me, you'll thank me later."

I wasn't sure what to say to that, so I just gave her a tight nod and headed for my bedroom.

Chapter 18

The morning light streamed through my window, further ensuring I wouldn't be able to fall asleep. Not that I would have been able to anyway ... not after that nightmare. Not after how I woke up standing in the corner of my room with the window open.

A storm is coming.

I shivered, wrapping my arms around my chest while prowling restlessly around my room. I had assumed once I was away from my mother, I would feel some sense of peace and relief, but instead, I felt worse. Now, I was trapped in my bedroom without coffee and only my thoughts to keep me company.

And they weren't good thoughts.

A storm is coming.

I raked my hands through my hair. Not this again. Hadn't I already dealt with all of this before? Wasn't it time to finally move on?

Maybe this was all just a product of my overactive imagination. Or yet another sign that my mother was right, and I wasn't getting better. I was still too caught up in the Church of the Forgotten investigation, and that was keeping me from getting better.

Maybe everyone was right, and what I really needed to do was walk away from all of it. No investigating, no talking about it, nothing. Just take a good long break.

Except ... I sucked in my breath, as the truth about my condition hit me square in the face.

I had tried taking a break for a few weeks. I hadn't been following the case. I wasn't investigating. I spent my days doing a little light cleaning and cooking while making an effort to keep from taxing my brain.

And I still wasn't any better.

The uneasy feeling that something was very, very wrong with me started creeping down my spine. *Why* wasn't I better? Why was it taking so long?

Was there something else seriously wrong with me?

Maybe whatever it was wouldn't be so bad. Maybe I just needed more time. Or more ... something.

Maybe. A lot of maybes, and no real answers.

And the worst part? Not only had I not gotten better during my little break, but someone murdered Edna while I was busy puttering around the house "taking it easy."

Over the past few weeks, everything had somehow gotten worse. Including me.

None of this was supposed to happen.

The words popped into my head, but it wasn't the voice from the shadow guy in my kitchen. It was Margot's, and it brought me back to the conversation we'd had while she sat on her cot in the community center gym.

This conversation is over.

I chewed on my bottom lip. Why would the dark shadow repeat Margot's statements? Was it just my brain trying to make sense of what Margot said?

Or was something else going on?

Not all things are equal. Some things are more dangerous than others. And one may kill you.

I suddenly knew exactly what I was going to do with my day. And it wasn't shopping.

***

From my spot behind a massive oak tree, I studied the community center. If memory served me right, in front of me should be a side door that led to the hallway with the locker rooms—the same side door I had used to take a quick break from the Zumba music some time ago.

Hopefully, it wouldn't be locked. But if it was, I did have a key to try. During that unfortunate Zumba class, Mia had introduced me to a few of the staff members, as they were all former tea clients of

Aunt Charlie's. One of them was a woman named June, who was in charge of cleaning the facility after hours.

Luckily for me, June didn't need much of an explanation as to why I wanted to borrow her keys, although I did have to listen to a ten-minute tirade about Redemption, the mayor, and the city council, as she was on unpaid leave until the community center was returned to its original function.

That was infinitely better than what happened with my mother. I basically took the coward's way out. Once I had my plan in place, I told my mother something had come up, so I would need a raincheck on the shopping date, and I had to leave *right now* ... and then, I ran out of the house before she could ask any questions.

It was a childish move. I knew it was, because it was precisely how I always reacted growing up, too. Even, I was ashamed to admit, into my twenties. Rather than stand up to her, I would try and deflect and ignore. And if that didn't work, I'd run away.

I shouldn't have done it. I knew I would have hell to pay when I saw her next, but I couldn't focus on that. I had to push down the squirming, uncomfortable shame around the fact that, at thirty-two years old, I was still allowing my mother to control me.

But enough. I had bigger problems to worry about. Like sneaking into the community center, finding Margot, and convincing her to talk to me, all without being detected.

Ugh. What had I gotten myself into?

The seemingly solid plan I'd formulated in my bedroom seemed idiotic now. This was never going to work.

But what choice did I have? I needed to talk to Margot, and if I simply marched through the front door like I had yesterday, I was likely going to get the same result. Instead, I thought up this bit of insanity.

It was still better than going shopping with my mother.

I eyed the community center one more time. Really, if I was going to do it, I needed to get moving. Standing there second-guessing myself was pointless. Since I had no other plan, it was either this or go back home. And as I wanted to put off going home for as long as possible, it was time.

I squared my shoulders, took one last deep breath, and headed toward the community center.

My feet crunched on the dry leaves, the sound echoing in the stillness. I adjusted the hood of my black hoodie—well, Mia's black hoodie—so it also covered her baseball cap I had borrowed. Mia didn't wear either of the items, so I didn't think she would miss them. The hoodie was a gift, and it was too big for her, but it fit me. She also wasn't much of a cap person. I had tucked my hair up under it and added a pair of oversized sunglasses to complete the look, even though the sun was barely more than a watery presence in the sky. As I walked, I was careful to hunch my shoulders and keep my face down.

I didn't think anyone would recognize me. At least, I hoped not.

The closer I got to the community center, the more my eyes darted around me, as if on their own accord as I hoped and prayed not to see anyone. My luck seemed to hold, as I made it to the side door without coming across a single person.

But that appeared to be the end of my luck. The door was locked.

I dug June's keys out of my pocket. I felt so exposed, trying to remember which key unlocked the side door. "You may have to jiggle it as well," June had said, as if I needed one more thing to remember.

There were so many keys on her keychain, finding the right one was an intimidating task. Not to mention how they merrily jingled as I shoved key after key into the lock. The sounds were so loud, I was sure someone was going to come investigate, and I had no idea what I would possibly say if I was caught. It would be bad enough if it was one of the Church of the Forgotten members, but if it was a cop …

I could just picture Daniel's face if he knew what I was doing.

The lock finally clicked open, and I immediately ducked inside, thankful for a reason to ignore all unwelcome thoughts about Daniel.

But my relief was short-lived. The next part, by far, was the most dangerous component of what I was doing.

The narrow hallway ended in a sharp left followed by a right before turning into the long, straight hallway, which was where I would find the locker rooms.

It was also a straight shot to the gym.

The chances of running into someone coming or going from the locker room were high, but I had no choice. I had to position myself somewhere where I would at least have the opportunity to run into Margot alone. Hiding in the women's locker room seemed like a good idea when I'd first thought of it.

But now that I was actually in the community center, it felt more like a suicide mission.

I almost left then. I went so far as to put my hand on the door. But when I tried to think of any other way to see Margot alone, I came up blank.

This was a ridiculous idea, yes. But ridiculous or not, it was the only one I had.

Moving swiftly before I could change my mind, I headed down the hallway, peeking around the corner before darting down each section. Back when the community center was a community center, this area wasn't used much other than for storage. I assumed that was still the case, but that didn't mean one of the members wouldn't decide to wander back here.

At least for the moment, though, I was still alone.

Maybe my luck was holding out.

I hurried to the next turn and peeked around it, thinking I still had one more turn before hitting the main hallway. But I immediately realized I had remembered wrong.

I was in the main hallway.

It was empty, but I could see the light at the end where the gym was. I could also see the women's locker room, which was closer to me than the men's. Still, it seemed at least a mile away.

Not just that, but I would be completely exposed for the entire distance. If anyone turned down the hallway, or even if they walked by the gym, they would be able to see me. There was nowhere for me to hide.

My heart was pounding so hard, I could hear the blood rushing in my ears. This was insane. I should thank my lucky stars no one had seen me yet, turn back around, and get the heck out.

But then, I wouldn't have what I came for.

And what if you're caught? Then what? Do you really think you're going to be able to find a way to talk to her alone if someone sees you running down this hallway?

I had no answer for the little voice inside me.

Nor did I have any other option. Especially since I had already come so far.

It was now or never.

Taking one last deep breath and forcing my brain to shut off all its panicked "what ifs," I half-crept, half-trotted down the hallway.

I was halfway to the women's locker room when the door to the men's locker room opened, and a man strode out.

I froze, a scream caught in my throat. He was going to see me. How could he not?

But he didn't. He immediately turned toward the gym and lumbered away. Maybe if he had turned his head a little more, he would have seen me out of the corner of his eye, but he didn't.

I watched him go, barely able to breathe, let alone move. What if he turned around? What if he turned his head when he reached the gym? What if … what if …

He reached the gym and disappeared to the right. Just like that, he was gone.

And I was still standing in the middle of the hallway, completely exposed, yet somehow undetected.

It was so sudden that for a moment, I didn't move … just stayed where I was with my mouth hanging open, until it occurred me that if I didn't get my butt in gear, I would no longer be undetected.

I dashed toward the women's locker room and quickly ducked inside. I didn't want to stand in the hallway any longer than necessary, but I also knew I had to be careful in case someone was in the locker room already. Luckily, there was a short hallway before it opened up into the main room, so I was able to flatten myself against the wall and edge my way to the opening. I strained my ears, trying to figure out if anyone was in there, but all I could hear was my own blood rushing and pounding heart.

I peeked around the corner. The first room was full of actual bright-yellow lockers, and it was empty. Next to the locker room were three hallways that formed a cross. To the right was a short alcove with toilets and sinks. Straight ahead led to the showers, and to the left was a dressing area with a couple of closed doors at the end.

I had officially reached the "fuzzy" part of my plan. While I knew I wanted to hide until Margot came in, assuming she eventually would and hopefully alone, I hadn't quite figured out where. In my bedroom, I surmised if there wasn't an obvious nook or corner to hide behind, I could possibly use one of the showers or a bathroom stall. My hope was that I would have a little bit of time to scout everything out and come up with the best solution.

But my hopes were dashed by the sound of the shower running.

Don't panic, I ordered myself, as I could feel my heartbeat and breathing accelerate. I certainly couldn't afford to hyperventilate.

I had to figure this out, and fast.

I skidded into the toilet area, thinking that a bathroom stall would be the quickest, easiest place to hide. I immediately realized that wouldn't work very well, as I wouldn't easily be able to see who was coming in or out, and if they skipped the toilets and just went for the shower, I wouldn't see them at all.

I raced out, my heart thumping so hard, I was sure whoever was in the shower was going to hear it, and ran to the two doors at the end of the dressing room. Both were locked.

Think, Becca. For a moment, my brain locked up, and I couldn't do anything but stand there like a rabbit staring back at a hungry wolf. There had to be something I could do. Maybe I could pick the lock …

Keys. I had keys!

I pulled June's circle of keys from my pocket. There were so many! How was I possibly going to find the right one before whoever it was finished her shower?

I was going to have to do it the hard way.

My hands were trembling so badly, I was sure I was going to drop them, but I managed to select a key and tried to fit it into the lock. Didn't work. Tried a second one. Didn't work.

My brain was screaming to hurry. Soon, I would have to abandon the whole plan, duck into a bathroom stall, and wait for the shower-taker to finish up. I tried a third key.

It slid inside and turned. Bingo.

I yanked open the door. It was a very small broom closet. The walls were lined with shelves holding cleaning supplies, toilet paper, and paper towels. On the floor was a mop and bucket that took up pretty much the entire space.

I was trying to figure out how I was possibly going to squeeze myself inside when I heard the shower turn off.

I was out of time.

As quietly as I possibly could, I jammed myself inside. I somehow managed to straddle the bucket, though it was extremely uncomfortable. I hoped against hope that I wouldn't have to hold that position for very long.

I kept the door open a crack, so I could see when the showerer finally left.

It felt like it took forever. The closet was hot and smelled of bleach and other chemicals, threatening to gag me. To offset it, I concentrated on taking shallow breaths from my mouth.

Finally, someone I didn't recognize came into view. Her hair was in a long, wet braid down her back, and she was carrying a bundle of clothes and a towel. She didn't even glance toward the closet, just shuffled out of the locker room.

I forced myself to stay where I was while I slowly counted to a hundred. When no one else appeared, I started to carefully rearrange myself in the closet. It took a bit to figure it out, but eventually, I discovered if I filled up the bucket with toilet paper, I could sit on it fairly comfortably and still see through the crack.

Once I was more or less settled, all I had to do was wait.

Which was easier said than done. I knew it would be boring, but I didn't realize *how* boring. I didn't want to use my phone, as I didn't want to risk the light of the screen, or any type of notification, giving me away. So, all I could do was sit there.

And think.

Not ideal.

The longer I sat, the more ridiculous my whole idea became. What if Margot never came in? Not a lot of women were. It was hard to know because I couldn't see a clock, but it felt like I was seeing maybe three or four women an hour. It was certainly plausible she wouldn't use the locker room at all.

Alternatively, what if it she did come in, but was with someone? Or what if she came in while someone else was already in? Then what?

And how long did I wait? Until dinner time? Longer? And would I be able to sneak out without getting caught?

I had no good answers for any of those questions. And the longer I sat, the more idiotic I felt.

There was no way this was going to work.

I was just about ready to throw in the towel and see if I could sneak back out when Margot walked in.

What Wasn't Forgotten

Chapter 19

I was so shocked that for a moment, I did nothing but stare at her, my mouth hanging open. Before I could collect myself, she disappeared into the toilet area, leaving me wondering if I had really seen her or hallucinated.

No, I wasn't going to second-guess myself. I was sure it was her.

I pushed the door open and stood up. My knees and legs were stiff, but I wanted to be ready when she emerged. The last thing I wanted was for her to disappear as quickly as she had arrived.

The moment she was ready to leave, she needed to see me.

When she finally stepped out from the toilet area, shaking her hands as if they were still damp, she jerked to a halt. Her expression went slack as she stared at me.

"Hi Margot," I said.

Almost immediately, her face shifted to something that looked like irritation and exasperation, with something else mixed in. Was it fear? I couldn't tell.

"I told you not to come back."

"I wouldn't have, if you had told me the truth. I know you're hiding something."

"You don't know anything," she practically spat.

Involuntarily, I took a step back. "I don't understand why you're being like this. I thought we were friends …"

Now, she came toward me, her hands clenched into fists. "We *are* friends, Becca. Why do you think I'm warning you to stay away?"

I did a double take at the sound of my name. My real name. "Then talk to me," I pleaded.

She shook her head violently, wisps of hair that had escaped her tight bun flying around her head. "I *can't*. Don't you understand?"

"I understand we're in danger. Both of us. Probably a lot more than just us, unless something changes. And the only way that happens is if you trust me—or someone—with the truth."

She stared at me for a moment, gnawing at her bottom lip. The silence stretched out for so long, I was sure she was going to refuse.

But then, she took a step back as her eyes darted around the room. "We can't talk here," she said abruptly. "Follow me."

She turned and strode out of the locker room. I was so surprised, it took me a moment to get my feet moving, and I hurried to catch up with her.

She held up a hand as she approached the open door, then leaned out and looked both ways. She gestured for me to follow and turned down the hallway, away from the gym and toward the way I had come.

We quickly trotted down the hallway and around the corner before she paused at one of the doors. Turning the knob, she poked her head in, then gestured again for me to follow her.

Apparently, I wasn't the only one to have done some exploring of the community center.

The room Margot brought me to was full of outdoor sports equipment. Field hockey nets were piled up precariously in one corner while another corner was full of a variety of balls—soccer balls, volleyballs, and footballs. There were colorful plastic cones stacked next to them, and in another corner, I noticed a collection of what I thought were croquet mallets.

Margot looked outside one final time before closing the door and coming to stand in front of me, arms folded across her chest. "Do you have any idea how dangerous it is for you to be here?"

"Please talk to me," I said. "Tell me what's going on. The sooner we get to the bottom of everything, the sooner it will be safer for all of us."

She looked away, huffing a long sigh. "It's not that easy."

"Why?"

She shook her head. "You don't understand. I *can't*."

"Why can't you?"

She didn't answer, just kept shaking her head. I took a step closer to her and put a hand on her arm. "Margot, please. Why do you think I snuck back in and hid in the bathroom? So no one would know I was here, and it would be safe for you to talk to me."

She snorted. "*Safe*. We're not safe. We'll never be safe."

"We have to at least try," I said. "And getting to the bottom of who killed Edna would be a good start."

She started shaking her head again. "Becca, you don't understand." She reached up to rub her temples. "Oh, this is such a mess." Her voice was low, almost as if she was talking to herself. "It wasn't supposed to be this way. None of this was supposed to happen." She began to pace, barely avoiding a couple of stray balls as she continued muttering to herself and scrubbing at her temples.

Watching her, it began to dawn on me that Mia might have had the right idea about the Church of the Forgotten members. "You knew." It was barely a whisper.

Her steps faltered, but she quickly recovered. "It's not what you think."

"Not what I think? Did you know about Zelda and Pamela or not?" I took a step back from her, the horror and stupidity of what I had gotten myself into beginning to sink in. And the worst part was, no one even knew where I was. I should have told someone. Maybe Daphne, although she probably would have insisted on coming with me. I could have at least left a note in my room.

I was such a fool.

Margot glanced at me, her expression unreadable. "It's more complicated than that."

I threw my hands up in the air. "What's complicated? It seems simple enough to me. Did you know that Eleanor murdered a woman and kidnapped her ten-year-old daughter, intending to force her to kill another ten-year-old in some sick sacrifice?"

She stopped pacing and glared at me. "See? This is precisely the problem."

"What's the problem?"

She jabbed a finger toward me. "You."

"Me?" I was flabbergasted. "How am I the problem? I'm trying to help."

"You're not helping." She resumed her pacing. "Sometimes in life, the only 'choice' you have is between bad options. So, you pick the least harmful one and make the best out of a bad situation. It's not what anyone wants to talk about, but life is hard, and sometimes, you just have to make do."

She continued pacing, her expression flat, but I had seen a flicker of shame behind it.

None of this was supposed to happen.

On one hand, it seemed so clear-cut. Margot was a member of a cult that murdered a woman, kidnapped her child, and intended to kidnap and kill another child.

But when I thought about her patience and kindness toward me as we sat in the sewing room, it seemed less clear. Why would someone make that choice? Especially someone who seemed to be a genuinely good person.

"What bad choice did you have to make?" I asked quietly.

Her eyes flickered toward me. "I don't need your pity."

"I'm not offering it."

She raised an eyebrow.

"I just want to know what's going on. That's it," I said. "You keep saying it wasn't supposed to happen. So, what WAS supposed to happen?"

She paced a little more, kicking one of the soccer balls out of the way. It bounced against the crochet mallets. "No one was supposed to get hurt. At least, that was my understanding." She swallowed hard, her throat bobbing. "Pamela was a mistake. At least that was what I had been told. No one meant to kill her. It was an accident."

"If it was an accident, why didn't you go to the cops?"

She shot me an exasperated look. "Becca, you're smarter than that. Do you really think the cops would have understood? They were already suspicious of us. We had to keep it under wraps."

"What about Zelda?"

She shrugged. "We had no choice. We had to keep her. She was ten years old, and someone had to be responsible for her."

The soccer ball rolled back to where Margot was pacing, so she kicked it again. This time, it hit one of the nets. "You do know Zelda has a father who would have taken her, right?" I asked.

Margot's brow furrowed. "I know that now. I didn't know that then. At the time, Eleanor said Zelda had no one else, so we owed it to her to take care of her."

"By keeping her chained up?"

Margot's cheeks flushed. "I didn't know she was being chained up, either. Not until ..." Her voice faded.

"The night I freed her," I finished.

Margot's cheeks turned redder. She opened her mouth, closed it, then released a deep sigh. "I didn't know for sure until that night. But ... I knew something was off before then. I knew ..." She stopped walking and seemed to collapse in on herself. Her shoulders slumped, and her head bowed. It was like watching a balloon deflate.

I almost felt sorry for her. Almost. "How long did you know?"

She kept her head down. "The first time Lily ... *Zelda* ran away. After Pamela ... well, Zelda also went missing. I was under the impression that Eleanor was taking care of her in her quarters. I figured she was letting the child grieve her mother in private. But after Zelda ran away, Eleanor was ... frantic. She was desperate to find her. I've never seen her so ... unhinged. I could understand being worried about Zelda—after all, she was only ten and had just lost her mother—but this was something else. Like an obsession." Margot shivered. "It didn't feel right. So, when they found Zelda, I offered to take care of her. I even told Eleanor that Zelda could stay in my room with me. But Eleanor said no, she would take care of her herself. And we just ... never saw her again. At the same time, she was ... well ... trying to kidnap that 1888er child—"

"You knew she was trying to kidnap Jill?" I asked.

"Not at the time," Margot said quickly. "It was like with Zelda. Eleanor said that Jill didn't have anyone else. That Penny was her only relative, and with Penny dead, the state was going to take her, and she was going to end up in foster care. So, we owed it to Jill to give her a good home."

"But Jill had a mother. Wendy was her mother, not Penny," I said.

"I know that now," Margot said. "But at the time, I believed what Eleanor said. You have to understand, that's how the Church of the Forgotten was created. We were all lost souls, forgotten by the world that broke us. Why wouldn't I believe Eleanor?"

I couldn't help but wonder what had broken Margot. "So, Eleanor was upset that she wasn't able to kidnap Jill."

Margot made a face at the word "kidnap," but she didn't correct me, as that was what Eleanor was technically trying to do. Luckily for Jill, Wendy managed to thwart Eleanor by sending Jill away. "It was just like when Zelda ran away ... she went a little crazy. She was so upset about it, which made no sense to me."

"Did you try talking to her?"

She rolled her eyes. "I did, but I didn't really get anywhere. Just the usual mumbo jumbo. At the time, I figured she was just in one of her moods. That would happen from time to time, you know ... she would get completely obsessed with someone or something, but it would eventually blow over and everything would go back to normal. I assumed that would happen in this case, too, and when it did, we would see Zelda again in the community and she would have a proper room, like the rest of us and all would be well. But, instead, you showed up and ... well ... you know the rest."

I barely heard the end of what Margot was saying. I was still stuck on the mumbo jumbo part. "Did you say ... 'mumbo jumbo'?"

Margot finally lifted her head and looked directly at me. "Of course. What would you call it?"

"I'm ... I'm not sure what we're talking about," I said.

She frowned at me. "Oh Becca. Come now. I know you don't believe in The One."

I stared at her. "No, I don't. But ... you don't either?"

She waved her hand. "Of course not. It's all silly."

I was having trouble getting my head around her words. "But then ... why would you stay at the Church of the Forgotten? Wasn't that the whole point? To bring back Lily?"

"Sure, but I never thought it was literal. I thought the whole thing was symbolic. The Church of the Forgotten is all about building up those who are forgotten by society. Those who slip through the cracks. At the Church of the Forgotten, we had a home. A purpose. Never in a million years would I think Eleanor was going to try and bring back Lily for real. We were a peaceful community. That was the point. No one was supposed to get hurt."

"But The Harvest," I started to say.

"Again, I didn't think it was real. I thought it would be a *symbolic* ritual. That was what Eleanor made me believe. Not that she was ever going …" she stopped talking, her shoulders heaving. "I still can't believe she would have gone through with it. Even if you hadn't freed Zelda, I can't believe she would have done it. There had to be a miscommunication somewhere along the way."

I couldn't imagine what the "miscommunication" could have possibly been, but at that point, it didn't matter. Deep down, Margot knew the truth. I could see it on her face, just like I could see how much she was trying to convince herself otherwise.

"If you didn't really believe in all of it, why did you join in the first place?"

Margot went still, except for her hands. They seemed to have developed a life of their own as they plucked frantically at her dress. "It was a long time ago." Her voice was so quiet, I could barely hear her, but I noticed that all the blood had drained from her face.

"I didn't mean to pry," I said, starting to feel alarmed. I took a step toward her, afraid she might pass out.

Her mouth twisted. "It doesn't matter now. It was another lifetime. I was married with a daughter. I was a stay-at-home mom. I used to do crafts with my little girl. It's how I got so good at sewing." Her expression softened at the memory. "We were expecting another child. We were happy. I was happy. But then, my daughter was diagnosed with cancer."

I pressed a hand to my mouth. "Oh no."

Margot nodded. "She was six."

"Oh, I'm so very, very sorry," I managed, even as I felt the inadequacy of the words.

She inclined her head. "She died." Her voice was flat. "And when she died, I died." Her hands were still twisting her dress. "I lost the baby. My marriage imploded. My husband couldn't handle it. One day, he went to work and never came home. Investigators eventually found his car parked near a railroad bridge near Sauk City. No note. No sign of him. He was presumed dead, but without a body, the insurance company refused to pay." She swallowed and turned to stare at the soccer nets. "To this day, I think he was trying to make it seem like he didn't commit suicide. He knew the insurance company wouldn't pay out if that's what he did, but they got the last laugh anyway." Her lips curled into a parody of a smile.

"So, there I was ... no husband, no children, and no way to pay bills. I hadn't had a job in years, since before I was married, and even then, my only experience was working in a mall as a salesclerk. It wasn't long before I was bankrupt and living on the streets. That's when Eleanor found me."

Margot took a deep breath and turned to face me. I had expected to see tears of grief, but instead, there was only resignation. "I have no family. No friends. No money. No way to support myself. I have nothing, without the Church of the Forgotten."

My eyes widened as it slowly sank in what she truly meant when she spoke about making a choice between bad options. "What are you going to do?"

She let out a laugh that was devoid of humor. "I'm a middle-aged woman who has spent more than half of her life in a cult. I have no job skills, no references, no family, no friends. What would you suggest?"

There was nothing I could say.

Chapter 20

I was still in a state of shock when I pulled into my driveway.

Margot and I parted ways shortly after she shared her story. She said she needed to get back before she was missed, and I needed to get out of there before I was caught. I was too shook up to question her. I couldn't even fathom what she had gone through, yet despite everything, she was still standing in front of me.

Who was I to judge the choices she made? Could I honestly say, given the circumstances, I would have done anything differently?

We were about to leave when she turned to me. "Becca, you need to be careful." Her voice was serious. "Promise me you won't come back here."

It occurred to me there was still so much I hadn't asked her. "Why am I in danger? What aren't you telling me?"

She pressed her lips together in a flat line. "It's complicated. There are things going on that even I'm not sure I believe. But …" she leaned closer to me, her lips brushing my ear, even though we were completely alone. I could smell her sweat mixed with the harsh chemicals of the cheap soap and shampoo she used. "It's not over. That, I'm sure of. The Church of the Forgotten members are determined to do whatever they can to not be forgotten."

"Is that why they killed Edna?"

Anger flashed in her eyes. "Edna should have known better. She knew the danger, yet she failed to take proper precautions to protect herself."

"Who killed her?"

Margot closed her eyes briefly. "I don't know. I have my suspicions, but I don't know for sure." She gave me a hard look. "That's why you need to be careful, too. Don't turn yourself into a target any more than you already have. And whatever you do, remember that things are not always as they seem."

"What does that mean?" I asked as Margot yanked open the door. "Is Edward behind all of this? Did he kill Edna? Or Gertrude?"

But Margot didn't answer. She simply strode down the hall, leaving me alone with my questions.

And I still had no answers.

I thought about checking in with Daniel, but I wasn't sure what I would even tell him. What did I learn, other than Margot's heartbreaking story? And how many other Church of the Forgotten members had equally horrible stories? I couldn't even tell him for sure who I thought might have killed Edna.

But that was only part of the reason for my hesitation. Over and over again, I kept seeing Daniel flashing me his lopsided grin as he apologized. I still wasn't sure how I felt about it. Or him. It seemed easier to stay away for a while. I had enough complications in my life. I didn't need even one more.

Arriving home, I opened the front door and heard my mother's voice coming from the kitchen, although I couldn't make out specific words. I wondered who she was talking to. Was Mia or Chrissy in there with her? I couldn't really see either of them voluntarily having a conversation with her ... unless they were planning on ganging up on me to find out where I had been all day. Ugh. I briefly considered sneaking upstairs and locking myself in my bedroom. After all, I was exhausted and starting to get another headache, and the last thing I wanted was to deal with another third-degree line of questioning.

I had just reached the staircase when I heard a voice answer my mother. A male voice.

What on earth?

At that moment, my mother's head poked out of the kitchen. "Oh, Rebecca. There you are. We were just talking about you." Her eyes shifted to my hand on the banister. "Aren't you coming into the kitchen? Why are you going upstairs first?"

"Um ..." My head was spinning. I had no idea what to say. "I ... just ..." I removed my hand from the banister. "No reason."

My mother's eyes narrowed like she didn't believe me, but always the perfect hostess, she didn't challenge me. "Well, then come on in and greet your guest." She stepped back and made a flourishing gesture with her arm, an expectant expression on her face.

My guest? What male guest was here? Oh man, if it was Daniel …

"Hello, Becca."

I blinked. Aiden was standing in the doorway, arms crossed over his chest. His gray eyes were flat as he studied at me.

Oh crap. All the texts I had ignored from him the night before and again this morning tumbled through my mind. I was a terrible friend. I made a mental note to get better at responding to texts if I didn't want any more surprise guests showing up on my doorstep.

"Oh, um … hi … um …" I stuttered. I had no idea what to say, especially with my mother hovering right next to us.

Luckily, Aiden decided to take pity on me. "Your mom has been catching me up on what's been happening with you, so I know you've had a busy twenty-four hours."

"Ah, yes." My eyes darted between my mom and Aiden. "Yes, I have."

"It's been so nice getting to know your friends," my mother chirped, putting a hand on Aiden's arm. "We had such a nice chat."

I bet she did. That was all I needed, my mother trying to set me up with Aiden.

Aiden smiled at my mother, but it was perfunctory. "I've really enjoyed getting to know you as well, but unfortunately, I have other plans tonight. Becca, walk me out?"

It wasn't exactly a question, but I nodded and turned back to the front door as Aiden followed me outside onto the porch.

A cold wind was stirring up the dead leaves in the driveway, sounding almost like the rattling of old bones. I wrapped my arms around myself as I faced Aiden. "Look, I'm really sorry," I began. "I was in the middle of something when I got your text last night …"

"I get it," he interrupted. "Your mother explained how she showed up on your doorstep unexpectedly and has been busy 'fixing' everything for you." His lips quirked up in a half-smile. "I'm not surprised you've been a bit … occupied."

A tiny smile touched my mouth. "That's one way to describe it."

His grin brightened for a moment before his expression turned serious. "Knowing what I know now, I wouldn't bother you with this, but …"

Oh no. I could feel my chest muscles start to tighten as my head began to throb. This couldn't be good.

"Unfortunately, I'm running out of time," he continued. "I have to make a decision in the next few days about whether I'm going to stay in Redemption or not."

"What's going on?" I asked. Maybe he wasn't asking what I thought he was. Maybe he just wanted my opinion on what he should do for the next phase of his life.

"Well, other than the obvious that I can't keep living in a hotel when I have a perfectly good apartment waiting for me back in Riverview," he said, "my old boss called me this past week and told me he wants me back. Enough to give me a promotion to boot."

"Wow, a promotion," I said, my voice sounding faint even to my ears. "Does it include a pay raise, too?"

His eyes became even more intense. "A big one. Bonuses, as well."

"Is that what you want?" My mind was still spinning.

His eyes didn't leave mine. "It depends. If there's nothing else in my life, then sure. I wouldn't mind making more money. But it would mean moving back to Riverview. It would also mean long hours and more travel. It would be … difficult to come visit Redemption on a regular basis."

My chest was so tight, I could barely breathe. "That would suck. We'd miss you."

He cocked his head. "*We?*"

"Daphne, Mia, and me. Well," I amended. "Maybe not Mia."

"You *and* Daphne?"

I tried to suck in my breath, but felt like I was breathing through a straw. "What are you asking me, Aiden?" My voice was barely a squeak. Goosebumps rose up on my arms, and I hugged myself more tightly.

His gaze became even more intense. "I'm asking if you would miss me."

The words seemed to hang between us. I didn't know how to answer him. On one hand, I kept thinking about that night when I snuck out of the Church of the Forgotten. The way he had looked at me. How he had my back throughout that entire ordeal. There was no question I had felt something for him, something more than friendship.

But then I thought about Daniel and his lopsided grin, and I didn't know what to do.

I swallowed hard. "Of course I would miss you. We're friends."

I knew it was a copout even before the words were out of my mouth, and seeing Aiden's face flatten made me feel like even more crap.

"Friends." There was a bitter note in his voice.

"Aiden, don't be like that." I pleaded, feeling worse and worse. "It wasn't that long ago that Daniel and I broke up, and it was a year before that when I got divorced. Again, I don't want to jump into another relationship that is destined to end badly, especially when I'm still recovering from everything I've been through."

He didn't answer. Instead, he turned his head toward the towering, swaying pine trees at the edge of my property. I bit the inside of my cheek, wanting to say something else, but not sure what. I wished I had done something—anything—differently, to have avoided standing on my cold front porch as darkness fell around me, the scent of decaying leaves in the air and the knowledge of breaking someone's heart—someone I truly cared about—heavy on my soul.

"I get that," he finally said, turning back to me. "I know this isn't the best timing. I know you're still hurting and healing. But Becca, I need to at least know if there's a chance for something more. If there is, I can be patient. You're worth waiting for. But if not, you need to be honest and tell me."

You're worth waiting for. The words felt like a knife twisting in my gut, but I wasn't sure why.

"I can do that," I said. "I'll need a little time though. Can I have a couple of days?"

His smile was sad. "Yes, you can have a couple of days." There was a finality in his voice that turned the knife a little harder.

"I'm just exhausted right now, and my head is pounding. Let me get some sleep and think about it." I felt like I was babbling, so I forced myself to close my mouth. Things were happening too fast. I needed some time to myself to sort out my feelings.

"Of course," he said again, stuffing his hands in his pockets. "Let me know when you can."

He turned and walked down the steps, disappearing into the dark. A wave of sudden panic seized my chest and throat, and I wanted to call him back. I wanted to tell him there *was* a chance … that I needed to move on from mooning over Daniel like some pathetic schoolgirl. I wanted to see if we could make it work.

But the words were trapped in my throat, so instead, I simply stood there watching him leave … and wondering if I had just made the biggest mistake of my life.

Chapter 21

"A storm is coming."

I was standing in a dark room I didn't recognize. In front of me stood the shadowy figure, its back to me. I was able to make out more details than before, like its strands of brown hair. Lightning flickered from somewhere, although there didn't appear to be a window, illuminating the figure even more. It seemed to be wearing jeans and a shirt.

"Who are you?" I asked.

The figure didn't turn. "You're not asking the right question."

"Then what *is* the right question?" I demanded. I was getting tired of all the riddles.

"That's not it either," the figure said.

"Oh, for Pete's sake," I snapped. "Why keep bothering me if you won't even tell me what you want?"

The figure finally turned to face me. I could see the faint details of a face start to emerge—high cheekbones, a strong jaw. There was something familiar about it. "I'm here to help you."

"Well, you're not doing a very good job of it. You won't even tell me who you are," I grumbled.

It cocked its head. "I live here. Same as you."

I folded my arms across my chest. "For how long?"

"Many years. Since before you were born." The lightning flickered again, and the figure turned toward it. "A storm is coming."

"You keep saying that. What does it even mean?"

I expected another snappy comeback, but the figure remained silent for a long moment. "You need to beware of the storm. I don't want to see you make the same mistake I did."

Something cold and slimy slithered around in my gut. "What mistake did you make?"

I could almost see its eyes glittering in its skull. "You need to wake up. NOW."

"Rebecca!"

A harsh light exploded across my face, nearly blinding me. I lifted my hand to protect my eyes, blinking violently.

"Rebecca!" The voice called again. "What are you doing down here?"

My head darted around, trying to make sense of where I was. My bare feet were against something smooth, cold, and hard. The air was cold and smelled damp.

"Rebecca? Are you okay?" The voice came closer, and I finally realized it was my mother. She was standing in the middle of the wooden steps that led to the basement.

The basement …

"Where am I?" I asked. My eyes finally focused, and I was able to look around. I was in the corner of the basement, where the concrete was a slightly different color than the rest of the floor, as it had been freshly poured within the past year.

"You're in the basement," my mother said, although I knew that now. "Why you're there, I don't know … it's the middle of the night!"

The middle of the night? "I … I don't understand," I said faintly as my stomach seemed to turn inside out. There was no reason for me to be in the basement in the middle of the night, yet there I was.

I couldn't deny it anymore. I was sleepwalking, and it was even worse than Mia's and Chrissy's episodes.

My body started trembling uncontrollably, and I could feel my knees start to give out.

"Oh my gosh. Rebecca!" Somehow, my mother had descended the rest of the stairs and crossed the room just in time to catch me midair as I collapsed. She wrapped her arm firmly around my waist. "Lean on me. Let's get you upstairs."

I couldn't even argue with her. My body, twitching and shuddering, felt foreign … like it wasn't my own. Somehow, despite my legs feeling practically useless, she managed to get us both upstairs.

She dragged me to the kitchen table and deposited me in a chair. "You rest. I'll make some tea."

Rest. I propped my head up with my hands so my mother couldn't see that I was desperately trying to keep from falling into hysterics. Where exactly would I go, after literally having to drag me up the stairs?

She wasn't speaking. There was no sound other than the banging that came with her bustling around the kitchen. Finally, she thrust a cup of hot tea in front of me and broke the silence. "Drink."

Obediently, I took a sip and winced. It was very sweet.

"It will help with the shock," she said, sitting down in front of me with her own mug.

She wasn't wrong. I took another tentative sip.

She watched me for a few minutes. "Better?"

I nodded as I placed my cup back down on the table. I could feel my trembling muscles start to relax. "Better."

"Good. Now, I want some answers."

I winced again. I really wasn't in any shape for this conversation. "Can't it wait until morning?"

My mother crossed her arms and leaned forward on the table. "I found you wandering around in the basement in the middle of the night, confused and disoriented. No, this can't wait until morning."

I rubbed my forehead, feeling the beginning of a headache forming behind my eyes. "There's nothing wrong. I'm fine. Truly."

Her eyebrows went up. "You think you're *fine*? You were in the basement! Why??"

I wondered if she would believe me if I told her I was down there investigating a noise. No, that wouldn't work. She'd probably think someone was trying to break in and call the police. "Sometimes I just go check things out to make sure everything is alright."

"In the middle of the night?"

I shrugged and picked up my cup. "Why not?"

My mother's eyes narrowed. "Why were the lights off then?"

Um. That was a good question. It was a wonder I hadn't broken my neck. "It's really nothing to worry about."

"How can I not worry? What is going on, Rebecca? What aren't you telling me?"

I let out a sigh as I rubbed my forehead again. As much as I didn't want to tell her the truth, I couldn't think of a plausible lie. "Honestly, it's not a big deal. It's just a little sleepwalking …"

"Sleepwalking?" My mother stared at me in horror. "You never used to sleepwalk. How long has it been going on?"

"Not long. Just a couple of weeks."

"This just started?" My mother was aghast. "Does your doctor know?"

"It's not uncommon to have sleep issues when you're healing from a trauma or concussion." Although, to be fair, my doctor hadn't said anything at all about sleepwalking. We only discussed me not being able to fall or stay asleep, and he let me know he could prescribe sleeping pills if it became a problem. I declined, but my mother didn't need to know all the particulars.

"I think walking up and down stairs while you're asleep is a very big problem," she said. "You could have fallen and broken your neck!"

"Honestly, it's not that big of a deal," I said again.

She shot me a look. "It *is* a big deal. It's been weeks now, and you're still not better." She scrubbed at her face, which caused her night cream to streak across her cheeks. "Rebecca, I think you need to seriously consider coming home to New York."

I jerked up. "What?"

She held a hand out. "Just for a visit. A few weeks. Maybe a month or two."

My eyes widened. "A month?"

"Just long enough to get better," she said quickly. "You can stay in your old room. It would be far safer for you, as we don't have stairs you could fall down. Or a basement, for that matter. And you wouldn't have to worry about anything other than getting better."

"I don't think that's necessary …" I started to say, but she cut me off again.

"You would also have access to the best doctors, including specialists in head trauma. I've already been in touch with Dr. Gannon …"

I stared at her. "You've been what?"

"I just wanted to see what our options are," she continued defensively. "I didn't make an appointment or anything like that. But he personally knows the head of Neurology at John Hopkins and was sure he could get you in ..."

I dropped my head into my hands. "Mom, I'm fine. I don't need all of this. It's way too much. I just need to rest." The last thing I wanted was to go back to New York and live with my parents. That would be awful on all sorts of levels.

"But baby ..." my mother tentatively put a hand over mine. "I know you keep saying that, but you're not getting better. If anything, you're getting worse."

"I'm not getting worse," I said, despite the fact that I couldn't help but wonder if I was lying to myself. Still, even if my mother was right and I *was* getting worse, I absolutely knew the cure wasn't moving in with my parents for a few weeks.

"You're sleepwalking, which you've never done before," she said. "Whatever is going on with you isn't normal." She tapped a fingernail on the table as her voice rose. "I know you know this. We raised you better than this. This nonsense has to stop."

Something stirred inside me, like it had been asleep and was finally waking up. "Nonsense?" My voice was mild, but if my mother was actually listening, she would have heard the edge to it.

"Yes. Nonsense! You're out here living in the middle of nowhere and taking care of everyone but yourself. No one here even lifts a hand to help you even though it's obvious to anyone with a half of brain that you're getting worse by the day. And on top of that, you're seeing substandard doctors who wouldn't know how to help you if the answers slapped them in the face!"

My back stiffened. "My doctor is not substandard."

"How do you know? Have you had a second opinion? Of course not." She didn't wait for me to answer.

"Actually, that's not true. I did get a second opinion. And I'm not taking care of everyone else at the expense of myself. Nothing you're saying is accurate."

But my mother wasn't listening. She was shaking her head as she picked up her mug. "I blame my sister. This house, this town, has always been bad news. But would she listen to reason? No, of course not."

I stared at my mother in disbelief. "What does Aunt Charlie have to do with any of this?"

Now it was my mother's turn to look at me in disbelief. "Are you kidding me? Your Aunt *Charlie* has everything to do with this!" She flung her arms around the room. "You wouldn't even be here if it wasn't for her. You wouldn't have gotten caught up in that dreadful cult and gotten hurt. You would have been safe and happy."

"*Safe?*" I couldn't believe my ears. "You think if I had stayed in New York, I would be safe and happy right now?"

"Of course. You would probably be married and maybe even pregnant …"

"Have you forgotten that both of my exes live in New York?" I asked.

"Well, of course there are some bad apples, but with my help …"

"Mom," I cut in. "You can't possibly believe it's that cut and dry. Terrible things happen to people in New York, just like they do here. You have no idea if I would have been safe and happy if I had stayed put."

"Well, you wouldn't be sleepwalking," she said, almost triumphantly. "That never would have happened. And that's why it's time to stop this nonsense and come home."

In that moment, something snapped inside me. "I *am* home."

She made a disgusted face. "This Podunk little town isn't home …"

"It *is* home. This is *my* home and *my* life, and you need to start respecting my wishes. Like not moving into a room I told you to stay out of."

She rolled her eyes. "Oh, for heaven's sake. We're back on that again? There's nothing wrong with that room …"

"It doesn't matter what you think," I shot back. "What matters is that this is my home, and I told you not to stay in that room. You ignored me and did it anyway."

"Only because it didn't make sense …"

I slammed my hand on the kitchen table, causing both mugs to rattle. Tea sloshed out of mine. "You're missing the point. It doesn't matter if it made sense or not. What matters is my home, my rules."

"Rebecca, you're being irrational. This is why I keep telling you that you need time to rest and recuperate. If you would just listen to me, you wouldn't be in this position."

"If you can't respect my wishes, then maybe you should think about going back to New York."

I wasn't sure which of us was more surprised that those words came out of my mouth. Her expression would have been comical, if I wasn't marinating in a stew of old, pent-up resentment and anger.

"How can you say something like that to me?" she finally managed when she could get her mouth to work again. "After all I've done for you?"

"None of which I asked for or told you to," I said.

Her eyes nearly bugged out of her face. "How dare you?" she said. "This never would have happened if you had stayed in New York. This town is a terrible influence on you."

"This town is my *home*," I spat back through gritted teeth.

She shook her head. "This is all my sister's fault. I never should have agreed to ..." she snapped her mouth shut before finishing.

I stared at her. "Agreed to what?"

"It doesn't matter. The damage is done," she said bitterly with a hard, pointed look in my direction. "There's no going back now, even if she was still here."

I felt like I had been slapped. "You're talking about my aunt. And your sister!"

She glared at me, a defiant look in her eyes. "Don't talk to me about my sister. I knew her better than you did."

In my mind's eye, I saw Aunt Charlie again, bustling around the kitchen, making me tea when I was having one of my headaches. My grief rose up, mixing with the anger and resentment, and it was like a fuse had been lit inside me. "You're absolutely right. You DID know her better than me. And boy, did you make sure of that."

Something shifted in her expression, and I detected an uneasiness in her eyes. "What are you talking about?"

I leaned forward. "Fifteen years. That's what I'm talking about. That's what you took from me. From her."

Her mouth worked. "Rebecca, I was protecting you. You almost died that night ..."

"*Protecting* me?" I let out a laugh that sounded more like a scream. "You weren't protecting me. If anything, you were protecting yourself."

Her face went white. My barb had struck home, though I couldn't even imagine what she was protecting herself from. "That's not true."

"You think denying me a relationship with my beloved aunt was for my protection? Fifteen years, mom. I didn't see her for *fifteen* years! And then it was too late, because she was dead!"

My mother's eyes darted around the kitchen. "Keep your voice down. It's still early. You don't want to wake everyone up."

I realized then I was shouting. Tears streamed down my cheeks. "She died alone," I said, forcing myself to speak more quietly. "In this house. And it didn't have to be like that."

My mother didn't respond. Instead, she bowed her head and stared at the table.

"Don't you ever think about that?" I asked, my voice breaking. "She was your sister."

"Of course I think about it," my mother rasped, her voice almost as broken as mine. She seemed to have collapsed in on herself, like a marionette with broken strings. "Every day I wonder what might have happened if things had turned out differently. If she hadn't been so ..." she shook her head tightly. "So darn stubborn."

I reached over to swipe the box of tissues off the counter. "Why wouldn't you let me see her? Why did you let me believe that it was somehow her fault that I almost died that night when I was sixteen?" There was a time when I couldn't remember a second of that long-ago night—it was also when my friend Jessica disappeared. But now that my memories had returned, they were burned into my brain. "You must have known she had nothing to do with it, but you still encouraged me to believe it. Why would you do that? To her? To me? What happened between you two?"

Before my eyes, my mother shrunk in on herself even more. "It was just ... sister stuff. It happened a long time ago. It's not important."

A memory flashed in my head ... something I had nearly forgotten about. "Did it have to do with her fiancé?"

My mother's head shot up. "You know about Alan?"

I felt like I had been punched in the gut. When Louise told us that my mother had sided with her sister's abusive fiancé rather than her sister, I didn't want to believe it. It had to be a misunderstanding. "Is he the one who abused her?"

Her eyes went wide before her hand snaked out and grabbed my arm. "Who told you that? What do you know about Alan?"

I was going to be sick. It was true. Despite all of my challenges and issues with my mother, I never believed she would sink so low. "How could you? How could you believe *him* over your own sister?"

Her hand tightened, digging her fingernails into my arm. "Rebecca, I need to know. Who told you about Alan?"

"Ow, you're hurting me. Stop it." She loosened her fingers just enough for me to pry her hand off as I pushed my chair back away from her. "I have a headache. I'm going upstairs."

"Rebecca, no. We need to talk about this."

I stood up. "What is there to talk about? You chose an abuser over your sister. I can't talk to you. I'm going upstairs."

She lunged toward me again, but must have seen something on my face, because she backed away. "Rebecca, that's not ... I didn't *choose* him. It's more complicated than that."

I let out a humorless laugh. "Of course it is. Just like it's probably her fault, too. Right."

"Rebecca, please. Listen to me ..."

I held a hand up. "Leave me alone. I'm done with this conversation. And if you want something to do, you might as well start packing your things. You're not welcome here anymore."

The blood leached out of my mother's face as she stared at me. Before she could speak again, I turned and headed up the stairs.

Chapter 22

It was nearly mid-morning, and Mia and Chrissy had already left the house when I heard a quiet knock on my door. "Rebecca? Are you sleeping?"

I was standing by the window facing the backyard, decidedly not sleeping. My head had been spinning for hours.

How could my mother have done that to Aunt Charlie? And how did I let her nearly take over my life ... again?

I wondered if there was something fundamentally broken in me.

The soft knock came again. "Rebecca? I brought you some coffee."

I toyed with the idea of simply ignoring her, despite the coffee, but I knew that was childish. If I truly wanted to be an adult, I needed to have a conversation with her.

Then, I could kick her out.

I rubbed the back of my neck before crossing the room and opening the door. Immediately, I was greeted with the smell of bacon and coffee, and I realized how hungry I was.

"Thanks," I said, trying to ignore the pathetic relieved expression on my mom's face.

I had expected her to push her way into my bedroom or force me to come downstairs, but instead, she just stood there, swaying back and forth. "Can we talk, Rebecca?" Her voice was hesitant. "I know you're not happy with me right now, and what I have to say will probably upset you even more. But there are things we need to talk about ... things I should have told you a long time ago."

I blinked at her. I had expected the "we need to talk" conversation, but the rest? "Um ... I guess so."

She nodded and took a couple of steps away from the door. "I'll wait for you in the kitchen."

"Okay," I said again, although it really wasn't. I had no idea what was going on, but I was starting to get a terrible feeling. I watched her leave as I took a long drink of coffee. She had made it the way I liked, with cream and sugar.

I took another sip before steeling myself and heading down to the kitchen.

The table was set for two. In the center was a platter of bacon, buttered toast, and hard-boiled eggs. My mother was pouring herself some tea, but she waved toward my spot. "Sit. Have some breakfast."

My mouth was watering, but still, I hesitated. That uneasy feeling had gotten stronger, and I had the strange sensation that if I did sit down in that chair and listen to whatever it was my mother wanted to tell me, my life as I knew it would be over.

Oh, don't be so dramatic, Becca, I thought, pushing the sense of foreboding away.

She nudged the platter toward me before scurrying away to fetch the coffeepot and refill my cup as I started piling bacon and toast on my plate. "I didn't think you knew how to cook bacon."

She laughed, but it was a little hysterical. "Mia helped me before she left for work, so I'm pretty sure it's all edible." She put the pot back before joining me at the table.

I picked up a piece of bacon and nibbled on it. As hungry as I was, I was also growing more and more uncomfortable. This wasn't how my mother acted. She was always confident, self-assured. This woman in front of me was a nervous wreck.

I was definitely getting a bad feeling.

She picked up her cup but just held it, without drinking. "Charlotte and I had a complicated relationship."

No kidding, I thought, and tried not to roll my eyes.

She swallowed hard. "It's true that I was … less than supportive when she first told me what happened with Alan. And," she held a hand up as I opened my mouth to speak. "I'm not proud of myself for that. I should have believed her."

My mouth stayed open, not because I was going to say anything, but because I was in shock.

She smiled briefly at my expression before becoming more serious. "Alan was a serious charmer. Not that that's an excuse, but he was. He knew exactly how to manipulate me. And it didn't help that I found Charlotte ... challenging. When she first told me what he did, I assumed she was exaggerating. Alan would never hurt anyone. I certainly couldn't imagine him pushing anyone down the stairs on purpose. I felt so strongly that it must have been an accident."

She squeezed her cup, as if trying to absorb its warmth. "But despite all our challenges, she was still my sister, and I loved her. So when she called me for money, I of course sent it to her, even though I thought she was being silly and dramatic and really just needed to come home."

Sounds familiar, I thought.

"Even if she ended up breaking it off with Alan, I felt she owed him a face-to-face conversation. Sneaking out of New York without telling anyone was just wrong. So ..." she paused and swallowed hard. "I started making a plan with Alan."

"You what?" In my agitation, I began absentmindedly breaking my bacon into tiny pieces.

Her lips were pressed together so tightly, they were white. "You have to understand ... I assumed it was just a lover's spat! I truly believed it was just some sort of misunderstanding that Charlotte blew out of proportion. Because that's what she did! And once she and Alan were able to talk about it face to face, they would work it out, and she would come home." She stared directly into my eyes. "That's all I ever wanted. For her to come home."

My chest was so tight, I could barely breathe. All the conversations I'd had with my mother since I moved to Redemption, all the times she had begged me to come home. For the first time, I could see it from her perspective ... how she must have felt like she was caught in some kind of time warp, reliving the same exact situation she'd found herself in with her sister years ago and getting the same results.

But ... she had also betrayed her sister. "You told Alan where to find her," I said, unable to keep the disgust from my voice.

"No!" She shook her head violently. "That was never the plan. She had sworn me to secrecy, and I wasn't going to betray that. The plan was for me to talk her into going somewhere romantic, and

Alan would ... well, he'd meet her there." She closed her eyes. "It sounds so stupid, I know. I don't know what I was thinking."

"So what happened?" I thought back to what Louise had said, but I didn't recall anything about Aunt Charlie leaving.

"Alan got into a fatal car accident before I could even say anything to Charlotte. At the time, I was beside myself. I felt like I had somehow contributed to his death, considering he was only in that area to scout out the perfect romantic spot. But ..." she paused and put her cup down. "Eventually, I started remembering things. Or maybe I should say I started putting things together. Like how Alan would often excuse himself to use the bathroom when he visited, and he would always be gone for what seemed like a long time. I started to wonder ... was he snooping around? I never hid the transfer confirmations of the money I sent to Charlotte. Could he have found them? Did he know where she was? Was that the real reason he was on the road that night ... because he was driving to Redemption to find her?

"But then I told myself it didn't matter. He was still dead. Knowing the reason why wasn't going to change anything. Still, it niggled at me. Especially when ..." her voice trailed off, and her gaze became fixed on the table.

Something was off. It was like the energy suddenly shifted, and the air became heavy. I got the sense that the dark being that I was sure had followed me home from the Church of the Forgotten had slipped into the kitchen and was watching me. Again.

I shivered, trying to brush off the sensation. I was letting my imagination get the best of me.

"Especially when what?"

It took my mother some time to answer. She seemed to be fighting with something in herself, and for a moment, I didn't think she'd answer at all. But finally, she took a deep breath, squared her shoulders, and looked up at me.

"Especially when she called to tell me she was pregnant."

Chapter 23

I was sure I'd misheard her. There was no way. Aunt Charlie never had kids. She had never even gotten married.

"I'm sorry, but could you repeat that? I thought you said Aunt Charlie was pregnant." I laughed a little at the end, mostly because it was just so absurd.

But my mother wasn't laughing. On the contrary, her face was deadly serious.

"When she finally called me, she was getting to the point she could no longer hide it. She was barely leaving the house because she didn't want anyone to know. She was buying her groceries in another town, and her so-called doctor worked at some clinic outside of Redemption, as well." She pursed her lips and shook her head. "Thank goodness Charlotte was so healthy. Otherwise, I don't know what would have happened."

I held up a hand. "Wait. I don't understand. Are you saying I have a cousin somewhere?"

My mother looked at me with eyes filled with a mixture of love, grief, and pity, and suddenly, I couldn't breathe. My breath seemed to lodge in my throat. Had the baby died? Was that where this was going?

"She asked me if she could come stay with me, just until the baby was born," my mother said quietly. "Then, she was going to give the baby up for adoption."

"Why would she do that?" Images of baking cookies with my aunt as we laughed about something stupid filled my head. "She would have been a great mother."

My mother looked even more sad. "I … I'm not really sure. I tried to convince her to keep the baby, but she was adamant. Said she had no business being a single mother, and it wouldn't be fair to the baby."

I couldn't imagine why my aunt would have thought that. Unless … "What about the father?" Redemption was a small town. Maybe the issue was with the father ... maybe it was him who really wanted to keep the baby a secret. Although ... if Aunt Charlie wanted the baby, I couldn't see her allowing a man to dictate what she'd do.

"I asked her about the father of her baby, but all she would say was that he wasn't in the picture. She wouldn't tell me who he was or what happened to him. I was always ..." she hesitated, shaking her head.

I opened my mouth to ask her what she was about to say, but she plowed ahead before I spoke. "When I finally realized she wasn't changing her mind about the adoption, I told her I'd take care of everything—including sending her a plane ticket. She protested, told me she could buy her own, but I insisted. Partly because ..." she swallowed and took another sip of tea. "Because I knew she wasn't going to be flying into JFK. If she was going to insist on putting this child up for adoption, then she absolutely couldn't stay with me."

"Why not?"

She looked at me like I had grown a second head. "What would people say? Our friends, our social circle, your father's clients? Not to mention our parents. Heavens, they would have been devastated if they knew Charlotte was giving her child up for adoption. I knew I had to keep it a secret."

Of course that would be her concern. Not her sister's welfare, but her standing in society. I felt hot then cold as all my own failures rose up inside me. I had always known that I was a disappointment to my mother, mostly because I was a constant embarrassment to her. I hadn't lived up to her expectations. Apparently, neither had my Aunt Charlie.

"So, I checked her into a very private, discreet clinic. If someone wanted a medical procedure without people knowing, this was the place to go. I also booked myself a room to stay with her. Charlotte wasn't thrilled about being there for several months until she gave birth, but she also knew she wasn't exactly in a position to complain." She paused and took another drink of tea. "It was all going to plan ... until Marguerite showed up."

"Aunt Marguerite?" I frowned. Aunt Marguerite was CB's mother. "Why was that a problem?"

My mother had started playing with her mug. "Your Aunt Marguerite desperately wanted a child, but unfortunately, her body had other ideas. She had several miscarriages, the last one occurring just a few months before Charlotte told me she was pregnant."

I was surprised. "I didn't realize Aunt Marguerite had so many problems getting pregnant before CB."

My mother didn't look at me. "She showed up at the clinic absolutely furious that Charlotte was pregnant and not her. It was bad enough I had had two children, but for Charlotte to be pregnant? Who wasn't even married and who didn't even *want* a child? She was beside herself."

"You hadn't told her?"

My mother shook her head. "I told her what I told everyone—that Charlotte was sick, and I was going to help take care of her for a few months here in Redemption. Charlotte used a version of that same lie, telling people she was coming to New York to take care of me. The only person who knew the truth was your father, and he swore he didn't tell Marguerite." She pressed her lips together and took another sip of tea. "Marguerite refused to tell me how she figured it out. I suspect she hired a private investigator, but that's neither here nor there. Once she arrived and realized Charlotte's intentions were to give her baby up for adoption … well, it was a mess. Charlotte was upset, as she hadn't wanted Marguerite to know. They were never close. Still, she also didn't want to add to Marguerite's pain. So, it was bad. A lot of yelling, a lot of blaming. A mess." She paused to let out a long sigh. She was still staring at the table.

"I don't remember whose idea it was … if maybe Charlotte said something in anger, or if Marguerite came up with it, but … well … Marguerite wanted to adopt Charlotte's baby."

My jaw dropped. "CB is … *Aunt Charlie's baby*?"

My mother closed her eyes and rubbed her temples. "Yes."

"And … you didn't tell me?" I thought about the last time I had seen CB in prison, when he said he knew things about the family that I didn't. "Did CB know?"

"It wouldn't surprise me," my mother grumbled. Her eyes remained closed, and she was still rubbing her temples. "There was a catch though."

There it was again—my breath trapped in my throat. "What catch?"

My mother took a long time to answer. I watched her as she fought to breathe normally, the sense of foreboding slowly rising up in me, threatening to swallow me whole. I was sure I didn't want to hear what she was about to say, but I also knew I must.

Finally, she opened her eyes and straightened up, looking me directly in the eyes. "Charlotte didn't have just one baby. She had twins."

My entire world seemed to tip sideways. I tried to say something, but nothing came out. I tried again. "Twins?" It was barely more than a whisper.

My mother's eyes never left mine as she slowly nodded. "Twins. A boy and a girl."

I couldn't breathe. I couldn't think.

"Even though Marguerite was desperate for a child, she refused to take them both. She only wanted one. But Charlotte refused to separate them. She would not even entertain the idea of putting one up for adoption and letting Marguerite adopt the other. So, the only option was ... for me to adopt one of them."

The edges of my vision were starting to go black. I swayed in my seat, feeling like somewhere along the way, I had fallen into a black hole and was now in a completely different reality where nothing made sense.

"I had always wanted a little girl," my mother continued, squeezing her mug so tight, her fingers turned white. "Don't get me wrong; I love my boys, but a little girl? That had always been my dream. Mother-daughter shopping trips and spa days and all the rest. But as much as I wanted a little girl of my own, and as much as I wanted to help Marguerite realize her dreams of becoming a mother, I had conditions. I didn't want people to know I had adopted my sister's child. Talk about a scandal. I wouldn't put my family through that. So, we decided to tell people that Marguerite and I both found ourselves pregnant at the same time, but unfortunately, both of us were also having issues with our pregnancies, so we decided to do something completely different and stay at the clinic together, so we could get the very best medical attention. I knew everyone would believe Marguerite would do something like that, especially with her history of miscarriages, so I figured people wouldn't look too closely into my motivations. And if anyone asked why we kept our pregnancies a secret, we both said we didn't want the pain of telling people we were pregnant only to then tell everyone we lost the babies, if that's how things ended up. I admit, I wasn't sure we would be able to pull it off, but surprisingly, it was easier than I expected. Although in retrospect, I suspect people thought the real reason why I did what I did was for Marguerite. Marguerite was a wreck back then, even more so than normal."

My mother ... wait, was she even my mother anymore?!? The words just kept pouring out of her mouth, but I could no longer process what she was saying. The black around my vision was starting to pulsate, matching the pounding in my head and the beating of my heart. It was like a marching band from hell had taken over my body, and all I could hear was the BAM BAM BAM of some diabolic drum.

"I wanted to make it a condition that Charlotte also tell us who the father was, but she flat out refused." The words kept coming, almost like she was babbling, despite my having *never*, in my entire life, known her to babble. "She wouldn't even talk about him, no matter what I said. I still think it was a mistake, as I kept telling her over and over. What if there was a health issue on his side of the family? Or something else we should be aware of? But it didn't matter what I said ... she wouldn't say a word. Even when I asked her directly about Alan, she wouldn't tell me."

Alan? Why were we talking about Alan when I still had so many questions about Aunt Charlie and my mother, or supposed mother, and what they had done? Was she trying to say that Alan was ... my father? Alan, the man who pushed his fiancé down the stairs? Who, if true, had also faked his own death, come to Redemption, and ...

No, I couldn't think about that now. I was having enough issues trying to get my head around who my mother was. I couldn't even begin to wade into the dark swampy waters of who my father might be.

"Rebecca?" The woman sitting across from me was looking at my anxiously. "Are you feeling okay? Do you need me to get you some …"

"Are you telling me that Aunt Charlie is my mother?" My voice was hoarse, like I had spent the last two hours screaming at the top of my lungs. A part of me wondered if I had.

She winced. Then, her face seemed to crumble in on itself. "Yes. That is what I'm saying. Charlotte is your mother."

Silence, other than the fiendish marching band banging away inside my head. I stared at the woman in front of me … the woman I had called "mother" for over thirty years.

The woman who was, essentially, a complete stranger.

"You lied to me." My voice didn't even sound like mine. It was lower, rougher … like nothing I had heard before.

"I didn't lie," she said. "I just … I just didn't tell you everything."

I held up a hand. "You lied. Don't try and sugarcoat it."

She gave me a helpless look. "I didn't lie about the important things."

My jaw dropped again. I couldn't even believe she'd said it. "*You think that me believing you are my mother for my entire life wasn't important?*"

"I AM your mother." Her voice was firm, but her chin trembled. "I raised you and took care of you. And I love you just as much as if I had given birth to you myself."

There were so many emotions roaring inside me, it was like a tornado. I couldn't even identify what I was feeling, other than the one single emotion that threatened to overtake me at any moment.

Rage.

I put my hands on the table and leaned forward. "You are NOT my mother."

A panicked look flickered in her eyes. "Rebecca, you don't mean that. You can't! I know this is a shock. Believe me, I wish there had been a better way to tell you, but I know once you've had some time to think about it, you'll come to your senses and realize that no matter what, I AM your mother. Your Aunt Charlotte also loved you ..."

I couldn't listen to another word. I had to get out. I needed to be alone. I needed to think. I needed to quiet the mess in my head so I COULD think. Right now, with the marching band in my head and the tornado of emotions in my chest, I couldn't process a single clear thought.

I staggered to my feet. "I have to go to my room."

My mother ... no, I guess my *aunt*, stood up as well. "Rebecca, don't go yet. Stay. Let me explain ..."

"You've explained enough," I rasped, lunging forward. My vision was going black again, and I was afraid I wasn't going to make it up the stairs before passing out.

"Rebecca, wait. I think you should sit down. You don't look good ..."

I opened my mouth to tell her I was fine, but instead, my entire breakfast spewed out of me and onto the floor.

What Wasn't Forgotten

Chapter 24

"Becca?" Mia's voice floated toward me, barely penetrating the bubble around me. "What are you doing out here?"

I continued staring straight ahead, toward the woods at the back of the property. The trees were a riot of color—blazing reds, golden yellows, and bright oranges. The wind stirred the piles of leaves that covered my lawn, rattling around like an army of skeletons about to attack. It even smelled like death and decay.

I couldn't move.

My mother wasn't my mother. My aunt wasn't my aunt.

The two women who claimed to love me more than anyone else in the world had been lying to me my entire life.

How was I supposed to deal with that?

Mia stepped into my line of vision, and I felt her fingers brush my cheek. "You're freezing! Why are you sitting out here in the cold? And why is your mother crying in her room?"

I gritted my teeth at the word "mother." "Can you ask Daphne to come here? And do you know where Chrissy is?"

Mia stared at me in confusion. "Uh … sure. But what's going on?"

"Can you get them both here? I can only say this once."

Her eyebrows went up. "Becca, what happened? Did something happen to your father or your brothers? Or …" her mouth went slack. "Is it you? Are you sick?" Her voice lowered to a hush. "Are you dying?"

"I'm not dying," I said, although a part of me thought it might be easier if I were.

Her brows knit together. "Did something happen between you and your mother?"

I almost laughed at the understatement. "Honestly, I can't do this twice. If you don't mind tracking down Daphne and Chrissy, I'll tell you all at the same time."

"Okay ... but can you at least come inside?"

"I'm fine." I wasn't fine. I was about as far away from "fine" as possible. But the idea of being back inside the house, breathing the same air that "mother"-turned-stranger was breathing, turned my stomach.

Mia looked like she wanted to say something, but instead, she moved out of my line of sight. I continued staring at the woods.

After getting sick, I initially went to my room, but found I couldn't stay there. My emotions were all over the place, along with my thoughts. I kept flipping back through my childhood, searching for any sign that I might have missed ... something, anything, that could have been a warning of the bomb that was just dropped on me.

But nothing stood out. Instead, all my childhood memories descended on me like a thick blanket, suffocating me. *My mother-turned-aunt comforting me when I had pneumonia and a high fever for days. My first day of school, when she held my hand tightly as we walked and told me about all the new friends I was going to make and how much fun I was going to have. How she defended me to my sixth-grade teacher, who had it in for me and told me I didn't have what it took to succeed in life.*

My relationship with her had always been complicated. For every memory I had of her sighing as she took in my appearance and asking me if it was really *too much to ask* that I keep from wrinkling my dress or fix my hair a little nicer, I had a warm one to offset it—her ordering takeout from my favorite restaurant when I was having a bad day, for example. It was incredibly complicated, because I knew she loved me, in her own way ... even if it didn't always feel like it.

There was a flicker in the woods in front of me, like something moving behind one of the trees. It was probably an animal. Maybe a deer, as it was too big for something like a squirrel or rabbit. Although a deer didn't seem quite right either. I strained my eyes, trying to get a better look.

"Becca, aren't you freezing?" Daphne dragged the metal chair across the cement patio closer to me. Her eyes were full of worry as she reached out to hug me.

"Honestly, I'm fine," I said. "It's not that cold out." It was probably in the fifties, maybe a little colder, but with the sun starting to descend, it would cool down quickly. I wasn't sure what I would do when that happened, as I didn't think I could bear being in the same house as ... *Annabelle*. I could feel myself choking on her name. If it came down to it, I figured I could always sleep in my car.

Mia reached over and pulled a knitted stocking cap over my head. "There, that should help keep you warm."

I made a face but left the hat on. I was too exhausted to fight about the cold. Besides, it *was* nice and warm.

Chrissy slid into the seat across from me, folding her arms across her chest. "What's going on, Becca? Why is Mrs. ... uh ..." she paused, furrowing her forehead. "Now I can't remember which last name she wants us to use."

"It doesn't matter," I said. "You'll understand in a minute."

Mia plopped down in the seat next to me. She had replaced her jacket with her winter coat, which was zipped up to her chin, and her neck was wrapped in a bright-red scarf. "Do you need anything?" she asked, her voice somewhat muffled behind the scarf. "A glass of water? More hot tea?"

"I'm good," I said, pushing away the mug that was already in front of me. Annabelle had brought it out a while ago—how long exactly, I wasn't sure, as time had ceased to have any meaning—as an excuse to beg me to come inside. I ignored her. She left it in front of me, which is where it sat, untouched, all day. I folded my hands across my lap and looked at each of them—Daphne, Chrissy, and Mia. All of them looked concerned, although Mia was looking at me like she was expecting me to keel over at any minute.

If they only knew the truth.

Well, it was time. Might as well stop procrastinating and spit it out.

"I spoke with my aunt today," I said.

Immediately, I saw Mia's and Daphne's eyes shift as they exchanged glances. "Your aunt? Are you talking about CB's mother?" Daphne asked, her voice cautious.

"No, I'm talking about my other aunt. The one in the house right now."

I watched as Mia's and Daphne's expressions turned uneasy. Chrissy, however, went in a totally different direction.

"Did someone else arrive unannounced?" she demanded. "What is it with your family just showing up uninvited?"

I could feel my lips twitch up in an almost-smile. "No, no one else came. I'm talking about the woman you all think is my mother. As it turns out, she's actually my aunt."

Now all three were staring at me like I had lost my mind. "What are you talking about?" Daphne asked. "How can she be your aunt?"

"Well, you typically become an aunt when your sister has children," I said.

"But that makes no sense," Mia said. "Who is your mother, then?"

I paused for a heartbeat. "Charlie."

Silence. The wind had picked up, blowing the dried leaves across the patio.

Daphne was the first to speak. "*Charlie* is your mother?"

"According to my moth- ... my aunt. The one crying in the house right now." I gestured with my thumb behind me.

"Then who is your father?" Mia asked.

"My *aunt* seems to think it's Alan," I said. My heart twisted inside me as an image of the man who raised me, the one who I thought was my father, filled my head. I could feel my throat start to close, and I pushed the image away. I was having enough trouble dealing with the maternal mess—I couldn't even begin to tackle the paternal.

"Who's Alan?" Chrissy asked.

Daphne's eyes went wide. "Alan? Charlie's fiancé who abused her?"

Chrissy gasped. "Your aunt ... err ... Charlie was engaged to a man who hurt her?"

"Apparently so."

"But he died, didn't he?" Mia asked, looking at Daphne. "In that car crash."

"Yeah, he did." Daphne chewed on her cheek. "Do you think she was pregnant before she showed up in Redemption?"

"I don't know. But wasn't she here for a while before Jesse disappeared? Could she have hidden her pregnancy for that long?" Mia was still talking to Daphne, like I wasn't sitting at the table with them, but she finally turned to me. "When is your birthday again? April, right?"

I stared at her. "I ... I don't know."

Mia looked at me in confusion. "What do you mean, you don't know?"

Daphne's eyes went wide in understanding. "If your moth ... err ... aunt lied about who your mother is, she could have lied about your real birthday, too."

"Especially considering CB and I have—well, we've always had—different birthdays," I said.

Mia gave me a strange look. "CB? What does he have to do with your birthday?"

"We're twins," I said. "So we should have the same birthday, obviously. But we don't."

Mia's jaw dropped. "CB is your twin?"

"You better start at the beginning," Daphne ordered.

So, I did. I told them everything my mother-turned-aunt told me. When I was finished, there was another long silence.

"And I thought my family was messed up," Chrissy muttered, rolling her eyes in typical teenage fashion.

"I guess I can see why you're sitting out here instead of in the house," Mia said, folding her arms across her chest with a shiver. "That is ... insane."

I had to agree.

"Although ..." Daphne said slowly. "It actually explains a lot of things. Remember how Louise said that Charlie had left Redemption for a while, and she thought Charlie was gone for good? That was probably when Charlie was at the clinic."

"Yeah, and that was months after Jesse disappeared," Mia said, counting on her fingers. "I don't think the timing works, for Charlie being pregnant when she arrived in Redemption."

"I don't think my ... aunt thought Charlie was pregnant when she arrived in Redemption," I said, thinking back to the flash of panic in her eyes when she talked about Alan. "It sounded like she thought Alan had faked his death and come here."

"What?" Mia stared at me, aghast. "He faked his death?"

"That's really screwed up," Chrissy said, shaking her head.

"I'll say," Mia agreed. "If he did that, then it probably means he ... ouch!" Daphne kicked her under the table. She glanced between me and Daphne and clapped her hand over her mouth. "Sorry. I shouldn't have said anything."

I pressed my lips together. "You can say it. If you thought it, you can bet I have, too."

Mia slowly lowered her hand. "If he came here after faking his death and found Charlie," Mia swallowed hard. "You could be a product of ..."

"Rape," I interrupted. "You can say it. Yes, my biological father would have been an abusive SOB."

"Oh Becca," Daphne said, reaching out to squeeze my hand. "I'm so sorry."

"That just sucks," Mia said. "Knowing that is who you're related to? I can't think of anything worse."

I balled my hands into tight fists. In my head, I saw myself standing in the basement. *I live here, same as you.* The familiarity of the shape of the eyes, the nose. I hadn't wanted to believe it. I still didn't want to believe it. But more and more, I couldn't deny the truth.

"I can." My voice was low, yet still seemed so much louder than it should be. The other three simply stared at me.

Daphne was the one who caught on first. "Jonathan," she breathed.

"The guy in the basement?" Chrissy asked.

I winced and squeezed my hands tighter. Chrissy noticed, and her cheeks colored in shame. "Sorry. I didn't mean it like that."

"Don't worry about it," I said. "It's not like it's not an accurate description."

"Jonathan makes a lot more sense," Mia said. "And not just from a timing perspective." She cocked her head and studied me. "I know what Jonathan did was ... awful. But if he was your father, at least you would have been conceived in love. Everyone who witnessed those two together said it was obvious they were wild about each other."

"He was still a murderer," I said. "Regardless of how they felt about each other."

"Yeah, but it might not have been his fault," Daphne said. "It wasn't like he spent his life killing people. It was only after all of them did that ritual. Maybe that was the cause of him losing it."

"Or the price of what they all did," Mia said, her voice dark.

I thought about the dark shadow that had been haunting my dreams. If Jonathan was ... possessed, I guess, for lack of a better word, and that was why he killed Jesse and that waitress before Charlie killed him and buried him in the basement, I wasn't sure it made anything better. Because then, there was a high likelihood he had been possessed when I was conceived ... and did I really want to go down that rabbit hole? That was a hard no.

"If I'm honest, right now, the identity of my father is the least of my concerns. I'm still trying to get my head around what my mother and aunt did," I said.

Daphne shot me a sympathetic look and squeezed my arm again. "Yeah, I get that. It's a lot to take in. All of it."

I nodded and tried to force my fists to loosen. My fingers were stiff and aching, so much so, I could barely move them. Or maybe that was just the cold. The temperature was starting to drop quickly now that the sun was barely a sliver over the horizon. As much as I wished otherwise, I was probably going to have to head into the house.

Mia cleared her throat, her eyes darting between me and the house. "What are you going to do about ... her?"

That was the million-dollar question. "I don't know yet," I said with a sigh as I reached up to rub my temples. Every time I thought about asking her to leave—at the very least, asking her to move into a hotel—the memory of her rubbing a cool washcloth over my burning forehead would bubble up again.

Why couldn't this be easier? It felt like it should be straightforward, but somehow, it wasn't.

Daphne gently squeezed my arm again. "She's your mother. It's normal for this to be confusing."

"She's NOT my mother," I spat, jerking my arm away. "Haven't you been listening?"

Daphne's expression softened even more. "She raised you and played the role of mother for over thirty years. Her not being your biological mother doesn't change that."

I couldn't believe what I was hearing. "She lied to me! Whose side are you on, anyway?"

"I'm on your side, of course. All I'm saying is it makes sense why you would be so ... conflicted right now."

The image of us in a rocking chair, cuddled up in her lap as we rocked. "You're right," I sighed, rubbing my temples. "I'm sorry. I shouldn't have snapped at you."

"You have nothing to apologize for," she said.

"I wonder why she told you now?" Mia mused. "She kept it a secret for so many years. Why now?"

"We had a bit of a ... fight, earlier," I said.

"It must have been something, for her to volunteer such a revelation," Mia said. "I mean, this is a *lot*."

Mia had a point. Why had she told me now? And why hadn't she, or Charlie, ever said anything before?

Mia shivered and wrapped her arms tighter around herself. "Look, I know you don't want to face her yet, but it's cold and dark. It's also dinner time. I'm hungry, and I'm sure you are, too. Have you even eaten anything today?"

"I didn't have much of an appetite," I said, even as my stomach growled at the mention of food.

"What if I go in first and ask your moth ... your aunt, to stay in her room until you've had a chance to eat? Would that work for you?"

I wanted to say no. A part of me would rather sit outside all night, no matter how cold or hungry I got, rather than risk seeing her. But I knew I was being childish and foolish. I needed to get warm, eat, and sleep.

"That works," I said.

What Wasn't Forgotten

Chapter 25

"Rebecca, we need to talk."

It was morning, and I was back outside in the same chair as the night before, except this time, I also had a very large cup of hot coffee. I was also more prepared, wearing my heaviest jacket and the same stocking hat Mia had found for me, and with a blanket over my lap. The sun had just broken the horizon, so even though it was light out, the rays had yet to warm the night's chill.

My aunt stood next to me, also dressed in multiple layers. She looked ... messy. Not nearly as pulled together as normal. Her face was pale and her eyes red-rimmed, but her expression was firm.

I let my eyes drift back to the woods and thought about my options. My knee-jerk reaction was to tell her to go away; it was way too early to have this conversation, especially since I had barely any coffee in my system yet. But another part of me was resigned. I still had questions, and she still had things to say. I might as well get it over with now, as nothing was going to move forward until I did. "My name isn't Rebecca. It's Becca. Rebecca died a year ago. She should have died long before that, but she's finally dead now."

My mother-turned-aunt's lips pressed together into a thin line. "Very well, Becca."

I jolted a little before hiding my face behind my coffee mug. I hadn't expected her to acquiesce so quickly. I tried to remember the last time, if ever, she had done that, but my mind was a complete blank.

She dragged a chair closer to me and sat down. I saw she had also brought a mug out with her, which she cupped in both hands.

"You need to know that this adoption almost didn't happen," she said. "A lot had to go right, and it almost didn't."

"Just jump right in, never mind what I want," I muttered, but there wasn't any heat to my words. I was exhausted and worn out, and frankly, sick of my thoughts and emotions.

She ignored me and plowed on. "We all had conditions. Me, Marguerite, and Charlotte. Marguerite's were the easiest. All she wanted was one baby and for everyone to think she had been the one to give birth. She didn't care what the sex was, although she was thrilled to have a little boy, nor much else. All she wanted was that baby, and there would be hell to pay if anyone got in her way … including her sisters." Something flickered across her face. It looked like pain, but it vanished too fast for me to be sure.

"I told you a couple of my conditions, but I didn't tell you what Charlotte's were." She paused and took a long drink of whatever was in her mug, which I assumed was tea. "Charlotte wanted to be a part of both of your lives—yours and CB's. She said she couldn't bear you being a part of her family without having a relationship with you. It would be different if you were adopted by a stranger, but being your aunt? That was too much. So, the moment you were old enough, you were to spend part of the summer with her."

That explained why my brothers never once visited Redemption. When I had asked why they didn't, I was told it was because they were boys, and I was a girl. I asked why CB was always there and was told that my Aunt Marguerite liked having a little time to herself. Knowing my aunt, I could believe it.

"I wasn't crazy about that condition. I thought if we were going to raise Charlotte's children as our own, that's what we should do … not ship them off to Wisconsin for the summer. But Charlotte insisted. Marguerite also thought it wasn't a big deal and kept telling me it would be good for the twins to spend their summers together. I reluctantly agreed. It was Charlotte's second condition that nearly derailed the whole plan."

She hesitated again, for so long, I finally glanced over at her. Her face was even paler, if that was possible, and her eyes had a glassy sheen to them that didn't look right. I opened my mouth to ask if she was feeling okay, but those weren't the words that came out of my mouth. "What was it?"

She didn't respond. Instead, she stared intently at the table, almost like she didn't hear me. The only sign of movement was her fingers turning white as she squeezed her coffee mug. "As soon as you were old enough to understand, Charlotte wanted to tell you the truth."

I snapped my head toward her. She was still not looking at me. "Charlie wanted us to know we were adopted?"

A barely perceptible nod. "As early as possible. Like around four or five years old."

The wind had picked up, rattling the leaves as they raced across the lawn and tangling my hair. "So why weren't we told?"

Another long pause. Finally, Annabelle took a deep breath, squared her shoulders, and lifted her chin to look at me. "Because *my* last condition was that you never be told."

Even though I should have known it was her all along—that she was the one who had kept all of this from me—it still felt like a punch in the gut. "But WHY?"

A faint, sad smile touched her lips. "I could tell you the same reasons I said back then, which is I didn't want to confuse you, and I thought it would be confusing to be calling me 'mother' and your biological mother 'aunt' if you knew. I could tell you that I was worried you and CB wouldn't keep it to yourselves, even if we told you not to tell anyone, and everyone would find out the truth ... and then we would have to explain why we had lied in the first place. Charlotte thought both of those situations could be handled, just as long as we went about everything properly. I didn't agree."

"Charlie was right," I said, feeling more deflated and sad than angry. In the end, all the adults had let me down. Even Charlie, who was initially trying to do the right thing. *Why did she back down?* "You should have told me."

She turned her head toward the woods again. "I know." Her voice was so quiet, I could barely hear her over the wind and rattling of leaves. "I'm not proud of the woman I was back then. At that time, I was more concerned about how things looked than doing the right thing. I was also ..." her voice faltered, and she cleared her throat. "I was also a coward. Deep down, I was afraid if you knew the truth, you wouldn't love me anymore."

Her eyes looked directly into me, and it occurred to me how different they were from mine. Mine were more like Charlie's—brown mixed with green and gold. Hers were dark brown, with no hint of the other colors. I wondered why I had never noticed that before, just as I wondered why I had never put it together that my hair was almost exactly like Charlie's. How could I have missed all the signs? I felt foolish. Yet again, I had been duped by someone I trusted. No wonder why I kept choosing the wrong men … the wrong relationships. My entire life had been built on a foundation of secrets and lies.

But as deep as that anger and betrayal cut, there was a part of me that wanted to reach out to the woman who had raised me. The pain in her voice hurt me almost as much as her lies had. How could it be possible, to want to both strike out at and comfort someone at the same time?

"You should have trusted me," I said, my voice hoarse with grief, sadness, and what-ifs. "You were my mother. You were the one raising me. Even if I had learned that Charlie had given birth to me, that wouldn't have changed who I called 'mom.'"

Her lips twisted. "I know. There are a lot of things I should have done differently." She dropped her gaze to the table. "A lot of things I regret."

Another long silence broken only by the crunching of leaves. I took a sip of cold coffee, wishing for a refill, but not wanting to break the spell that had been woven around us. Annabelle had never confided in me like this before, and I was afraid if I broke the spell, I would never hear the whole truth.

"So what happened? Why did Charlie eventually agree not to tell us?" Even saying the words hurt. Why would she abandon us like that? It was difficult enough knowing she didn't love us enough to keep us with her, but for her to also agree to not telling us? That pain cut just as deep as what my mother-turned-aunt had done.

She turned back to me, her gaze steady. "She didn't."

I frowned. "I'm sorry? I don't understand."

"She didn't agree. Wouldn't agree. She insisted you be told as vehemently as I insisted you never be told. Neither one of us were willing to negotiate, so Charlotte said the adoption was off. Marguerite was beside herself, but she couldn't convince either of us to budge.

Charlotte started researching adoption agencies, and I figured it was for the best, in the end. This idea of bringing an infant home and passing it off as our own ... the more I thought about it, the more far-fetched it all seemed. Helping Charlotte find one or two solid families made far more sense.

"Until Marguerite tried to kill herself by swallowing a bottle of pills with a fifth of vodka."

I gasped as my hands jerked, spilling cold coffee over my fingers. "She what?"

Annabelle pressed her lips together. "It wasn't a 'serious' attempt, according to the medical professionals. They called it 'a cry for help.'" She had set her mug down to make air quotes with her fingers. "Not only did she have a room next to the clinic, like I did, but she called both Charlotte and me to tell us that she had just swallowed the pills. Of course, we both immediately got her admitted so they could pump her stomach, which they did. She was fine, made a full recovery."

"A full recovery," I echoed. I didn't think I could feel worse about this whole sordid situation, but I was wrong. A collage of CB-centered memories flipped through my head—playing at the park, giggling with him at family meals, him refilling my wine glass at a very upscale wine bar after discovering my first husband had been cheating on me, sitting across from me in the jail cell, dressed in orange, a dark peculiar expression on his face. Would CB had ended up there if he hadn't been raised by my crazy, manipulative aunt? "You let her adopt CB after she tried to kill herself?!" The anger that I thought I was too exhausted to feel started burning inside me again.

Annabelle let out a long, heavy sigh. "Part of the agreement was that she needed to get therapy."

"Therapy?" I almost laughed. "You thought that would be enough?"

"We hoped it would. Times were different back then."

"People who tried to commit suicide were allowed to adopt back then?"

She rubbed her forehead. "It wasn't like that. We knew Marguerite wasn't going to keep trying to kill herself if she had a baby."

"So, she pretended to kill herself in order to manipulate you." I shook my head, wondering how two intelligent women—Annabelle and Charlie—had allowed all of this to happen. "You really think that was better?"

"It turned out fine in the end," she insisted. "Marguerite never tried to kill herself again."

"CB is in jail right now for kidnapping and murder," I said. "Can you really say it all turned out *fine?*"

Annabelle's entire body seemed to deflate in her chair. She clutched at her mug, her fingers turning white again. "You have to understand. It was what we had grown up with. Marguerite had always been a little … unstable, but that was just the way she was. We thought she would be fine, and when she had her moments, Don could step in."

"Unstable?" The edge sharpened. "Again, you gave her an infant knowing that?"

"It wasn't like that. Neither one of us thought she would ever hurt a baby. Being a mother was always her dream!" Here, she paused, stared into her mug. "In retrospect, I can see now that 'obsession' is probably more accurate a word." Her voice broke. "There's a lot I would do differently if I had to do it again, and I suspect Charlotte would feel the same. But at the time, neither one of us could bear the thought of our sister killing herself because we couldn't work out an adoption agreement that we could all live with."

I sucked in my breath. Like a scene in a movie, I could picture it in my head. Charlie and my mother-turned-aunt sitting beside Marguerite's hospital bed, listening to the beeping of the machines as the guilt and fear over what had almost happened drowned them.

It wasn't right. Especially knowing what ultimately happened to CB. But could I blame them?

I could understand their justifications. How Marguerite wasn't alone. She had Don. She had her grandparents. She had Annabelle. She was wealthy enough to hire help.

And she wanted this more than anything.

"We finally agreed we would tell you and CB when you became adults. Neither one of us was happy, but it was better than the alternative. And Marguerite was beyond thrilled."

I frowned. "An adult? I'm thirty-two years old. I've been an adult for well over a decade. You couldn't have told me a little earlier?"

She shot me an unreadable look. "You almost dying when you were sixteen changed everything."

I stilled. Of course. As it would.

She sighed heavily. "I was so angry with Charlotte when I got the call. Angry and terrified. For years, I had dreaded the day when we would tell you the truth, as I was so worried I would lose you. Then, to really almost lose you? I couldn't bear it. So, I told Charlotte the deal was off. Not only was she not going to see you again, but I also had no intention of ever telling you the truth, at that point.

"Charlotte was ... upset, of course. We argued some, but not as much as you might think. She told me I couldn't do that, that it wasn't fair. I told her she lost any say on the matter when she allowed you and CB to have an unsupervised party full of teenagers and alcohol on her property. She couldn't really respond to that, especially since you had almost died, and your friend had disappeared. The whole thing was a train wreck. I knew ..." she swallowed hard. "I knew Charlotte felt terrible about what happened. I knew she loved you and CB dearly. I even knew it wasn't her fault. I had gone through the same thing with your brothers years before, so I knew I was being a hypocrite. But ..." Here, she paused thoughtfully. "I saw an opening. I knew Charlotte had her hands full with the police and the community, and I knew she was beating herself up over what happened. So, I used it." She gazed off toward the woods. "I used my sister's suffering to protect myself. To keep myself from suffering. And I'm not sure I can ever forgive myself for that."

We were quiet for a long time. I thought about the last time I saw Charlie. I remembered the desperation in her eyes when she tried to see me, and how Annabelle wouldn't let her come near. At the time, I was fine with not seeing her. Not only was I sick, but I had a black hole where my memory should have been, and I allowed

Annabelle to brainwash me into thinking everything was Charlie's fault.

But now, knowing the truth ... she was my mother, and I refused to ever see her or talk to her again. The fact I didn't know felt like a cold comfort. I cherished the wonderful memories I had of her, but now more than ever, I wished I had made a point of seeing her again.

I wondered if I would ever be able to forgive myself, either.

"Why are you telling me all of this now?"

She was still looking at the woods, but I saw her flinch. "About a year before Charlotte died, she called me. It was unexpected. She rarely called me after the first couple of years, just like I hadn't called her. I told myself it was better that way." She shook her head, her expression indicating what seemed like self-loathing. "Anyway, when I picked up the phone, I had expected another argument about seeing you or telling you the truth, but that wasn't what happened. Instead, she asked me to make her a promise. I asked her what the promise was, first, of course. She was silent for a long moment before she asked me."

My mother-turned-aunt stopped speaking inhaled deeply before sliding a long, thin envelope out of her pocket and setting it on the table.

"She told me she was mailing me a letter that I was to give to you after her death, when I told you the truth."

I shivered as the feeling of icy fingers slid down my back. My hands trembled, sloshing more cold coffee out of the cup. In that instant, I understood the saying, "Someone just walked over my grave."

"I told her she was being ridiculous. She was the younger sister, for heaven's sake. She should outlive me, not the other way around. She said be that as it may, I needed to promise her. I again told her she was being silly and hung up. A few days later, a packaged arrived in the mail. A note for me and this." She tapped the envelope. I could see *Becca* written in Charlie's familiar handwriting on the outside. "She said ..." her voice thickened, and she paused for a moment. "She said she forgave me for everything, and she knew deep down that I loved you and her. She said she was sure I would do the right thing after her death even without a promise. I ... I was so furious, I wanted to burn it. But I didn't. I tucked it away and convinced myself Charlotte was being just as dramatic and foolish as always. I still have no idea if she knew she was sick when she called me that day or not."

I stared at the envelope, but I didn't touch it. "But you still waited to tell me. It's been almost two years since her death."

She raised her hands and gestured around the yard. "What did you expect me to do? She willed you this house. She lured you out here, away from me! If I told you, you might never come home, and I would lose you forever. I couldn't let that happen." Her voice was getting more and more agitated, until she forced herself to stop and take a breath.

"But your mother knew me well." Her voice was quieter, and she lowered her hands. "She knew the guilt would devour me alive. It was just a matter of time."

She turned to look me directly in the eyes. "I started to tell myself I would tell you the truth as soon as you came back to New York. I just had to be patient. But," she shrugged as a faint, wry smile touched her lips. "You're a lot like your mother. I think I've always known you weren't coming home, but I didn't want to admit it to myself. I kept putting it off and putting it off. But when the news broke that you were involved with the cult and had been attacked, that was it. I knew I couldn't wait. If you ..." her voice broke. "If something happened to you, and I never had the chance to come clean and do the right thing for both you and my sister, I knew I would never be able to live with myself. So, I booked a plane ticket, then called to tell you I was coming."

I furrowed my brow. "Wait. You booked your ticket first?"

Her look was knowing. "If I had asked, you would have said no. And I wasn't waiting any longer. It was time. Even if ..." her chest caved as she collapsed on herself, but after a moment, she straightened back up, her expression determined but resigned. Only her eyes looked bleak. "Even if you never want to see me again, I needed to do this."

She pushed her chair back with a clatter and stiffly rose to her feet. She reached down and pushed the envelope toward me. "I'll pack my things and move to a hotel later today. There's no reason for you to be forced to sit outside of your own home. If you need anything, you have my number." With that, she turned on her heel and disappeared into the house.

Leaving me alone with my thoughts. And the letter.

Chapter 26

I watched the sun begin its descent over the horizon, an untouched glass of wine in front of me alongside the unopened letter from Charlie.

Annabelle was still in the house, I assumed making dinner, or, more precisely, reheating whatever the personal chef had prepared earlier.

After about an hour of sitting outside with my cold coffee, I had gone in to get a fresh cup and tell her she didn't have to leave.

I found her in front of her half-packed suitcase, mopping her face with a balled-up tissue. She startled when she saw me, pressing a hand to her chest. "Oh, you scared me." She tried to give me a watery smile, but it fell flat. "I shouldn't be too much longer …"

"Stay," I said. She stilled. "If you want," I added.

She looked at me then. I noticed how much older she appeared without her normal, carefully made-up face. Wrinkles bracketed her lips and purple bags hung beneath her eyes. "I don't want to chase you out of your home."

"You're not." I waved my hand around the room. "This is Charlie's home. I'd be outside regardless of you being here or not."

I could see the faint traces of hope start to bloom in her eyes, and I quickly turned away. I was already twisted up enough inside, and somehow, seeing that made me feel even worse. "Even so, why would you want me to stay?"

I didn't answer. I wasn't sure how to answer. How could I tell her about the memories that kept haunting me … the times when she was a true mother to me? Those precious moments when I could feel her love for me?

Not to mention that despite everything she had done, a part of me still loved her and wanted her in my life. I didn't even know what to do with that part.

"I don't really know," I finally answered, and as the words left my lips, I realized how true they were. "I don't know what I'm thinking or feeling right now. I'm still trying to sort through it all. But it … it doesn't feel necessary for you to stay in a hotel. At least not right now."

"If you're sure," she said, her voice almost halting. "I don't mind …"

"I'm sure," I said even as my eyes fell on the very bed she had moved from the attic against my wishes. The spark of anger ignited inside me yet again. Why did I just tell her to stay? I should have let her go, but it was too late now.

She must have seen something in my expression, because she fished her phone out of her pocket. "I'll get the bed moved back up to the attic today."

I looked at her in surprise. "I thought you didn't want to be in the attic."

She gave me a wry smile. "I don't. But as someone pointed out, it's not my house, and I should honor the owner's wishes."

I shot her a small smile back. "Thank you."

She inclined her head and held her phone up. "Since I'm making calls anyway, would you like me to cancel either the housekeeper or the personal chef? Both of them are scheduled to come today, but I'll cancel them both and compensate them for their time, if you'd like."

I had completely forgotten about them. It felt like a lifetime before, when she told me she had hired them. And now I wondered why I had gotten so upset about it. Yes, it was invasive, and yes, she should have checked with me, and yes, it complicated things with Chrissy. But she was trying to get me some help. And who wouldn't be happy with a housekeeper? Did it really matter if a stranger cleaned my house? What did I have to hide, anyway? Maybe that was precisely what the house needed—a good, deep cleaning to remove all the secrets and lies and betrayals that lived within its walls.

"No, that's fine. If you trust they'll do a good job, then I trust them."

Her face flushed pink with pleasure, and she busied herself with her phone.

I wondered when was the last time anyone had told her they appreciated what she had done for them. I had been so busy mentally cataloguing all the ways she had let me down over the years ... maybe I should have given some thought to the ways *I* had let *her* down, too.

As I watched the sun slowly set, my coffee replaced with wine, I wondered if I could give Charlie the same benefit of the doubt.

It was strange, because while I wasn't as angry at her as I was with my mother-turned-aunt, I still felt ... betrayed by her, in a different way. As upset as I was with Annabelle, I at least could understand where she was coming from. She was trying to protect me, in her own messed-up way, and preserve our mother-daughter relationship.

But Charlie? Why didn't she try harder to see me? Why didn't she try harder to get her sister to tell me the truth?

Why did she just ... give up?

Did she not love me? Was I not important enough to her?

All my life, I felt like I wasn't enough. Not put together enough, not smart enough, not pretty enough, not witty enough. Annabelle played a big part in that, as she was always trying to turn me into something I wasn't.

But Charlie? I always felt like I could be myself with her. That she loved and accepted me the way I was. I didn't have to try so hard. She just wanted me to be me.

But now, knowing the truth and how she didn't fight for me ... had I been wrong? Had everything in my life been one massive lie?

The thought made me sick. It made me even more sick to think that I would open Charlie's letter to find only a mess of excuses and half-baked apologies.

I didn't think I could handle it.

"Mia told me I would find you out here." The deep voice made me jump, and I turned to see Daniel striding across the yard in my direction.

I sat up a little straighter, wishing I had interrupted my brooding at some point to take a shower and maybe put a nicer shirt on. "What are you doing here?"

"Looking for you." He was wearing tight jeans and a dark-blue hoodie that brought out the blue in his eyes and emphasized his broad chest.

I wanted to roll my eyes. "Why?"

He pulled out one of the chairs and sat down, stretching out his long legs. "When you weren't answering your phone, I reached out to Mia."

I had completely forgotten about my phone. I wondered how many other messages I had missed. "I suppose she told you what happened."

He shook his head. "She didn't think it was her place." He cocked his head. "She also said to be patient, as you might not want to talk about it."

I could feel my eyes fill with tears, and I quickly looked away. Mia was such a good friend. She always had my back, even when I didn't think she did.

"I'm here if you want to talk," he said, his voice quiet. "If you don't, that's okay, too. I can talk, or we can just sit here in silence. And if you want me to leave, just say the word. I just wanted to make sure you were okay."

I almost laughed. I wasn't sure if I would ever be okay again. I definitely didn't think I would ever be the same again.

But maybe that wasn't a bad thing.

I looked at him, sprawled out in the chair, and a wave of grief rose up out of nowhere, nearly swamping me. I wanted nothing more than to wind the clock back to when we were still together, so I could crawl into his lap and have him put his arms around me as I poured out the whole sordid story. Or maybe I could just go back in time to when he was breaking up with me, and rather than getting angry and storming away, I could have stayed and talked about it. Maybe then, things would be different …

No. I wasn't going to do that anymore. Yes, Daniel was the one who broke up with me, but that didn't mean I was blameless in the matter. I needed to own my mistakes and screwups. He was right—I had hidden things from him, not telling him the full story. And maybe, if I had been honest and upfront, the whole last few months would have turned out differently. Yes, Daniel didn't like me to get involved in cases, but maybe if I had been straight with him, we could have come to a compromise that would have worked for both of us. Maybe if we had been communicating like adults, the whole initial screwup—when Daniel raided the Church of the Forgotten based on what I thought I heard in the barn—wouldn't have ended in such a disaster. Maybe if we had been working together, we could have come up with a different plan, a better one, that would have not only saved Zelda, but also put the masterminds of the whole thing behind bars.

Maybe my actions caused more problems than solutions.

And it wasn't just Daniel. It was Mia, too. Maybe if I had been honest and open with her, she never would have joined the Church of the Forgotten. Maybe she would have told Daniel and me, and Daphne too, about Waylon whispering sweet poison into her ear, and Daniel could have investigated him or tailed him before he convinced Mia to join the Church of the Forgotten. Really, the more I thought about it, the more I couldn't believe I had fallen into such a deep, dark pit that I truly thought Mia was against me. How did that happen?

Maybe all of this was an enormous wake-up call. Maybe it was time to own up to my past mistakes and make different choices. Maybe instead of feeling like I was the one who was broken and weak, the one who kept making the same bad choices with relationships and who couldn't sense people's true nature, it was time to shift my perspective.

I wasn't broken. I wasn't weak. And the reason why I had bad luck with relationships was because I either wasn't listening to my intuition when it told me something was off, or my actions were part of the problem.

Maybe it was time for a new Becca.

Daniel was still studying me, his dark-blue eyes steady and calm. I could feel that familiar prickling of energy between us. It was always there, ever since we were kids.

If only that had been enough.

"You really don't have to tell me," he said. "I meant what I said. We can just sit here in silence or talk about something else. Or if there's something else you need, just let me know."

I took a deep, shaky breath, inhaling the sharp bite in the autumn air. "No, I want to tell you. But I have to warn you ... it's a crazy story."

A hint of a smile touched his lips. "I'm a cop. I eat crazy stories for breakfast."

"Not this crazy," I said. "Trust me."

"Always," he said with a crooked grin.

My heart stuttered in my chest, and a fresh wave of tears threatened to flow. I quickly blinked them back. If I started crying, I would never get the story out. "Alright then. Just keep in mind, I warned you."

And I started to talk. Somewhere in the middle, the tears started to flow, and by the end, I was in his lap, his arms around me as I bawled into his dark-blue hoodie.

He didn't rush me or ask questions. He simply held me, rubbing a hand lightly up and down my back until I had cried out all my tears, and then, he kept holding me. The warm, familiar scent of his shampoo and soap mixed with his essence was all around me, and all I wanted was him.

I reached up and tried to mop my face without getting his sweatshirt more wet than it already was. "Sorry. I've made a mess of your hoodie."

"Nothing a toss in the washing machine won't fix," he said easily.

I smiled into his chest. "I'm sure you have tons of questions, so if you want to ask, I promise I won't cry anymore."

"I don't have any questions that need to be asked right now," he said before pausing for a moment, his hand stilling on my back. "Actually, I do have one." His voice was hesitant. "Are you and Aiden dating?"

Aiden. My eyes popped open. Oh no. I had completely forgotten about him. Again. Man, what an awful friend I was. Although, to be fair, I had been busy picking up the pieces of my life that had been turned upside down.

But ... that wasn't completely right, either. If I was going to be honest, I might as well start now, no matter how uncomfortable or unwelcome the truth might be.

While I hadn't thought about Aiden at all, I *had* thought about Daniel. Multiple times.

Oh boy.

"I guess I got my answer," Daniel said as I sat up in his lap. His hands had dropped to his sides, and I was suddenly cold, much colder than I had been sitting by myself in my own chair. He had a wry expression on his face as he looked at me.

"No, it's not what you think," I said. "He ..." I swallowed and tried again. "He asked me if I would be interested in dating him at some point, even if it wasn't now. He was willing to give me time, but he wanted to know if he at least had a chance."

Daniel's eyes sharpened. "And what did you say?"

"I told him I needed to think about it. He agreed, but I had to get back to him in a few days. He has to make a decision about his job. So, I said I would, but ... well ..." I shook my head in self-disgust. "I'm probably going to find a text from him on my phone, too."

Daniel's eyes hadn't left mine. "Did you make a decision?"

I drew in a shaky breath. He was staring at me so intensely, it was difficult to get air into my lungs. "Yes."

"And?"

It's time, Becca. Time to tell stop hiding. "Aiden is a friend. A good friend. Maybe, if things were different, I would be open to dating him, but not now."

Daniel put his hands on my arms, drawing me closer to me. "What would have to be different for you to date him?" He was so close, I could feel his breath on my lips. My head was spinning, and every part of me tingled.

"I would have to be over you."

He froze. And for one horrible second, I was sure I had completely misjudged the situation. He wasn't interested in me after all. He was just being nice because we were friends ...

Then his lips came down on mine.

The kiss was everything I could have wanted. Passionate, familiar, sweet. It was like we had never broken up and were discovering something new.

I don't know how far it would have gone if his phone hadn't buzzed.

He muttered a curse under his breath as he broke the kiss. "Sorry. I have to take this." He dug into his pocket for his phone while I took a few deep breaths to center myself. My emotions were all over the place, and I felt completely out of control.

He stared at the screen, and I could practically see his cop face snap back into place. "I have to go."

"What happened?"

He pressed his lips together as he eyed me over his phone, his expression unreadable. "Margot is dead."

I gasped. "Margot? Oh no ..."

"I know." His voice was grim.

"What happened?"

He hesitated, and for a moment, I thought he wasn't going to answer, but then he seemed to change his mind. "The same as Edna."

I thought about the last time I saw her, standing in that crowded room surrounded by sports equipment. *Don't turn yourself into a target any more than you already have.*

She was protecting me.

Was that what killed her?

"I have to come with you," I said.

Daniel's eyes flashed. "Absolutely not."

"But ..."

"No buts." His voice was firm, but his hands on my arms were gentle. "Look, this is all ... not happening the way I pictured it. Things need to be different. You need to trust me when I tell you something isn't a good idea or is too dangerous, just like I need to stop shutting you out. I know this, and I am working on it, which is why you have to listen to me when I tell you that you are in no shape to come with me tonight to a crime scene. Even if it wasn't nuts to allow a civilian to join me."

I opened my mouth to argue with him, then closed it. He was right. I was an exhausted, emotional wreck. I had no business going anywhere.

More than that, I needed to trust him.

It was a difficult pill to swallow, but if I was going to be a new Becca—one with healthier, happier relationships—I was going to have to compromise. And that included being better about keeping him in the loop, especially about things that directly impacted active investigations.

"I want to talk about this more, but right now, I really have to go." He squeezed my arms and started to move me off his lap.

I swallowed and put a hand on his chest. "Wait. I have something to tell you. About Margot."

He stilled. "I'm not going to like this, am I?"

I sighed. "Probably not. And I'm going to capitulate that I was wrong for not telling you sooner, and I too am committed to doing a better job trusting you in the future. Also, I will fully accept any and all yelling you feel is justified."

He leaned back in his chair and closed his eyes, letting go of my arm to pinch his nose. "Unfortunately, the yelling is going to have to wait, as I'm going to have to get out of here right after you tell me whatever it is you did."

"It wasn't that bad," I muttered.

He opened one eye. "I'll be the judge of that."

Chapter 27

I tried to keep my story short and sweet, not just because he had to leave, but also because despite what I said about the yelling, I did want to keep it to a minimum.

But Daniel was having none of it. Unlike when I told him about my family's convoluted history and he just let me talk, this time, he couldn't stop interrupting me.

"I can't believe you broke into the community center." He raked a hand through his hair.

"I didn't break in," I said indignantly. "I told you, I had a key."

He shot me a look. "You had no business using that key, and you know it."

"Well, how else was I supposed to get in without people seeing me?"

"You weren't. That's the point."

"But then ..." my voice trailed off. I was going to say how else would I protect Margot, but as it turned out, I hadn't been able to do that at all.

"We're definitely going to have a conversation about this," he grumbled. "After the yelling. But right now, I have to go. Unless there's anything else you need to tell me?" He raised an eyebrow.

"No, I think that's it," I said after a moment.

He didn't look convinced. "You sure?"

Something was niggling at me, but for the life of me, I couldn't put my finger on what it was. My brain was too tired to work properly anymore. "I'm sure." I sounded more confident than I felt. "But if I think of anything else, I'll call you," I added. Mentally, I gave myself a little pat on the back. The old Becca would not have said that.

Something flickered across his face, and I wondered if he was thinking the same thing. He reached up to cup my cheek. "I know it's been a rough few days, and you're still not a hundred percent. So, if something else does come up, let me know."

His fingers were so warm on my skin. I closed my eyes briefly, wishing he could stay longer. Even if it meant more yelling. "I promise."

He leaned forward and gave me another kiss, lingering longer than he probably should have, considering the circumstances, and when he broke it off, I was even more flushed and out of breath. "I'll call you." His voice was rough and unsteady.

"I'll make sure I have my phone with me," I said.

He chuckled as he helped me off his lap before standing himself. His phone buzzed again, and he rolled his eyes as he looked at it. "I better take this."

I nodded as he turned and loped away, phone pressed to his ear. I watched him until he disappeared around the corner of my house.

Could this be real? Were we truly back together? I almost felt like I was in shock. So many things—big, life-changing things—had happened over the past few days, I didn't know what to think or feel.

Except for one thing, I thought as my gaze fell on the unopened envelope still lying on the beveled-glass table next to the full glass of wine. *I'm not opening that letter today.*

I'd had enough excitement. I didn't need any more.

I swept the letter up and into my pocket and was about to pick up my wine when something flickered in the corner of my eye. I glanced over and saw it again—a movement in the woods.

Cold prickles began to race down my back. I shivered and folded my arms across my chest. The sun had nearly set, casting long shadows across the yard. It was probably nothing. The light playing tricks. Or maybe an animal had darted behind the trees.

An animal …

The niggling was back, but this time, I was remembering a couple of days before when I'd seen something in the woods. I thought it was an animal then, too. And that, of course, made sense.

But …

My mind flashed back to Penny's memorial service, standing in her backyard and seeing Zelda hiding in the woods. Of course, I hadn't known at the time it was Zelda, but that was neither here nor there.

I took a step toward the woods before remembering I didn't have my phone. I brushed it off, figuring it didn't matter. I was in my own backyard, for goodness' sake.

But then I heard Margot's voice in my head, telling me to be careful.

I froze. She never did explain exactly why I needed to be careful ... just that I was in danger.

I scooped up my wine, then turned and darted into the house, trying to keep from spilling it in my hurry. My phone was in the kitchen, which was empty, but filled with the scents of beef, onions, garlic, and tomatoes. I grabbed it and dashed back outside, hoping if there was someone in the woods, they wouldn't disappear before I got back out there.

Leaves and grass crunched under my feet as I cut across the backyard. The wind had died down, but the temperature had started dropping as the sun disappeared. There was a heaviness to the air that felt like rain heading our way. I could smell it in the air, heavy, swollen, and ready to let loose.

A storm is coming.

I pushed that thought down, along with the prickling sensation that someone was watching me. The evening was quiet and still, no sign of life whatsoever. Maybe it was all in my head. Whatever I thought I saw in the woods, and even the uneasiness that stirred in me now, was just a byproduct of the insanity I had gone through the past few days.

Maybe. But somehow, I didn't believe it.

I reached the edge of the woods and paused, peering through the trees. I could see nothing but darkness.

Visions of my sixteen-year-old self wandering in these very woods floated through my head, and with them, images of Jessica, of CB ...

I shoved my hand through my hair, willing myself to stop thinking about that night. Instead, my mind started replaying the images of Zelda in the woods, the fearful look in her eyes as she backed away from me ...

This wasn't helping. I should just go back to the house, have some dinner, and get some sleep. I could always come back in the morning when the sun was out if I wanted to do some exploring.

The trees seemed to sway in the nonexistent wind, mocking me.

That niggling sensation returned, and I found myself thinking of Margot again. Why did she think I was in danger? Was it just about revenge? Or was there something else going on?

When I had told Daniel, I had glossed over the part about my being in danger. In that moment, it didn't seem as important as telling him what Margot had said about knowing about Zelda and Pamela. If Margot knew, others probably did, too. And maybe that was the reason she was killed.

But now, standing in my own backyard next to the woods that had once haunted me for fifteen years, I wasn't so sure.

Margot's words rang in my head:

It's not over. The Church of the Forgotten are determined to do whatever they can to not be forgotten.

What wasn't over? Who was killing the members? And was it to cover up a murder and kidnapping, or for some other reason?

Maybe ... something worse?

From a distance, a jagged streak of lightning sliced through the night sky. It reminded me of the night I had snuck out of the Church of the Forgotten, when one of the buildings had caught fire. If that hadn't happened, Eleanor likely wouldn't have caught me, and maybe I would have found a different way to get Zelda out without alerting the whole community and starting the chain of events that ended in Edna's and Margot's murder.

Eleanor.

"We have uncovered no evidence that suggests Eleanor didn't die in that fire," Daniel had said.

What an odd, careful statement. Almost like he didn't actually think Eleanor was dead after all. And if Eleanor wasn't dead ...

I swiped at my phone, my fingers stiff and numb, even though I didn't think it was quite that cold out. It took a couple of tries before I was able to find his contact info.

He picked up almost immediately. "Becca? Is everything okay?"

My lips were as numb as my fingers. "Did Eleanor die in that fire?"

There was a moment of startled silence. "Did Margot tell you that?"

I briefly squeezed my eyes shut. "Is she alive?"

I heard him curse under his breath. "What did Margot say to you?"

The woods seemed to be mocking me, inviting me to come closer, to peer more deeply into the darkness. I glanced around quickly, feeling exposed and vulnerable, before starting to back away toward the house. "Nothing. Margot didn't say anything."

"Then who?"

"No one said anything. Other than you, that night when you first came to tell us that Edna was dead."

Another brief pause. "Becca, what's going on? Why are you asking me about this right now?"

I had reached the table and chair I had spent so many hours brooding in and risked a quick look over my shoulder. Everything looked the same. Nothing was chasing me.

Still, I knew I wouldn't breathe easier until I got inside.

"First, you have to tell me why you didn't tell us that Eleanor was still alive."

"I don't know if she is. There's some ... discrepancies, but that doesn't necessarily mean she's alive."

"What discrepancies?"

"It's too complicated to get into now. I promise I'll explain everything later, but right now, you need to tell me why you're asking about this."

A part of me wanted to argue with him. Or scream. Or maybe both. Eleanor might be alive, and he didn't tell me? How could he keep that from me?

But before I could say anything, he started talking. "Why do you think I called Mia today? I was going to tell you earlier, but … well … it seemed more important to be there for you."

I slumped against the door, feeling all the anger and righteousness drain out of me. He was trying to change. I had to give him the benefit of the doubt.

"Trust me," he said softly. "Now, will you tell me what I want to know, please?"

I straightened up and ran a hand through my hair. "It's hard to explain. Margot was … she wouldn't tell me why she thought I was in danger, but she seemed overly concerned …"

"Wait. You didn't tell me Margot thought you were in danger."

I had reached the back door, but I didn't go inside, as I didn't want to have this conversation in front of my mother-turned-aunt. Instead, I leaned against it, pressing my back against the solid wood so I could look over the entire backyard. Everything still appeared completely normal. Maybe I was just losing it. "I know. I should have probably told you, but at the time, what she said about the church seemed more important. I didn't think I was really in danger. Not here, anyway. At the community center is a different story, but …" I knew I was babbling, but I couldn't stop.

"Becca, what did she say?"

"She said I had made myself a target. I asked her why, but she wouldn't tell me. Maybe it's revenge? For destroying the church?"

As if Daniel could sense my fear, he switched gears. "What's going on, Becca? Did something happen? Something you're not telling me?"

I stared at the woods. It was too dark to see them clearly anymore, let alone make out anyone lurking behind the trees. "No. Not really. I just have a bad feeling."

"Becca, I don't want you going anywhere tonight. Can you just stay in and keep your doors locked and your alarm system on? Have Mia stay in with you, too, okay? I'll swing by in the morning to check things out."

Instantly, my chest loosened. There would be four of us in the house, and everything would be fine. "Yes, I can do that."

"If you see anything strange, anything at all, call me. Okay? I don't care how late it is."

"Okay," I said, feeling a rush of warmth flood my chest. I wasn't alone. Daniel was back.

Maybe everything was finally going to be okay.

Chapter 28

"You didn't listen to me."

I was sitting at the kitchen table across from the shadowy figure. Darkness surrounded the single, small pool of light that illuminated us.

"Listen to you about what? You didn't tell me anything," I said crossly.

"That's because you refused to listen." Its features were more defined than normal. I could almost make out a pair of dark eyes, high, defined cheekbones, and a full mouth.

"Listen to what? You talk in riddles."

The figure suddenly slammed its hands onto the table, making me jump. Puffs of dust floated up into the air. "You refuse to see what's right in front of you." The figure leaned closer to me, so close, I could smell its rotting, decaying breath. *"You refuse to see the truth."*

I wanted to lean back. I wanted to leave. But I couldn't move. I couldn't even breathe. I could only stare into those eyes that were somehow so cold and yet so familiar ...

"You're Jonathan Decker, aren't you?"

Its full lips pulled back into a caricature of a smile, revealing a mouth full of broken teeth. "Ah, so you actually figured one thing out."

His face was somehow both loathsome and compelling ... like just beneath the horror he had become was the attractive, loving man Charlie had fallen in love with. "You're my father, aren't you?"

The smile shifted, becoming more real and less inhumane. "Finally. I was starting to really wonder about your intelligence. I was hoping that didn't come from my side of the family."

I blinked. I didn't expect the scary dark shadowy figure to have a sense of humor.

His smile brightened as if he could read my mind before he slowly lowered himself into his seat. "You're a lot like her, you know.

Which is why Annabelle struggled so much with you over the years. It would have been easier for everyone if you had been more like me."

I wasn't sure what to say to that. "Um ... but didn't you kill people?"

He turned to look out the window. "I made a lot of mistakes."

Quite the understatement, I thought. Along with killing two people, he was also married when he met Charlie. I had a sick feeling that I too could be counted as one of his "mistakes." "Like getting involved with Charlie."

He jerked back toward me. "I will never regret falling in love with Charlie. Never." His voice was fierce and his eyes intense. "Could I have handled things differently? Absolutely." He paused then, and something changed. "And unfortunately, like father, like daughter. You're about to make one of the same mistakes we did."

An icy finger trailed down my spine. "What mistake?"

A bolt of lightning flashed through the window, causing the room around us to flicker. He turned to the window again.

"A storm is coming."

That icy finger grew and wrapped around my chest, constricting, keeping me from breathing. "What storm? What mistake?"

More bursts of lightning followed by the crackle of thunder. I could see Jonathan talking, his lips moving, but I couldn't hear anything over the noise. "What are you saying? I can't hear you ..."

His face contorted in the flickering light, like a Halloween monster in a cheap horror film. His voice was going in and out, like a radio station losing a signal. I could only pick out a few words in between the static. "Don't go downstairs."

"What?" That didn't make any sense. Go downstairs where? I must not have heard him right.

An emotion that looked like grief seemed to shimmer on his face. "It's too late. You need to wake up. Now."

My eyes flew open at the same time a spear of lightning arced through my window. The thunder that followed was deafening, and rain was pounding on the roof and against the window.

A storm is coming.

Enough. I had to pull myself together. Obviously, I had incorporated the storm outside into my dream. Nothing more ominous than that. Instead of freaking myself out, what I needed to do was calm myself down, so I could fall back asleep ...

Thump.

I shot up in bed so suddenly, I woke Oscar, who opened one green eye to glare at me. That noise had come from downstairs. I was sure of it. Was there someone down there?

I sat there as quietly as I could, even trying to hold my breath as I strained my ears to listen. Sweat dripped off my forehead and trickled down my cheek, but no other sounds came.

Was it just the house settling? It didn't sound like it. I was very familiar with its creaks and groans, and whatever was downstairs sounded very different. Was it from the storm? Possibly. Maybe a branch hit the side of the house. Or maybe the storm woke up one of my housemates, and they were wandering around downstairs.

I should probably go check it out. That would be the smart thing. Then I would know for sure and could go back to sleep. Maybe I could get a cup of tea while I was at it.

I slid my legs out of the bed and stood up, but immediately hesitated.

Don't go downstairs.

Oh, for heaven's sake ... it was just a dream. It wasn't real. Dream Jonathan had no idea what was going on in my house. And what had he even meant, anyway? He could have been talking about the basement. Or some other downstairs.

Still ... I chewed on my bottom lip, feeling uneasy. Whatever the noise was, it was louder than a footstep. But what else could it be? I had an alarm system. It wasn't like someone could just break in.

The last thing Daniel said to me floated through my brain—to call him if anything strange happened, no matter how late it was. Maybe that's what I should do, even though I felt foolish even considering it. I was sure it was nothing. More likely, either my mother-turned-aunt was wandering around, or a branch from the storm was hitting the house. Why would I drag Daniel out of bed for nothing?

But in that moment, I realized I didn't care. Every part of me wanted to see him, to feel his warm arms around me. I also knew Daniel wouldn't care. In fact, he would probably see it as a huge breakthrough in our relationship, that I would trust him enough to call him.

Decision made. I looked around my room ... only to remember that I'd left my phone downstairs. I closed my eyes. Oh, for cripes' sake. Now I had to go down there. Ugh.

I crossed the room and opened the door. Behind me, I heard a soft thump and saw that Oscar had jumped off the bed and was trotting after me.

Well, at least I wouldn't be alone. I eased the door open to keep from waking anyone else up and started down the hall.

Almost immediately, I heard it. It sounded like voices, but I couldn't be sure. I also couldn't make out any words.

But who would be talking to who?

All the bedroom doors were shut, which didn't mean anything. They could have closed their doors before going downstairs, of course. But I didn't like it. Something didn't feel right.

After a moment, I retreated into my room to grab my baseball bat. Well, Charlie's baseball bat. I had inherited it with the rest of the house. I hefted it, feeling a little silly, and knowing I was about to feel a lot sillier when I found Mia and Annabelle in the kitchen chatting.

That didn't stop me from bringing the bat.

I crept down the hallway, trying to make as little noise as possible, even while telling myself I was overreacting. There was no way someone had broken into the house. I had locked all the doors and activated the alarm system before going to bed. No one could have gotten inside undetected.

Not even Eleanor.

My heart was pounding in my chest as I eased my way down the stairs. The lights were all off in the living room and kitchen, but that didn't necessarily mean there was no one there. I didn't always turn the light on in the middle of the night. I could hear someone moving around the kitchen (probably making tea, I told myself) and another breathy sound I couldn't identify. Rain was still pelting down, making it more difficult to decipher exactly what was going on in the kitchen.

You're probably going to give someone a heart attack, brandishing a bat like this, I told myself. Regardless, I couldn't release it even if I wanted to. I was clutching it in a death grip.

I made it down the steps, my back pressed against the wall, and listened carefully. Still couldn't hear anything specific. Actually, I couldn't hear anything at all, other than the sounds of the storm.

Had I imagined it? Was it just a combination of the storm and my nightmares and frayed nerves?

No, I couldn't have imagined it. I couldn't have.

I squeezed my eyes shut and really wished Daniel was with me. I *had* to stop leaving my phone in the kitchen!

That was neither here nor there, at that point. I either needed to check out the kitchen or go back to bed. Seeing as I already knew there was no way I would be able to sit in my bedroom without knowing if there was anyone downstairs, I was clear on what I had to do.

I sucked in a quiet breath, counted to three, and lunged around the corner.

I stopped dead.

Lightning flashed through the window, just like in my dream, filling the kitchen with a jagged, strobing light ... and illuminating two distinct figures. One was my mother-turned-aunt, sitting in one of the chairs, her face partially hidden. But the other ...

Was dressed in a long, old-fashioned muslin dress with little embroidered flowers.

Another lightning bolt shot its light through the window, and all I could see was Eleanor's face.

Eleanor, alive and glaring at me, her eyes full of hatred and madness.

"Oh, there you are," she said, but there was something wrong with her voice. It didn't sound like her at all. It sounded like ... my mind scrambled, went blank. "That will save me a trip up the stairs," she continued, before flipping on the kitchen light.

I shielded my eyes from the brightness, but not before realizing my mistake. It wasn't Eleanor in my kitchen.

It was Gertrude.

And she was holding a gun.

Chapter 29

"Don't just stand there. Come in," Gertrude said, gesturing with the gun. She glanced at my baseball bat and smirked. "Haven't you ever heard the adage, 'Never bring a baseball bat to a gunfight?'" She snickered at her own joke, before her eyes turned serious. "Drop it."

I let go of the bat, but otherwise didn't move. It clattered as it hit the floor. "What are you doing here?" Was this the reason why Jonathan told me not to go downstairs?

And by not calling Daniel first, had I made the mistake Jonathan had warned me about?

She looked at me strangely. "What do you think I'm doing? I'm righting a wrong."

Next to her, Annabelle stared at me, her face smeared with cold cream and eyes wide and pleading. Now that my vision had adjusted, I could see she was gagged with what appeared to be a kitchen towel. I recognized the cheery sunflowers, which added to the surrealism.

"Look, I'm sorry for what happened to the Church of the Forgotten," I said, trying to buy some time for Mia—or maybe Chrissy, although she slept like the dead—to wake up and realize something was wrong. Both of them likely had cell phones in their rooms, unlike me. If I got through this, I was going to chain my phone to my body. "That wasn't my intention ..."

Her expression shifted to incredulous. "You think I'm stupid? That was EXACTLY what you intended."

I shook my head. "No, I just wanted to rescue Zelda. That was it. I promise."

Gertrude took a step toward me, her eyes glittering with unholy light. "You never believed. You made a mockery of The One. You will be punished," she hissed.

I took a step backward, keeping half an eye on my mother-turned-aunt. Maybe if I talked really loudly, or even started yelling, it would be enough to wake Mia or Chrissy ...

Gertrude read my thoughts. "Don't bother. You won't wake either of them."

My heart flew up and lodged in my throat. Was she saying what I thought she was? "What did you do to them?"

She smirked. "They're both fine. For now, at least. I only drugged them."

My jaw dropped. "You ... *drugged* them? With what?"

She shrugged. "First a little chloroform, then a little injection. It wasn't difficult." Her eyes suddenly hardened, and she jerked her chin over her shoulder. "Your mother was supposed to be in bed, too ... not wandering around down here. I had to tie her up and gag her to keep her quiet." Behind her, Annabelle let out a garbled moan.

"Why didn't you drug me too?"

She looked at me incredulously, as though she couldn't believe how stupid I was. "Because *you're* the one who needs to pay. Why else would I have done all of this?" She waved the gun around the house, and my heart nearly stopped beating, terrified it would accidentally go off. "Come on now. It's time to come into the kitchen."

I wasn't sure if I could make my legs work properly, but I knew I had to. Maybe if I dove at her, I could somehow wrestle the gun away from her ...

Again, she seemed to read my mind and backed into the kitchen, keeping the gun trained on me.

She smiled, the stuff of nightmares.

I slowly shuffled forward, trying desperately to figure a way out. If I could somehow get to my phone, although I doubted she would let me anywhere near it, I could call Daniel.

Although ... an icy knot was forming in the pit of my stomach. Shouldn't Daniel know Gertrude was missing? They should have accounted for everyone at the community center, since they were still actively investigating Margot's murder. Right?

"Did you kill Margot? And Edna?" I asked, already knowing the answer.

Gertrude gave me a smug look, and without hesitation, said, "Of course."

"Why?"

She narrowed her eyes. "Because they were traitors. Just like you."

"How were they traitors?"

"Because they were going to tell."

"Tell what?"

An evil smile spread across her face. "That I wasn't me."

Understanding rose up inside me like bile. My mind flashed to the photo in the file at the police station—I knew there was something wrong with it. "Someone was pretending to be you to the police."

"Finally! Here I thought you were supposed to be so smart … it sure took you long enough." She rolled her eyes.

"But why would you do that? The police didn't find everyone. Why didn't you just … disappear?"

She looked at me with disdain. "You don't think they're still looking for the ones who disappeared that night? Them believing I was in the community center was the perfect cover."

"But all the other members know whoever is pretending to be you isn't you."

"Not all," she said. "I told Janice to keep a low profile. She didn't tell anyone she was pretending to be me, but it wouldn't have mattered if she did. The Church of the Forgotten knows how to keep secrets. Even if they hadn't known the details, they would have immediately understood I had been called to a higher purpose that required me to hide my identity."

"But you just said Edna and Margot were going to tell the cops."

Her forehead wrinkled as she frowned slightly, though it smoothed out only a moment later. "Your traitorous ways infected us. You're like a *disease*," she emphasized the last word as her expression turned to utter disgust. "Unfortunately, Edna and Margot succumbed, which left me with no choice."

I thought I was going to be sick. *Things are not as they seem*, Margot had said. Was this what she was talking about? That Gertrude had forced some other member to be her, so she could freely move around, undetected?

My mind raced as sweat began gathering at the back of my neck. I couldn't count on any outside help. Daniel wasn't coming; heck, Daniel didn't even know that Gertrude wasn't there. Mia and Chrissy were drugged. Hopefully, that was all, but I couldn't go there. My mother-turned-aunt was tied up and gagged.

There was only me.

And I needed a weapon.

But what? My eyes desperately scanned the room, but nothing stood out. A knife would be ideal, but getting my hands on one was a whole other story—despite seeing them nestled just out of reach in their wooden block. If only I still had the bat, I could use that … though Gertrude had made a valid point when she called me out for literally bringing a bat to a gunfight.

At that exact moment, my foot nudged the bat where I had dropped it, and my mother-turned-aunt made another garbled noise as her eyes rolled to the back of her head.

"Quiet," Gertrude snapped before reeling back and slapping her.

"Hey," I yelled while nudging the bat under the table with my foot. With any luck, Gertrude would forget I even had it. "She has nothing to do with this."

Gertrude looked at me with insane eyes. "She's your mother," she said. Apparently, that was reason enough.

"She had NOTHING to do with my actions," I said. Glancing back at Annabelle, I suddenly wondered why she was gagged. After all, Gertrude claimed she didn't need to gag me, since I couldn't wake anyone up.

I couldn't help but ask. Gertrude glared at my mother-turned-aunt before saying, "She annoyed me."

Annabelle made that strange noise again. She didn't look right; her face was too pale, and the towel in her mouth was soaked with drool. I suddenly realized the towel was covering both her mouth and her nose, and she might very well be suffocating. Either that or having a heart attack.

The fear that had been gripping my chest since the moment I realized there were people in the kitchen exploded inside me. "Take off the gag!" I ordered, fear making my voice sound even harsher than I intended.

Gertrude shot me a look of disdain. "You don't make the rules here. Remember?" She tapped her gun.

I took a step toward her, anger and fear colliding inside me. "Something is wrong with her! Take the gag off. Right. NOW."

Something flickered in Gertrude's eyes so fast, I couldn't read it, and she turned to Annabelle. "Fine." She yanked the gag off, and my mother-turned-aunt let out a strangled noise before slumping over in her chair. "Happy? It's not like she's got long to live anyway."

I ignored her and started to move toward the woman who I now finally realized was, unequivocally, my mother.

Yes, Charlie may have given birth to me, but she was the one who raised me. For better or worse, she was my mother, and I was her daughter. "Mom, are you okay?"

Gertrude waved the gun at me again before I could reach her. "Oh no you don't. Stay where you are. You got what you wanted."

My mother was breathing hard, her chin covered with drool and snot, but she managed to raise her head to look at me. "I'm fine. Don't worry about me."

"Enough of the family reunion," Gertrude snapped as she gestured toward a chair with the gun. "We've got things to do. *Sit down*."

I didn't move. "What things? What's going on?"

Gertrude's eyes hardened. "Sit. Down." Next to her, my mother let out a soft moan.

I remained standing. Something inside me had shifted and just like that, I was done. A part of me knew it was insane—I knew she would have no qualms about shooting me or my mother, so I shouldn't be antagonizing her. But I didn't care.

I was done being the victim.

I stared at her, my gaze unblinking. "Not until you tell me what's going on. Who are you doing this for? Eleanor?"

Gertrude's face went white with rage. "Don't you dare say her name!" she shrieked. Her eyes were wild as she pointed the gun at me. "You don't EVER say her name. You are not worthy of her name!"

"I was worthy enough for her to *give* me her name," I taunted right back.

Her head snapped back as if I had slapped her. Her eyes were rolling around in their sockets, reminding me of a horse before it tried to buck its rider off. For a moment, I thought I had pushed her too far. I tensed, expecting her to start shooting.

Instead, she let out a scream.

My mother's face blanched as she cowered in the corner. "That should have been me!" Spittle shot out of her mouth. "After everything I did ... *I* should have been the one to carry on her name, her work. She was like a mother to me! I gave her everything ... everything! I am the true heir. Not a traitor like you." She was so distraught, she was pacing back and forth, her face distorted with rage.

It slowly dawned on me that she had referred to Eleanor in the past tense. "Wait ... is Eleanor dead?"

Gertrude jerked her head back around to glare at me. "I told you not to say her name!"

"But is she dead??"

"Of course she's dead!" Gertrude yelled, one hand waving the gun, the other tugging at her hair. "I killed her."

Thunder crashed in the distance, as if to put an exclamation point on what she said. Next to me, I heard my mother suck in her breath. All I could do was stare at Gertrude, wondering if I had fallen into some alternative reality. "You ... you killed Eleanor?"

"If you don't stop saying her name ..." Gertrude threatened, shaking her gun at me. "I had no choice! And it's *your* fault."

"How could that possibly be my fault?" The sweat that was trickling down the back of my neck turned to ice.

Gertrude was delusional. I had always known she was crazy, but this was on another level. I was starting to get a sick feeling that I wasn't getting out of this alive.

But maybe I could save my family and friend.

"You infected her!" The thunder crashed again, and the rain pounded outside. "Just like you infected everyone else! You are a disease, and everyone who comes anywhere near you is cursed."

"I don't know what you're talking about," I shouted over the storm, over the hammering of my heart. "Eleanor had me locked up in my room! YOU were guarding me! And she was probably going to keep me locked up if I hadn't gotten away."

"That's exactly my point," Gertrude shouted back. Her face was red and splotchy as she flung her arms, and the gun, all over the place while pacing frantically. Again, I prayed the gun wouldn't go off accidentally. "She should have killed you, not locked you up ... not set up the ritual to have you join us. Not given you *her name*."

"That's what it all comes down to, doesn't it? Eleanor gave me her name and not you."

"Stop it!" she shrieked. "You don't know anything! You don't *understand* anything."

She was so incensed, she was no longer even looking at me. She continued pacing, her limbs lashing out sporadically.

And I realized it was my chance.

I dove at her before she even realized I was moving. She turned to me, her mouth dropping open in a surprised "O" as she tried to swing the gun toward me. I was too fast, though, and I grabbed her arm as I hit her square in the chest. The gun went off with a bang, right next to my ear, and I heard my mother scream.

We tumbled to the floor, both of us scrambling for the gun. Something crashed on the floor near us, and in a swift movement, I was on top of her and nearly pinned her down. Suddenly, she flipped me over and cracked my head against the floor. Pain shot through my skull, and the edges of my vision turned black. I panicked. I was going to pass out in my own kitchen, trapped with a madwoman.

"Idiot!" Gertrude yelled as she roughly grabbed my shoulder and wrenched me over, nearly pulling my arm out of the socket. I tried to hit her, but she knocked my hand away as she straddled me, sitting on my stomach, and pushed the gun against my cheek. I could feel the cold steel kiss my skin, and I went still.

"Finally, you're behaving." She blew a lock of hair out of her eyes and glared at me. "Luckily, your little stunt didn't cause any real damage."

I held up my hands, palms up, as I laid my head against the cold floor. Pain radiated across my temples, and I figured I was either about to die or was suffering a concussion with imminent, permanent brain damage. "Fine. You got me. Let my mother and the other two go. I'm who you want ... you don't need to hurt them."

A slow, sinister smile spread across her face. "Oh, but you're wrong. I do need to hurt them. And that's your fault, too."

"Why is it my fault?" I demanded, trying not to reveal the panic blossoming inside me. I couldn't let this happen. I had to save them.

"Because YOU–" she shoved the gun harder against my cheek, "forced me to kill Eleanor. And she was the only real mother I ever knew." She said the last part so quietly, I had to strain to hear her.

"That makes no sense," I argued. "Eleanor died in a fire she started. Or are you saying you started the fire?"

That fanatical light was back in her eyes. "Yes, I started the fire. But that's not how Eleanor died."

If Eleanor didn't die in the fire ... oh no. My throat closed up, and it was all I could do to force the words out. "Whose body was it?" I croaked, even though I was sure I knew. I could picture her cheery smile as she handed me her water that hot summer day.

"Who do you think? Trudy. That *bitch*." She spat. I could feel the spray of spittle on my forehead, but I didn't care. *Oh Trudy. I'm so sorry. You tried to do the right thing.*

"She had already called the cops by the time I caught her, but I made her pay." Her eyes glistened. "Eleanor grabbed what she could, while I concentrated on the house. Luckily, it was so old, it didn't take much to get it burn." She glanced around the kitchen. "Just like this house." Her voice was thoughtful.

A hot spike of dread stabbed my chest. "I still don't understand. Why would you kill her?"

She snapped her head toward me again, her eyes wild. "Because she wouldn't stop talking about you! You were her obsession! I wanted to kill you and end all of this, but no. She wouldn't hear of it. She still wanted you to join the Church of the Forgotten. She was sure if she could force you to do the ritual, The One would do the rest. After all, you were living in Lily's house. You had dreams about Lily. She was convinced you were Chosen by The One, and once you became a full-fledged member, everything would fall into place."

It was even nuttier than I'd imagined. How delusional would Eleanor have to be to think that, after everything that had happened, I would somehow willingly join the Church of the Forgotten?

"I couldn't make her see reason. It didn't matter what I said ... she was sure this was what The One wanted. But how could that be? *I* should have been the Chosen. *I* was loyal and faithful. Not you! You were the traitor. The *betrayer*. You shouldn't have been rewarded. *I* should have!

"Finally, one night I couldn't stand it anymore. I was trying to make dinner, and she was going on and on, and I finally turned and just ..." she swallowed, and I saw a sheen of tears in her eyes. "I didn't mean to hit her so hard. She just crumbled to the floor. I thought I killed her, but when I realized she was still alive, I strangled her. I had to put her out of her misery, you see. Because she still wasn't listening ... she wasn't listening to what The One wanted. It was the only way to get through to her."

It was all I could do to not gape at her. "What did you do then?"

She shrugged. "What could I do? I brought her back to the Church of the Forgotten and buried her. I had to time it when the cops weren't there, but I managed." Her face softened slightly. "She deserved to be buried there. She did so much good for The One. She deserved that."

I wasn't sure what to say.

She dashed a hand over her eyes. "Well, all that's in the past. Now, it's time to look forward ... to new beginnings."

The stake of dread started twisting inside of me again. "What do you mean?"

She didn't answer immediately. Instead, she shoved the gun more tightly against my face as she rose up slightly and fumbled with something on the kitchen counter above us. "There it is." Her voice was triumphant as she sat back down on my stomach with a thud. She flashed me a wicked grin as she revealed what was in her hand.

A lighter.

All the air seemed to leave my body. The metal glinted dully in the light.

"What are you going to do with that?" I breathed.

She waved it at me, taunting me. "I'm going to burn down your house, of course." Her voice was sing-songy.

I couldn't breathe. I couldn't think. She was going to burn down my house with my mother, Mia, and Chrissy inside. "But why? This is Lily's house. Why would you do that?"

She snorted. "This *isn't* Lily's house. Lily lived on the land, not in this house, you fool. I'm going to burn it down and build something brand new."

"That's ridiculous," I said, trying to keep myself from hyperventilating. "The cops will be looking for you. You certainly won't be able to buy it."

"Maybe not now," she said. "But someday. I suspect no one else is going to want this place. Why would they? A haunted house that has brought nothing but tragedy to anyone who has lived here. First Martha and her poor maid Nellie, then you. You, who went off the deep end and killed your mother, stepdaughter, and friend before killing yourself and burning down your house."

"That's crazy," I scoffed. "No one will believe it."

Her eyes danced. "You want to bet? Once Daniel gets the suicide text from your phone, they will. After all, you've been acting … peculiar, since returning from the Church of the Forgotten. Forgetting stuff. Misplacing things. You haven't been yourself. And it's not like you don't have a history of, well, mental illness."

My mouth dropped open. "How do you know I've forgotten things?"

She laughed. "Because I drugged your ibuprofen, silly! It was easy to do, just like it was easy to figure out your alarm system. Did you know that Chrissy has the code written on a note on her phone?" She shook her head. "This is why technology is going to destroy the world. All I had to do was take her phone and keys while she was working, make a copy, and replace them both."

I gaped at her. "You did this to me? This was all you?"

"Of course. Although ..." she frowned. "It was initially Eleanor's idea. She thought drugging you would soften you up for the Church of the Forgotten." Her frown deepened before she shook her head. "Well, never mind that. Shall we begin?" She flicked the lighter, and a small flame appeared.

A dull roar sounded in my ears, and I couldn't tear my eyes off the small, orange flame as it danced in the slight breeze. I could smell the sulfur.

"Gertrude, you don't have to do this," I begged as she moved the lighter across her body toward the curtains.

"Oh, but I do," she said, as her lips twisted in a slow, cruel smile.

And then, everything turned upside down.

What Wasn't Forgotten

Chapter 30

"Drop the gun!"

Gertrude froze. My mother was standing behind her, an arm wrapped around her neck and what looked like a jagged piece of red glass pressed against her throat.

"Mom?" I was having trouble processing the scene in front of me.

There was blood on Gertrude's neck, which made me think my mother had already cut her. But then I realized it was coming from my mother, running down her arm and dripping from her fingers onto Gertrude's chest.

Her face was grim.

"You're bleeding," I stated inanely.

Her eyes flickered toward me. "Before you came downstairs, we were having a bit of a tussle." She jerked the piece of glass, making Gertrude wince. "At one point, a coffee mug fell to the floor and broke. When you attacked Gertrude, I was able to tip my chair over so it fell near the shards, and I cut myself loose."

Apparently, she had also cut her fingers to ribbons in the process. I looked at the shard she was holding and tried to picture the mug it would have come from, as I didn't own a red coffee mug. But then I realized it was red because it was smeared with her blood.

My mother's eyes went back to Gertrude, and she shoved the shard against her neck again. A red drop welled at the tip as it broke the skin, and Gertrude let out a hiss of pain. "I said, drop the gun," my mother repeated, her voice like steel.

"You wouldn't dare," Gertrude breathed, thrusting the tip of the gun barrel into my cheek again. In the other hand, she still held the lit lighter, the flame flickering even though there appeared to be no air movement. "It wouldn't take much from me to pull the trigger right now."

My mother's eyes went cold—colder than I had ever seen in my life. "You pull the trigger, you're dead. Now drop it." Her voice was as hard as her eyes, and her expression ... well, it was terrifying.

In that moment, I caught a glimpse of the woman who would do anything, including commit murder, to save her family. This was the woman who had sent her younger sister money, even though she didn't believe her story, and agreed to a crazy adoption scheme to protect both of her sisters ... the woman who raised her sister's child as her own, even when she was forced to face that truth every time she looked into her daughter's face and saw her sister looking back at her. This was the woman who had found the strength to get on a plane and bring her adopted daughter a letter that might destroy their relationship forever ... because she knew it had to be done.

This was the woman who was willing to kill to protect me as fiercely as she would have my brothers.

She truly was my mother.

Gertrude's eyes went blank, and I felt the pressure of the gun barrel lessen. For a moment, I couldn't believe it—my mother had done it. Gertrude was surrendering.

But then, something flashed in Gertrude's eyes, and I suddenly realized it was a trap. Gertrude wasn't surrendering.

She was aiming the gun at my mother's head.

I didn't think, simply reacted. I lunged forward, grabbing the gun with both hands. She tried to jerk it away, and it went off again as I slammed her arm to the ground. She let out a shriek, though it was hard to say whether from frustration, pain, or both. I pried her fingers off the handle, then grabbed it myself, my own hands slippery with sweat, to point it at her.

"Get off ..." I started to yell, but abruptly stopped.

She was staring at me, her eyes wide and glassy. One of her hands was at her throat, trying to staunch the flow of dark-red, thick blood that was pouring out of an obvious wound. "Elle ..." Her voice was garbled as a pulse of blood flowed through her fingers, soaking her muslin dress.

My mother was on the floor beside Gertrude, a dazed expression on her face. She was still holding the bloody shard. I wondered if she had meant to cut Gertrude, or if it was an accident ... something that happened in the heat of the moment when we were scrambling for the gun.

Even though Gertrude was still sitting on my stomach, I managed to sit up and press my own hand against her neck, praying the pressure would help. "Mom, call the cops! And get something to help stop the bleeding." My fingers were warm and sticky as I pressed against the wound as hard as I could. Gertrude's mouth opened and closed, but she made no sound.

My mother didn't move. Her face was pale and remote.

"Mom!" I yelled, wondering if she was in shock. "Mom! I need help!"

Those words finally cut through whatever haze she was in. She blinked a few times before scrambling to her feet. "Of course. I'll find my phone."

"And a towel," I said. Gertrude was staring at me, her eyes wide and terrified.

As soon as I had the towel in hand, I quickly wound it around her neck. It was covered with sunflowers, which were quickly turning crimson. It took me a moment to realize it was the same towel that Gertrude used to gag my mother earlier.

"You're going to be okay," I said, adjusting her hands and the towel. But even as I said it, I could feel a sick knot tighten in my stomach. She was losing so much blood. I didn't see how we could save her.

Then, I smelled the burning.

"What's that smell?" My mother asked, wrinkling her nose. Her hands were shaking as she attempted to dial her cell phone.

My eyes skimmed the room, landing on the curtain that was going up in flames. Gertrude must have thrown the lighter while we were fighting for the gun. "Fire!" I yelled.

My mother jerked her head up. "What? Oh no." Her mouth went slack as she saw the flames and nearly dropped her phone.

Water. I needed water. I twisted around, desperately trying to find some within reach. Gertrude was still on my stomach, but I was scared that pushing her off would be the end of her. Luckily, Oscar's water dish was close by and I was able to snag it. The weight on my stomach lessened, and by the time I had turned around, Gertrude had already tipped over and was lying on her side, her mouth still working silently like a fish out of water.

"Hang on, Gertrude," I called, throwing the water at the curtain and successfully dousing some of the flames as they scurried up the side. "Keep putting pressure on your neck," I instructed as I scrambled to my feet. I couldn't ignore the irony—if she hadn't thrown the lighter, I'd be able to focus on saving her life instead of trying to keep us all from being burned alive.

I stumbled to the kitchen sink to refill the water dish. I also filled one of the pots that was drying in the rack next to the sink. Behind me, I could hear my mother talking to the 911 operator, begging for her to hurry.

I plugged the drain and left the water on to fill the sink as I raced back to the curtain, dumping the water from the water dish first. The flames hissed as the water transformed the heat into steam, which mixed with the smoke. The air filled with the odor of charred fabric, and I coughed.

I was just about to empty the pot on the rest of the flames when I paused, staring at the orange and yellow glow.

Would it be so bad if I let the house burn?

I had no idea where that thought had come from, but now that it was there, I couldn't shake it.

A haunted house that has brought nothing but tragedy to all who have lived here.

The truth was, Gertrude had a point. My house had seen more than its share of trouble. Maybe it would be better for everyone if I just …

Let it burn.

There was still time. I could get everyone out. Even if Chrissy and Mia were drugged, between my mother and I, we could drag them out.

And once we were all safely outside, I could watch as the flames burned away all the horror and wickedness that had been committed within the walls of Redemption's most haunted house. I could start fresh … build a new house that wasn't tainted by the evil that had been done …

A sharp pain dug into my calf. I gasped as I took a step back, my first thought being that I was burned.

But I wasn't. It was Oscar. He was holding up a paw and glaring at me. I noticed three deep scratches on my leg.

He let out a harsh meow and moved his paw toward me, like he was going to scratch me again.

I jumped back, water sloshing out of the pot and onto the curtain. Suddenly, the flog cleared from my mind.

What was I doing? *This was MY home.*

And I was going to take it back.

"Becca!" My mother was shouting at me. "What are you doing? Dump the water!" She had retrieved the baseball bat and was swinging at the fire.

I threw the rest of the water from the pot and ran back to refill it from the overflowing sink, trying not to trip on a motionless Gertrude. By the time the cops and firefighters arrived, my mother and I had pretty much put it out.

"Becca!" Daniel was pushing his way through the crowd, his face pale. "Becca! Are you okay?"

I stared at him, his hair sticking up and his wrinkled shirt that looked like he had fished it up from off the floor as he jumped out of bed and hightailed it over.

The tight knot that had been living inside me for months finally started to loosen and unwind.

This was what I had always wanted.

"I am now," I said as I fell into his arms.

What Wasn't Forgotten

Chapter 31

It was time.

I stared at the sealed envelope lying on my bed, knowing it was time to finally open it but unable to make my body move.

It had been two exhausting and stressful days since Gertrude tried to kill me and set fire to my house. Along with having to deal with my home becoming a crime scene ... again! ... I had to squeeze in multiple doctor appointments and tests. In the end, they decided I was fine, but said to continue to take it easy and let them know if my symptoms worsened.

So far, everything seemed fine. Throwing out my ibuprofen (actually, throwing out every single unopened bottle of medication in my medicine cabinet in case Gertrude had drugged more than what she'd admitted to) seemed to do the trick. That and knowing the Church of the Forgotten investigation was finally closed.

Once word got out about Gertrude's death, it didn't take long for the other members of the Church of the Forgotten to begin coming forward and telling the cops what they knew about Pamela's death and Zelda's kidnapping, including who had been a part of it. Edward had been involved, which was no surprise to me, but I didn't know any of the others.

As it turned out, Gertrude was even more feared than Eleanor, which I found hard to believe. But for all of Eleanor's flaws, she was at least considered to be, for the most part, mentally stable and fair.

Gertrude was neither. No one wanted to cross her, because they knew what she was capable of.

But with her death, the spell appeared to have been broken.

The large majority of the Church of the Forgotten members were innocent, and for them, it was time for a new start. The problem was, that meant figuring out how to live in the same world that broke them. And with the community center no longer being used as a makeshift shelter, that process needed to happen fast. Luckily, though, a few nonprofit organizations had already reached out to the members to help them get back on their feet, according to Daniel.

It was finally over.

At least ... no, I wasn't going to think about that. It *was* over. The storm had passed.

And I, too, was ready for a fresh start.

But before that could happen, I needed to let go of the past.

I took one last sip of tea, feeling the warmth move through my body before setting the mug aside and picking up the letter.

Dearest Becca,

If you're reading this, that means one of two things—either your mother told you the truth about your birth, or you've discovered this letter on your own.

I'm praying it's the first—that Annabelle did the right thing. But in case it's the second, you should brace yourself.

Yes, I am your birth mother, and Annabelle is your adoptive mother.

How is that possible? Well, it's a long and complicated story. But the short version is, I was pregnant with twins, and your Aunt Marguerite was desperate for a child. She adopted CB (yes, he's your brother), and Annabelle adopted you.

I'm truly sorry if this is how you're first finding this out. I wish with all of my heart things could have been different ... that I could have been there with you, in person, when you were told.

Alas, things don't always work out as we hope. So, we just have to muddle along and do the best we can. And that includes Annabelle. She did the best she could, too, Becca ... even if her best wasn't telling you.

And if that's the case, please don't be mad at her. She loves you dearly. I suppose that particular conversation was just too difficult and painful for her to have. I can't blame her for not wanting to have it, as I too have allowed my fear to cloud my judgement and cause me to make terrible choices. What Annabelle did for me and Marguerite was truly heroic— beyond what any sister could ever be expected to. She's the strongest woman I've ever known, even if we don't see eye to eye much of the time. But what she did was ... she stepped up in way most people never would.

And for that, I will always be grateful to her. She truly is your mother.

That said, I'm sure you want to know why I did it—why would I ever let my two sisters raise my children?

It wasn't because I didn't love you enough. On the contrary, I loved you and your brother SO much. All I wanted was for you both to have the best life possible.

And I didn't think I could give that to you.

If you haven't already guessed, Jonathan is your father. Yes, Jonathan Decker, the man I poisoned and buried in the basement. I poisoned him because I had no other choice—he was possessed and killing people. I could see no other way to stop him.

I had been so in love with him. Before the darkness took him, he was a wonderful man—kind and loving and supportive. He would have been thrilled to have had you as his daughter. Just as I am.

You were conceived in love. Try and hold on to that, rather than focusing on the unforgivable things he did. We both made so many mistakes. Terrible mistakes.

But giving birth to you and your brother wasn't one of them.

Raising you, however, was a different story.

I know this must be difficult for you to take in, but try and picture it. I was pregnant and alone, living in a small town. Jonathan was gone. Jesse was gone. And I was the only one who knew the truth about what happened to them. Plenty of people had their suspicions, of course. Louise being one of them.

There were also a lot of people who thought I had something to do with their disappearances. And, as you now know, they weren't wrong.

If they had known I was pregnant, they would have all guessed that Jonathan was the father. And the speculation and gossip ... well, I couldn't subject you to that. Imagine growing up under that cloud of suspicion—knowing that your father not only cheated on his wife with your mother, but that he also disappeared with his best friend ... and that your mother was the main suspect.

That would have been bad enough. What would have been worse would be you or CB asking me for the truth: did I have something to do with your father's disappearance?

And what would have been my answer?

Would I have lied to you? Would I have evaded answering by giving you a non-answer?

Or would I have told you the truth?

The truth was out of the question. There was no way I would make my own children complicit in my crimes.

So, that left living a lie. And you could say that's what I chose after all.

But I don't see it that way.

I chose adoption to give you a better life. To keep you from living under that cloud of suspicion.

I always hoped the lie would be temporary. I hoped I would be able to tell you the truth. By the time I did, I figured it would be long enough after Jonathan's disappearance to avoid dredging up all the old scandal.

Unfortunately, that didn't happen, and I'm so sorry that I failed you in this.

I'm so very, very sorry that my decisions and actions brought you pain.

While I don't think I deserve it, I hope that someday, you'll be able to forgive me for everything I did, and everything I didn't do. Not for my sake, but for yours.

Above all, remember how much I love you. I will always be both your birth mother and your beloved aunt ... just like Annabelle will always be your birth aunt and the mother who raised you.

Charlie

Before I had even finished reading, I was crying. I have no idea how long I sat on the edge of the bed, allowing the tears to flow.

For the past I should have had. That Charlie should have had. And that my mother should have had.

Once I finally had no tears left, I went to the bathroom to wash my face and brush my hair. Then, I poked around in my dresser until I found what I was looking for.

Next, I headed downstairs to the kitchen.

My mother was sitting at the table, a cup of tea in front of her. Her fingers were covered with soft white bandages and her expression was fixed yet unfocused. She startled when I walked in.

"Oh, Becca. You surprised me," she said, pressing a hand to her chest. "Do you need something? Would you like me to make you some tea?"

I didn't answer. Instead, I slid into the seat next to her. She looked older than I remembered. Even though she was still completely made up, I could see the puffiness under the foundation and the tiny wrinkles by her lips. Her hair was pulled back in a loose ponytail, and a few stray hairs curled around her face. It made her look softer, more approachable, than when she wore it in her customary bun.

"Alan wasn't my father," I said quietly.

Her eyes widened with surprise. "Is that ... was that in her letter?"

I nodded and placed both of Charlie's letters on the table. "My father's name was Jonathan Decker. He was the one found buried in the basement." I deliberately didn't remind my mother that the reason Jonathan was in the basement was because Charlie killed him.

I took a breath, bracing myself for her reaction. I wasn't sure what I expected—maybe something along the lines of "How could Charlotte possibly have gotten herself involved with a man like that?"

But that didn't happen. Instead, she made a strange sound, like something between a gasp and a squeak, before collapsing forward and covering her face with her hands. Her breathing was irregular, almost like she was hyperventilating. I feared she might be having a heart attack.

I quickly leaned forward and put my hand on her arm. "Mom? Are you okay? Do I need to call an ambulance?"

"No, no," she said, her voice hitching. "I'll be okay. Just ... I need a minute."

I rubbed her back slowly as she worked to get her breathing under control. When she finally raised her head, I noticed her eyeliner had pooled into dark circles under her eyes, and her lipstick had smeared.

"I'm just ..." her chest heaved. "I was sure that Alan had killed Jonathan."

I gaped at her. "What?"

She nodded. "Not for a moment did I think Charlotte could have killed that man. Especially if she loved him. Not my sister. I thought …" she turned her head and breathed intentionally, still trying to get back in control. "There was one day at the clinic … she was taking a nap, and I heard her screaming about Alan. When I asked her about it, she insisted it didn't mean anything. She said it was just a nightmare from before she left New York. But … there was something off when she said it. I knew she was hiding something from me; I just didn't know what. And then, when it came out that they had found that man in her basement, I just assumed …" she gave her head a quick shake and pressed her fingers against her temples. "Now I don't know what to think."

We had never really talked about what I found in the basement. I was sure she must have known. The story had been too crazy not to have gotten a significant amount of media attention. I hadn't really considered *why* we hadn't talked about it, though. I was honestly just relieved not to have that conversation with her.

But now, I was realizing it had less to do with me and more to do with Charlie.

Gently, I pushed the two letters toward her. "These are the letters Charlie left me. This first one I discovered after I found Jonathan in the basement. You can see the full explanation of why she had to kill him. I think … I think it will make more sense for you to read it yourself."

She lifted her face from her hands again and reached out to gently touch the paper. "What's the rest of it?"

"It's the letter you brought me. I assumed you didn't read it?"

She shook her head, her expression puzzled. "Why would you let me read her letter to you?"

I gave her a small smile. "She loved you a lot, you know. I know she told you that in her letter to you, but … I thought you might want to see what she told me about you. And for you to hear her reasons directly from her."

She cocked her head. "Are you sure?"

I nodded. "I know she confused and frustrated you, much like I confuse and frustrate you."

She started shaking her head violently. "Oh, Becca, that's not true …"

I put my hand on hers. "It wasn't just you. You confused and frustrated me, as well." I gave her a small smile. "I just thought maybe reading Charlie's letters might help. That's all."

She studied me for a moment before giving me a slight nod. "I'd like that."

I leaned over to give her a kiss on the cheek, surprising myself almost as much as her. We weren't a very affectionate family. But I could see by her faint blush that was pleased.

When I left, tears were already pouring down her face as she slowly pulled the letters closer to her.

What Wasn't Forgotten

Chapter 32

"So when do I need to be out of here?"

I looked at Mia in surprise. We were in the kitchen with our laptops open; Mia was working on school stuff, and I was researching materials I needed for the house. It had been several days since Gertrude had attacked us, and I was anxious to erase every trace of her ever being in my home. "Who said you need to leave?"

She shot me a look. "Come on, Becca. I'm not an idiot. I know Daniel is moving in. I'm just not sure when."

I could feel my cheeks warm. "Even if he does, you don't have to leave."

She snorted. "Yeah, like I want to be a third wheel."

"What are you talking about? You'll never be a third wheel."

She gave me a sideways smile as she shook her head. "I appreciate the sentiment, but again, I'm not an idiot. Besides, if nothing else, it's going to get mighty crowded in here with the two of you and Chrissy."

"Who will be leaving for culinary school when she graduates," I said. "But that aside, nothing is going to happen very fast. Daniel is going to put his house on the market, but before he does that, he needs to do some work on it first. And once that's done, then he's got a list of projects for this house."

Mia looked intrigued. "Really? What's on the list?"

I shut the laptop and sat back in my chair. "Well, for starters, he's got to fix the two bullet holes." I waved toward the ceiling and wall. "He'll do some minor repairs over the next few days. But he's thinking it might be time to modernize the kitchen."

Mia nodded thoughtfully. "Not a bad idea."

"He also wants to add an addition off the laundry room. One of those mother-in-law suites—it'll have a bedroom, full bath, and sitting room."

She grinned. "I guess he and Annabelle are getting along pretty famously?"

I rolled my eyes and smiled back. "It's actually not just for her. Even if we do reclaim the room at the top of the stairs, which I'm determined to do—it's silly to waste that space. Either way, it would be good to have more room for kids."

Her eyes widened as she sat up. "You two are talking about having kids?"

I nodded, even as I felt my flush deepen. "I've realized how much I like having Chrissy around. I know I didn't raise her, but being a mother figure to her makes me think it would be nice to have a few of my own." That was true, but it wasn't the entire story. It was also time for me to commit, fully commit, to a relationship and family. I had realized that one of the reasons why my first two marriages had collapsed was because I hadn't fully committed to either of them. Although, to be fair, my marriage to Stefan never stood a chance no matter what I did or didn't do. Regardless, I still made the same mistakes as I had in my first marriage—I hid parts of myself and never fully communicated.

Just like I did with Daniel.

If I wanted things to be different, I needed to be different. And even though I was terrified of making yet another mistake and finding my heart broken and life in shambles for a third time, I needed to be fully in.

"You're going to make a great mom," Mia said, interrupting my thoughts.

My flush deepened, and I quickly looked down at the table. "I hope so." I took a sip of tea, swallowing hard, and continued. "So, between Chrissy, our kids, a studio for me, and a place for mom to stay and visit, even if Daniel remodels the attic, which he's also talking about doing, I'm sure we'll be able to use the space. In the meantime, the plan is to do the mother-in-law addition first, so if you want to stay there, you are welcome to."

She stared at me. "You would do that for me?" Her voice was wondering.

I frowned. "Of course. Why wouldn't I?"

She looked stunned. "I just … I guess no one has ever done anything like that for me before."

I shrugged. "Well, that's their loss."

I opened up my laptop and went back to my research, leaving Mia to mull over my words in the quiet.

After a few moments, she cleared her throat. "How exactly do you plan on reclaiming the room at the top of the stairs?"

I sighed and ran a hand through my hair. "Good question. It's not just the room at the top of the stairs, although that's the focus. It's the whole house. I'm done letting outside influences dictate what I do or don't do with my own home. I know there has been a lot of tragedy within these walls, but there's also been a lot of joy and love." My throat hitched as images of Charlie flickered through my head. "And I plan on bringing a lot more of the latter into this place, by raising my family here." My voice was fierce.

"Makes sense," Mia said. "So, what's your plan?"

I gestured toward my computer. "Well, that's one of the things I've been researching. To start, I've asked a Catholic priest to bless the whole house, minimally, and do an exorcism if needed. Depending on how that goes, I'll decide what comes next."

Mia raised an eyebrow. "An exorcism?"

I stared back. "Do you have a better explanation for Lily?"

She chewed on her lip for a moment before giving me a slanted smile. "Guess not."

Just then, there was a knock at the door. Mia started to get up, but I waved at her, a knot forming in my gut. "I'll get it."

She sniffed. "It's probably Daniel anyway."

I grinned at her as I headed to the door, even as the knot tightened inside me. I had a feeling it wasn't Daniel.

And it wasn't. It was Aiden.

"Aiden. I'm so glad to see you. Come on in." I held the door open wider. I had texted him earlier, wanting to set up a time to see him, and he texted back he would stop by later in the day.

He shook his head. He was wearing a pair of jeans, an old Packers sweatshirt, and a blue jacket. His face was tired, but his gray eyes were clear. "I've come to say goodbye."

"Goodbye?" Even though I knew it was coming, I still felt my stomach sink. I stepped out onto the porch and pulled the door behind me. Instantly, I realized why he was wearing both a sweatshirt and a jacket, as the cold autumn wind had a bite to it. I wrapped my arms around myself, trying not to shiver. "I'm sorry."

He shook his head again, a lock of brown hair falling across his forehead. "You don't have anything to be sorry about."

"But I do. I should have … done something. I don't know. I certainly should have said something sooner."

A faint, sad smile crossed his lips. "First off, I know you've been a bit busy, so I get it. And second, this isn't a surprise. It was pretty obvious you were still hung up on Daniel, just like he was still hung up on you. I had hoped things might change, but I can't say any of it is a shock."

I hugged myself tighter. "I never wanted to hurt you." The words felt inane the moment they left my lips. I wished there was something else I could say … something that wouldn't sound cliche. Something that would actually make it easier for him.

"I know," he said softly.

For a moment, we just stared at each other. I couldn't help but wonder if things would be different if Daniel wasn't back in the picture. On the other hand, I might still feel the same way—while I really liked him, he just wasn't the one.

"I better go," he said, taking a step backward. "I hope it all works out for you, Becca. Truly."

"The same to you," I said. "You deserve someone who is hopelessly in love with you. And I hope you find her."

That got a smile out of him. "You're absolutely right." He sounded almost like the old, teasing, charming Aiden … the man who had been such a good friend to me when I needed one most.

I would always be grateful to him for that.

He started to walk down the porch steps, but when he reached the last one, he paused and turned back to look at me. "Oh, I wanted to tell you. I took that promotion after all."

"Oh." I was surprised. I had assumed he would open his own firm. He was certainly talented enough to do it.

He bobbed his head. "Yeah, it seemed like the best way."

I furrowed my brow. "The best way?"

His eyes narrowed. "I never could figure out how Sharon from the Redemption Historical Society had gotten all of those insurance companies to pay out from those fires. It turns out, some of the upper management may have been in on the scheme."

I widened my eyes. "They were being bribed?"

His mouth flattened. "Looks like it. No proof, though. At least not yet." He smiled, a slow, calculating smile. "You might be hearing from me again someday, Becca."

"I'm counting on it," I said, smiling back, although it was a little forced.

I watched as he walked down the driveway, the cold wind mussing his brown hair, the blue jacket emphasizing his broad shoulders. Gray clouds scuttled across the sky, and even though it was early, a taste of snow was in the air.

The uneasy feeling was back, even though I tried to tamp it down. There was always something peculiar going on with Redemption, whether it was Aiden telling me about insurance scams or what Daniel had told me a few days ago.

About finding the bodies at the Hoffman Farm.

He said it probably didn't mean anything. The bodies were old. They would have been buried there years ago, long before the Church of the Forgotten showed up.

They might have even been there before Old Man Hoffman bought the farm.

Obviously, there was no connection between the bodies and what was going on in the present. It was just another example of Redemption strangeness.

And yet … why was it that every time I thought I had finally solved the mysteries of Redemption, another one popped up?

The door opened, and Mia's head poked out. "Becca? What are you doing out here? And with no coat?"

"Good question," I said, relieved Mia had interrupted the dark turn my thoughts had taken.

The reality was, I needed to focus on the future, not the past.

My future. Not the house's, or Redemption's.

Mine.

I turned, smiled, and followed Mia inside … into my future.

A note from Michele

While this is the last book in the Secrets of Redemption series, the story of Redemption is far from over. Keep going with *The Vanished Ones,* Book 1 in the spin-off series, The Mysteries of Redemption.

There's a killer on the loose and Zoey's sister has disappeared. The problem is Zoey doesn't know if her sister is a victim … or the killer.

Learn more here:
MPWnovels.com/book/the-vanished-ones/

***

You can also check out exclusive bonus content, including a short novella told from Charlie's point of view during her pregnancy and adoption called *What Charlie Did*. Here's the link:
MPWnovels.com/what-wasnt-forgotten-bonus-content/

The bonus content reveals hints, clues, and sneak peeks you won't get just by reading the books, so you'll definitely want to take a look. You're going to discover a side of Redemption that is only available here.

***

If you enjoyed *What Wasn't Forgotten,* it would be wonderful if you would take a few minutes to leave a review and rating on Goodreads:

goodreads.com/book/show/202371995-what-wasn-t-forgotten
or Bookbub:
bookbub.com/books/what-wasn-t-forgotten-secrets-of-redemption-book-9-by-michele-pariza-wacek

(Feel free to follow me on any of those platforms as well.) I thank you and other readers will thank you (as your reviews will help other readers find my books.)

All my series are interrelated and interconnected. Along with my psychological thrillers, I also have a cozy mystery series that takes place in the 1990s and stars Aunt Charlie. (It's called the Charlie Kingsley Mysteries series.)

You can learn more about Redemption and my other series at MPWNovels.com. You'll also discover a lot of other fun stuff such as giveaways, puzzles, recipes and more.

And while you're waiting for The Mysteries of Redemption, you might want to check out the Charlie Kingsley Mysteries—a funny, twisty cozy mystery series set in the 1990s and featuring Charlie (of course). You can learn more about the series here:

MPWnovels.com/book-series/charlie-kingsley-whodonit-mysteries/

Books and series by Michele Pariza Wacek

***Secrets of Redemption* series**
(Pychological Thrillers)
The flagship series that started it all.
https://MPWnovels.com/r/rd_wwf

Mysteries of Redemption
(Psychological Thrillers)
A spin-off from the Secrets of Redemption series.
https://MPWnovels.com/r/mr_wwf

Charlie Kingsley Mysteries
(Cozy Mysteries)
See all of Charlie's adventures here.
https://MPWnovels.com/r/ck_wwf

Redemption Detective Agency
(Cozy Mysteries)
A spin-off from the Charlie Kingsley series.
https://MPWnovels.com/r/da_wwf

Riverview Mysteries
(standalone Pychological Thrillers)
These stories take place in Riverview, which is near Redemption.
https://MPWnovels.com/r/rm_wwf

Access your free exclusive bonus scenes from *What Wasn't Forgotten* right here:

https://MPWNovels.com/r/whatwasnt-bonus

Acknowledgements

It's a team effort to birth a book, and I'd like to take a moment to thank everyone who helped.

About Michele

A USA Today Bestselling, award-winning author, Michele taught herself to read at 3 years old because she wanted to write stories so badly. It took some time (and some detours) but she does spend much of her time writing stories now. Mystery stories, to be exact. They're clean and twisty, and range from psychological thrillers to cozies, with a dash of romance and supernatural thrown into the mix. If that wasn't enough, she posts lots of fun things on her blog, including short stories, puzzles, recipes and more, at MPWNovels.com.

Michele grew up in Wisconsin, (hence why all her books take place there), and still visits regularly, but she herself escaped the cold and now lives in the mountains of Prescott, Arizona with her husband and southern squirrel hunter Cassie.

When she's not writing, she's usually reading, hanging out with her dog, or watching the Food Network and imagining she's an awesome cook. (Spoiler alert, she's not. Luckily for the whole family, Mr. PW is in charge of the cooking.)

Michele Pariza Wacek

Made in the USA
Monee, IL
14 July 2024